Between Us

Also by Geraldine Kaye

Late in the Day

Between Us

Geraldine Kaye

review

First published in 1998
by HEADLINE BOOK PUBLISHING

A HEADLINE REVIEW hardback

10 9 8 7 6 5 4 3 2 1

Kaye, Geraldine, 1925–
Between us
1. Domestic fiction
I. Title
823.9'14[F]

ISBN 0 7472 1909 5

Typeset by Avon Dataset Ltd, Bidford-on-Avon, Warks

Printed and bound in Great Britain by
Clays Ltd, St Ives PLC.

HEADLINE BOOK PUBLISHING
A division of Hodder Headline PLC
338 Euston Road
London NW1 3BH

To my Children, Miranda Peake,
Jerry and Matthew Kaye, with love.

PART ONE

Heatwave

CHAPTER ONE

IT WAS SIX o'clock when Lydia Kemp woke that morning, and already hot. French windows opened on to a veranda and in summer she positioned the bed so she could look straight out at the June garden below. Foolish to sleep with French windows open, especially in a spacious area of Bristol like Stoke Bishop, the neighbours said. But the open window was something Edward had never permitted. Lydia smiled and ignored them. Was it what people called midsummer madness?

Besides, a heatwave of such length and intensity seemed a meteorological aberration and gave her a reckless feeling that anything might happen and probably would. How could shutting doors and windows keep out pollution, global warming, the drowning of the world, the shortage of water and everything?

The house had been built in the thirties with gables and exposed timbers, sub-Lutyens according to Ed, but for reasons unknown, the garden had never been cultivated. Lydia remembered the rough grass of twenty years ago, full of buttercups and moon-daisies and sloping away from the house. The previous owners had brought a pony over from somewhere to graze it, according to Margaret next door, but ponies were no part of Edward's plan.

Ed liked order, rationality, expertise. He invited a garden designer in; earth unmoved for hundreds of years was levelled by a mechanical digger into two flat spaces in a few hours. The top part, eventually contained by an ornamental wall, had a lawn and a wide bed planted with forsythia, pieris, ceanothus – trouble-free shrubs selected to flower in sequence. Wide steps led down to the lower part, a rose garden on the left and a small orchard right, privacy secured by a hedge all round to meet the wall and wrought-iron gates on the avenue in front.

Ed had mowed the lawn and clipped the hedge for the first ten years, Lydia for the last ten. Had she clipped it for the last time? she wondered, rising and pulling on her wrap.

The cistus was covered with today's pink buds. She had put the white peony tree in herself, dismaying Ed with the shrub's great untidy blooms like crumpled tissues, teasing him with surreptitious packets of seeds scattered to make sudden purple or yellow patches. Colour was the best part of life and should be celebrated; Lydia had felt that since her first box of crayons. Annie, her younger daughter, was the same.

If Lydia had reaped the benefit of the designer garden, she had eventually reaped the whirlwind too – all that lawn mowing and hedge clipping. Her son, William, had done it later on but never very well. Beyond the hedge at the end was the wild wood, a strip of land between the gardens of Cedar and Chestnut Avenues with no access, left by some planning oversight, the secret refuge of neighbourhood children.

Margaret's garden, next door, was entirely filled with a blue-tiled oblong pool and early as it was Margaret herself was already clicking back the bolts in her downstairs French windows. Lydia stepped back, not wanting to intrude on this private early morning swim. She turned to the wardrobe, glancing in the mirror. She looked tired, dark under the eyes. Well, she *was* tired with the prospect of exam papers to mark all weekend – Years Seven, Eight and Nine, three sets each.

Still, it was for the last time.

She had taught French at Stoke Bishop High School for the ten years since the end of the marriage. She had managed all right, since Ed, an accountant, made her a housekeeping allowance by standing order and continued to pay the mortgage as well as the children's school fees – Marina and William's, that is. He had never fully acknowledged Annie's existence. 'Can't you get anything right?' he had said angrily when she announced her final pregnancy. He hated the mess of babyhood, nappies, little throw-ups on his jacket. Marina and William were past all that; Annie was the last straw. Annie had made out on state education – probably where she'd get the most help with her dyslexia, the neighbours suggested kindly.

If only Annie would phone, Lydia thought. How many times had she told her she could always reverse the charges?

* * *

4

Annie Kemp knew the journey was over. The train had been at Waterloo station for almost an hour. She had cleaned her teeth, consumed the coffee and biscuits provided for overnight travellers, put on the new earrings Clover had given her and was sitting on her bunk when the attendant knocked on the door.

'You OK, miss?'

'Course I'm OK,' Annie said grumpily.

A pause. 'Getting off then?'

'Give us a chance.' Annie tucked the blue bottle of mouthwash into her haversack, a friend for last month's blue bottle at home alone and a handy size for specimens. 'What's the hassle?' she added, unlocking the door. 'Chucking us out this time in the morning? Train on fire?'

'Only doing my job, miss.'

She loved the journey though, Penzance to London in a first-class sleeper. Like sex, the rocking-horse swing of it all night long and the clicketty-click of the wheels. Last time Dr Rinde-Smith said they mustn't have sex for a whole month. Like a spot of blood was the end of the world. Jarvis went ballistic.

The Spensers paid her fare, paid everything. Like you could buy people, doctors, anything you wanted if you got the dosh. Only £3.25 an hour, her wages at that crappy hotel, and her accommodation of course. She had done that job for Jarvis too.

The trouble was she had to see Dr Rinde-Smith this morning and the clinic didn't open until ten o'clock.

'Damn birds!' Dr Rinde-Smith peered at his watch: half-past six. Saturday was Annie Kemp. Healthy primigravida, no contrain-dications, chambermaid, no current sexual partner, so she'd said. How was he to know it was a lie?

The divorce had been painful but Lydia had got over it. In the long run she found its disadvantages – the empty bed, driving herself home after parties, the necessity for a full-time job – counted less than the advantage of freedom from Ed's constant criticism, his exaggerated sense of order and irritation at her lack of it. He had been an only child. She had never been quite good enough for Edward, just as she had never been quite good enough for Mother.

The children had survived, even prospered, away from Ed's eagle eye. Conscientious, he had visited every Saturday at first, but with Marina's ballet exams, homework and teenage social life, this had dwindled to phone calls.

Richard had dwindled too. 'Working hard at my marriage' was the way he put it. She had been desperately in love with Richard for three weeks and Ed, discovering, had left at once.

He had set up with and ultimately married Leonie, a young woman in his office, so quickly that Lydia had half-suspected another pregnancy. But no child had emerged then or since. Ed bought a flat in Clevedon and nowadays she didn't see him from one year to the next except by accident.

Now the children had left home, the house was deliciously quiet. No sound but the birds in the garden and the faint splash of Margaret swimming. A moment of perfection, 'a moment of illumination' Virginia Woolf might call it. But it couldn't go on. Lydia, making coffee and wandering out to the terrace where the white table and chairs invited summer breakfast, knew that. Would Marina and Jeremy like to have the white garden furniture when the house was sold? she wondered. Next door the other way, the heatwave had already drawn the Newton children out to play.

After breakfast Lydia carried her briefcase with the exam papers upstairs to her study, William's old bedroom, which overlooked the garden. 'Why should William get the best bedroom?' Marina had said, six years old. 'Need it for my railway, don't I?' William had replied, and so he did. Better for everybody than railway lines trailing trippily across the hall.

For Lydia the children would always live in Cedar Avenue.

Downstairs the phone was ringing. Bound to be Mother this time of day, she thought, running down.

'Lydia?' Ed said.

'That's me,' she said briskly. Ed's voice was always a small shock. 'Good morning.'

'Going to be another very hot day.'

'Yes. Heatwave.'

'You all right?'

'Fine, thanks. *Très bien.*'

6

'Good. Er ... about the house. I've made arrangements with the estate agents, Belstones, to market it.'

'I could have done that,' Lydia said, aware of a clutch in her throat.

'You could,' Ed agreed. 'But you didn't, though I think I did remind you *spring* was the best time for selling ... Anyway I've instructed Belstones myself now. OK?'

'Sorry. I've been so busy. I mean it's exams at school at the moment and they all have to be marked and—'

'Quite,' Ed interrupted. 'The point is the chap'll probably be coming to look round and measure up *et cetera*.'

'I see.' Lydia paused. 'Can't say I like the thought of other people living in my house.'

'*Our* house,' Ed corrected. 'It's what we agreed: you would stay in the house until the children left home.'

'I know.'

'Marina's been married for five years, for God's sake,' Ed said. 'And Annie's been at art school since last September.'

'Yes,' Lydia said, and again her throat tightened. 'She hardly ever writes.'

'Writing's not her thing, is it?' Ed said.

'But she didn't come home in the Easter vac. Do you think she's all right?' Lydia said. The children still seemed to live inside her head, a way of keeping them safe, but sometimes she wondered if they might be safer out of it.

'The girl's twenty, Lydia, busy with her love life, I expect. Anyway, I'm phoning to let you know Belstones will be putting up a "For Sale" sign this weekend. All right?'

'I suppose ...' Lydia said. But what if something went wrong and one of the children wanted to come home?

'Where do you think of moving to?' Ed asked in a softer tone. 'I mean the house may go quite quickly.'

'I haven't really thought,' she said casually. But what was the point of aggravating him on purpose?

'Well, you'd better start *really* thinking. Belstones reckon we should get around £300,000, and minus the outstanding mortgage and conveyancing, *et cetera*, I reckon we should clear £120,000 each. You'll want to live near the job, I suppose?'

'I'm giving up my job at the end of term,' Lydia said.

'Redundant?' Ed sounded concerned.

'No, I gave notice.' She enjoyed shocking him.

'So what have you got in mind?' Ed was wary now. 'I understand teaching jobs aren't that easy to come by.'

'That's right,' Lydia said. Ed was sensible and maybe it wasn't sensible for a woman of her age to give up her job in the present climate. The trouble was she was tired of being sensible. She had been *sensible* for the children for twenty-six of the forty-six years of her life, even longer if you counted all that extra milk she'd drunk when she was expecting Marina. Now she was acting impulsively, not from boldness but because if she thought about it, she might easily lose heart.

'So what are you going to do?'

'Not sure,' she said. It was nothing to do with Ed anyway.

'You do realise I cancelled the standing order last September when Annie left?' he said. Actually she hadn't realised. She filed bank statements methodically but never had time to look at them. 'You're on your own,' Ed added on a note of triumph.

'Yes,' Lydia said. There was a long pause.

'So what will you do?'

'Just what I want,' Lydia said. '*Je m'en fiche.*'

Why should she tell him of the posse of letters and CVs she had dispatched to all the French publishers she could think of, as well as appropriate English ones, offering her services as a translator? Let Ed play ant to her grasshopper if it pleased him. It was nothing to her.

'You'll put your capital into a flat if you've got any sense. What would you think if I just gave up work?'

'But you wouldn't, would you?' Lydia said. *Couldn't* would be more accurate, she thought.

'Please understand you can't depend on me any more. It's over.'

'It was over a long time ago,' Lydia said. 'And I have got a mountain of exam papers, so if you'll excuse me . . .'

She put down the phone. Her voice was calm but her hands were shaking. Why did she let Ed get to her?

She was tired of teaching. Teaching and running the house and dealing with the children on her own had been too much. But now that was over too and the children seemed *all right*, though it was best not to probe.

Marina, twenty-six with a good maths degree, was an actuary for an insurance firm, and had been married to Jeremy for five years. It was disappointing she wasn't pregnant, but she didn't seem to want to talk about it.

William, a year younger, had qualified as a solicitor and been taken on as an assistant by a respected local firm. His salary was meagre but his live-in girlfriend, Ruby, worked as a nanny and helped with the rent of the house at Pill.

Annie's most remarkable feature was her lustrous and frizzy fair hair. 'Nothing like that in my family,' Ed had remarked suspiciously. But after some judicious and expensive coaching, Annie had got into Filton College for her art foundation year, and then surprised everybody by getting a place at Penzance Art School. Lydia had been delighted because so many people dismissed Annie, and because at her age Lydia had wanted to go to art school herself. But Mother had insisted that reading modern languages was a safer proposition jobwise, for a girl who didn't have her own father to fall back on after all.

Mother was right, of course; Mother was always right. It was Lydia's own fault that she couldn't quite forgive her.

Before lunch the telephone rang again. Annie, Lydia thought, running downstairs.

'Hello, it's me,' Margaret said. 'I'm asking you round for a drink. Now if it's the right time.'

'Now is perfect,' Lydia said. 'But I can't stay long, I've got these exam papers . . .'

She put down the phone and looked at herself in the mirror, combed her straight fairish hair and hooked in her new earrings, dangling glass droplets like frozen tears.

Margaret's front door stood wide open in the hot sunlight.

'Come in, my dear,' Margaret called. The long sitting room gave on to the terrace and blue pool beyond. There were two huge pink sofas at present littered with packaging and tissue paper. Were the curtains patterned with pink roses meant to compensate for the absence of a proper garden? Lydia wondered. The room also featured two walnut tallboys, and a floor polished by an electric polisher and Mrs Crabbe, who came three times a week in a white

Mini and was ridiculously overpaid, the neighbours said, especially since the parquet was hidden by a flourish of Chinese rugs, rose pink and swimming-pool blue. Everything in Margaret's sitting room, except the tallboys, was virgin new.

'Champagne?' Margaret asked.

'Gracious! Are we celebrating?'

'Certainly,' Margaret said, smiling rather wider than her plump face could readily accommodate. 'Bertie and I are getting married on Tuesday. Isn't it wonderful?'

'Marvellous!' How old was Margaret? Her seventieth birthday party had been several years ago.

'Tuesday. Down at Rye, where Bertie's daughter lives. You remember Bertie, you met him at Christmas?'

'Congratulations!' Lydia said, rooting in her memory for the face of a small white-haired man with whom she had exchanged a few words. Hadn't his eyes been a rather bright blue?

'Thank you, dear,' Margaret said, all complaisance. 'I've never been so happy, falling in love at my time of life. We met on my cruise to Madeira in November.'

'Shipboard romance?' Lydia said, hoping Bertie wasn't an adventurer. Margaret was rich and kind but no judge of character. The window-cleaner she'd introduced to Cedar Avenue had form for house-breaking.

'Yes, well, Bertie's a widower and I'm twice widowed and we got on like a house on fire straight away.' Margaret was, Lydia suspected, being a touch disingenuous.

'That's lovely!' Lydia said. 'And Bertie's retired?'

'Retired with a good pension and a flair for stocks and shares. He reads the *Financial Times* and the *Economist* every day.'

'Goodness!' Lydia, sipping champagne, was not entirely reassured. 'What did Bertie do before he retired?'

'Not sure I really know,' Margaret said. 'We don't talk about the past much, more about the future, the two of us together. Did you know ninety per cent of people think they have an above-average sense of humour? Bertie told me that. He's brilliant, you know, just didn't have the opportunity. And I particularly want to thank you, Lydia.'

'Thank me? What have I done?'

'Well . . .' Margaret paused and glanced down at her considerable bosom. 'That plastic surgery I was going to have, reducing this to manageable proportions. The surgeon did agree it was a lot to carry round in hot weather. But you were so against it. *Mutilation*, you said, and somehow that word stuck in my head and put me right off. And now I've met Bertie I'm so happy not to have lost any part of my erogenous zones.'

'Really, I . . .' Lydia said, embarrassed. But why should she be if Margaret wasn't?

'Shall I show you my treasures?' Margaret swung round to the packages. 'I had to send away, they just didn't have anything my size in Clifton.' She spread a lacy nightie in oyster silk and another in a froth of sea green across the sofa. 'I dare say a young thing like you will think it's a silly extravagance at my age but I've been so economical with lingerie lately. Nothing but cotton knicks from Marks and Spencer's. More champagne?'

'I mustn't,' Lydia said. 'By the way, Belstones are putting a "For Sale" sign on my house this weekend.'

'Oh, my dear . . .' Margaret's face fell. 'I shall miss you.'

'These things happen.' Lydia shrugged and stood up.

'But you've put so much *into* that garden,' Margaret said, following her into the hall. 'And Bertie was so looking forward to meeting you again. Let's hope the house doesn't sell for a very long time, or am I being selfish?'

'Course not,' Lydia said. 'Take care now.'

Back home she cut herself a piece of cheese, collected an apple and returned to the study. She had managed to congratulate Margaret, but she was disconcerted to find the friend she had known for so long had changed overnight from a wilful and eccentric widow to a lovesick ninny. She also found the situation distasteful, which prejudice, she realised, did not reflect well on her. Would she be forced to contemplate Margaret's sex life in her role as confidante?

Lydia dropped the remains of her apple into the wastepaper basket, sighed and turned back to the exam papers. She had done Year Seven, top set. People talked about teachers' long holidays but nobody talked about whole weekends given to marking. She was slow – 'morbidly conscientious' Izzy called it. Izzy taught dance and drama at the same school and did everything at high speed.

How had she coped ten years ago? Lydia wondered. The children were young then; Marina had tried to help but her efforts at cooking were usually rejected by the other two, resulting in tantrums. William had been a dab hand at baked beans 'improved' with a spoonful of brown sugar, probably still was. Certainly Ruby appeared to leave the cooking to him.

But why hadn't Annie phoned? There had been that bad patch in the winter, February and March, when Lydia had been worried sick, had even thought of driving down. She supposed it had been a love affair gone wrong; girls that age were so silly. Annie had always been secretive but at least she had gone on the Pill at sixteen. 'You have to let them grow up,' Margaret had said, irritating from a childless woman. 'You spoil Annie rotten,' Ed had said just before he left. Had Annie precipitated the end of the marriage as much as Richard?

When the train slid out of Waterloo station just before midnight, Annie was already stretched out on her bunk. The clinic had been OK, Dr Rinde-Smith rabbiting on about 'discretion' and 'contract' but he did say she and Jarvis could do it again. Tomorrow she would be back at the café, loving him to bits.

Annie slept.

Lydia sighed and fitted Year Seven, all three sets, back in her briefcase. It was cooler now. She stared at the darkening garden. A scatter of cistus petals she knew to be pink lay white on the gunmetal lawn she knew to be green. And suddenly she knew too that the loss of the garden, the core of her, was not just a hiccup – not like the children growing and going, a mixture of sadness and relief – but a calamity.

'*Quelle catastrophe!*' she whispered into the night.

CHAPTER TWO

L YDIA DREAMED. A word struggled into her mouth but her lips were as soft as duster cloth and she couldn't make a shape.

'Tell me . . .' she muttered, waking to distant church bells. If Annie phoned it was often on Sunday.

The train had just pulled into Penzance station. Carriage doors flung back, feet stepping away down the platform.

Annie humped her haversack over her shoulder. Like Jarvis said, she ought to phone Ma and be done with it. Easy to say. Would Jarvis be there to meet her this morning? Did he love her as much as she loved him? First-class sleeper to London and back was OK, but she was only doing it for Jarvis.

Downstairs the phone was ringing. What a nerve. Running downstairs Lydia glanced at her watch; it was later than she'd realised and already hot.

'Hello, Lydia?'

'Richard?' His voice, deep and sonorous, a Shakespearean actor's voice, the same yet not quite the same. 'Been a long time.' A year, she guessed, since he'd called to tell her he had moved to Bath, a call so different from the snatched whispers and 'got-to-go-nows' of the loving time it was almost an insult. Whatever there had been between them, her divorce killed it.

'How are you?' Richard said. 'I moved to Bath, you know.'

'Yes. You phoned . . . about a year ago. I'm fine but busy marking exam papers.'

'You career girls!' Richard said. He had always been unaware of changing mores. It wouldn't occur to him that nowadays the use of *girls* to middle-aged women was anything other than a compliment.

'I'm on my own now,' he said, his voice falling, and she knew that too, though for the past nine years their communication had been confined to Christmas cards with postscripts.

Four years ago a postscript had told her of his open-heart surgery. What did that mean exactly? she had asked Miss Tucker, the biology teacher at school. 'Bypass operation, cleaned up the atheroma in your friend's valve. Should be good for a few years if that's what you're after,' she added with a sharp glance. 'Thanks,' Lydia, who hadn't been after anything, had said. A year and a half ago Richard's postscript announced the death of his wife and his early retirement from the medical profession.

'I expect you saw Alison's obituary in the *Telegraph*,' Richard said.

'No, but you told me. I wrote to say how sorry I was.'

'Thanks, I remember now, course you did. It's been a difficult time, losing her . . . Nothing seems worthwhile.'

'You've had your share of traumas.' She was surprised though. Richard had always seemed different from other people – insouciant, invulnerable. It was why she had loved him. Now his buoyancy had collapsed.

'Anyway,' he said, pushing his voice up a degree, 'I want to see you, Lydia. I thought we might have dinner at that Llandroger place . . .'

'Good idea,' she said, not sure it was. 'But I am very busy. Exams this week and teaching again next . . .'

'I meant tonight.' His voice had firmed.

'Sorry,' she said. The effrontery of it! The second phone call in eight years and he expected her to drop everything. 'Marking has to be done . . .'

'Surely you're entitled to time off on a Sunday evening?' he said, attempting a jocular tone.

'That's not the point,' Lydia said. You did get over people sooner or later; she had got over Richard. There was bleak satisfaction in that. 'Teaching starts as exams finish.'

'You don't have to dress up or anything.'

'No really, I can't. Sorry.'

'I'm sorry too, Lydia . . .' he was saying, but her phone had already gone down.

As Lydia dressed, she thought about Richard as he had been when she'd met him. Sturdily built with thick brown hair curling along his forehead like a bull calf's, a roving grey eye and a whiteness of skin which made him look exceptionally clean and innocent. His reputation with women preceded him and was a turn-on: some atavistic female response to ensure a wide scattering of seed, Lydia supposed. They had met in the BBC canteen. She had been taking part in a Radio 3 discussion on French poetry, Richard, a GP, recording a series of talks for *Woman's Hour* called 'The Wakeful Baby'.

He was staying at the Overseas Club and, exhilarated by her broadcast and the visit to London, she got into his taxi and shortly after into his bed. It was not the kind of thing she did. Despite his reputation, his loving was energetic rather than remarkable but he had a humanity, a concern for the female person, a kindness and sweetness which pleased her. Nothing seemed to throw him – was that due to his experience of medical emergencies?

She had fallen in love and after that had pursued him beyond sense or discretion, meeting him for afternoons in local hotels. Richard had taken care to avoid Chippenham where he was in general practice but he'd talked a lot about his wife, a habit Lydia had found embarrassing. 'Suppose Alison finds out?' she'd enquired once. Had she hoped to startle him into some wild declaration? 'Oh, I always tell her everything, matter of principle,' he'd said with an air of moral superiority. 'The marriage is good every way but this one.' She'd been lying in his arms at the time. 'Matter of fact I find having a relationship improves the home stretch, haven't you discovered that?'

Lydia had been shocked and bewildered. What exactly was between them? she wondered, stiffening as his questing fingers pushed down her thigh. Was she naïve to have thought it was special, as overwhelming for him as it was for her? Had she avoided making love with Edward, ignored his irritation, just to find herself acting poultice to a sick marriage bed?

The affair might well have ended there, and perhaps Richard had intended that it should. But Ed found out, smashed the last three glasses of the wedding present dozen, swore at her all night and in the morning packed his bags and went. He was within his rights and his personality precluded compromise.

It was the end of over sixteen years of marriage.

Lydia sighed and settled at her desk. She had finished Year Nine, top set, when the phone rang. Annie?

'I'm phoning from the hospital,' Mother said in her telephone voice. 'I tried to phone yesterday but there was such a queue. I'm going home today.' The voice lowered. 'Just letting you know but don't tell James.'

'Will you be all right by yourself at The Cottage?' Lydia said. 'Anyway, James won't phone me, he never does.'

'You never know what he'll get up to nowadays. I'm not an invalid, dear, but I needed "a complete and well-deserved rest" as Dr Hardy put it. "That's what you need, Mrs Price," he said, "a complete and well-deserved rest." ' How come she always knew exactly what Mother was going to say? Lydia wondered. 'Taxi's fetching me, and I've a home help three times a week for shopping so I'll manage and—'

'You could come and stay here,' Lydia said, touched by her mother's courage despite herself. 'But you'd be on your own except at weekends.'

'Kent is a long way from you, dear, especially in this heatwave. I'll be all right. Tuesday's Vera's bridge afternoon and I hate missing. Things all right with you?'

'Fine. I'm marking exam papers at the moment.'

'Lucky you had a good education,' Mother said. 'Made sure my daughters had an education to fall back on. Just as well in your case, Lyddy. If only James would stay at The Lilacs . . .'

'He's bound to find out sooner or later.'

'Long as it's *later*,' Mother said.

Lydia combed her fingers through her hair. The hall mirror hung on a darkish wall, kinder to the image although a mirror in a friend's house had shattered that illusion. For years you worried about your children and no sooner had they settled, in so far as any young adult these days could be said to settle, than your mother required attention, and there was James as well.

Their father had died when Lydia was five. Her mother had married James when Lydia was fourteen and her sister, Unity, sixteen. Unity had married an American and lived out there.

At least the children were getting on with their own lives, Lydia thought, reaching for Year Nine, middle set. Marina had beauty, intelligence and the application to make the most of both. Marina would make out, whatever happened, and if Lydia had reservations about the Georgian house, a Grade II listed building Marina and Jeremy had recently bought at Frenchay – pretentious and impractical for a young couple was her private opinion – she she kept them to herself. Sometimes she wondered if she could be jealous.

That Sunday morning Marina kneeled by the path, planting out mauve violas and watching Jeremy replace the twenty-year-old crazy paving round the sundial with eighteenth-century flagstones, authentic according to the demolition contractor, and expensive. They were two of the things they had in common, history and gardens, though she hadn't realised at first.

Because of the time of the month, Jeremy had wanted her to sit in a deckchair and just watch but she couldn't do that. Jeremy liked to do things his way, slowly, carefully, perfectly. Marina had thought *slowly carefully perfectly* belonged to her until she married Jeremy.

'All right?' he gasped, sliding a flagstone on to its prepared bed.

'You know Ma's white table and chairs? Be good here,' Marina said. 'She won't need them when the house goes.'

'Depends where she moves to,' Jeremy said, breathless.

'Not likely to have such a big garden. I'll make tea,' Marina said. She went inside and switched on the kettle. Suddenly she didn't feel at all well.

It was a design fault, Lydia thought, back at her desk later that afternoon, that she couldn't see the roses in the rose garden unless she stood up. It was cooler now. She had almost finished Year Nine, when the phone rang.

'Thought you'd like to know I'm home at The Cottage,' Mother said jauntily. 'Mrs Gibbs left milk in the fridge.'

'Good for Mrs Gibbs and good for you, Mother,' Lydia said maintaining the jaunty tone. 'Everything all right?'

'Guess what was waiting for me in the porch? A lovely, lovely bunch of flowers sent by Interflora. Three carnations, two lilies, lots of pinks, ferns, sweet William and four beautiful roses. Guess who sent them.'

'Unity?' Lydia said.

'Never forgets, does she? I've taken a fish pie out of the freezer – freezer section of my fridge I should say – so I'm all right. Vera is putting her head in later.'

'Oh good. Well, take care, Mother. I've still got loads of papers to correct . . .'

'Good job you had a good education.'

'Good night, dear.'

'Jeremy?' Marina said, coming out with two cups of tea, white bone china on a pale blue tray.

'What?' he said, and saw her eyes fill with tears.

'I'm bleeding,' she said. 'I'm sorry. I try so hard.'

'That's half the trouble, love.' He folded his arms round her. 'Women don't have to try, they just *are*.'

'I'm no good to anybody,' she said, as tears rivered down her cheeks. 'Nothing but trouble.'

'Now you're being ridiculous, sweetheart,' he said, carefully keeping his earthy hands off her red and white check shirt. 'It's a setback, that's all. Don't let's make it a drama.'

Lydia finished Year Nine and went out to the garden. Hoses had been banned for weeks. She was leaning into the butt, scooping water from the bottom, when the front doorbell rang.

'Who on earth . . . ?' she muttered going back to the house. For a moment she didn't recognise him.

'Richard? I wasn't expecting . . .'

'No?' His expression was apologetic, his eyes shifted to the carrier he was holding and now held out towards her.

'Brought you a takeaway. Thought it would save you having to . . . Hope it's all right.'

'I'm sure it's all right. What is it?' Lydia said, taking it. She *was* pleased to see him now he was there but it wasn't just his voice that had changed, his whole manner was different. How could the man-about-town, debonair in his bright-buttoned blazer, have metamorphosed into this dismal figure in a shabby cotton jacket which didn't meet across his belly, his grey hair straggling across his forehead and shoulders needing a brush?

'It's moussaka,' he said.

'How kind. Come in the kitchen while I get plates. Have a drink? Red plonk on the side; no retsina, I'm afraid.'

'Red plonk's fine,' he said. She poured two glasses. 'Hot, isn't it?' She gathered cutlery and salad. 'We'll eat outside.'

'Can I help? Let me help,' he said, hovering in the way.

'Haven't you done enough?' she said sharply. Their eyes met and suddenly her heart was thudding in her chest. Could he be thinking what she was thinking: that if she had never met him she would still be married to Ed, comfortably off and living for ever in Cedar Avenue? 'Falling in love is the best thing in life,' Richard used to say. 'Fun and games for grown-ups.' Lydia had thought she could handle what was between them ten years ago; she had thought she was grown up.

'Shall I lead the way?' she said, moving out to the terrace.

'Didn't know you were a gardener.' Richard glanced round.

'Have to be,' Lydia said, spooning moussaka. 'Help yourself to tomato salad.' Did he know anything about her?

'It's good to be eating something you didn't cook yourself,' he said. His right hand gripped his left wrist under the table, taking his own pulse, Lydia supposed.

'Anyway, how are you?' she asked.

'Better than I was two hours ago,' Richard said, releasing his wrist. Was he talking about his heart or his mood?

'You've had a difficult time,' she said. Had he dropped by to tell her about his grief, appoint her his counsellor?

'I miss her so,' he muttered. 'It's been too much. I lost everything all at once, the practice, my health, my wife. I mean I had a life, enjoyed every minute of it – work, patients, family – and suddenly wham.' He brought his hand down hard on the table so the glasses jumped, slopping red drops on the smooth whiteness. 'Now it's gone. Alison's been dead for twenty months but it doesn't get better. I live in a desert. I feel so . . . so . . .' He was blinking rapidly.

'Don't, Richard,' Lydia said firmly. 'Please don't.'

'Sorry,' he muttered.

'It will get better,' she said, her tone gentle now. 'You've got your flat sorted, haven't you? What about your children? Sean was

19

at the Royal College of Music last time I heard. Doesn't he play the sax?'

'Don't see a lot of him nowadays,' Richard said, blowing his nose. He had always loved talking about Sean. 'He's composing now, film music. Well paid but it's getting the commissions.'

'And what about Fen?' Lydia said.

'Married a dentist,' he said. 'Got a little boy. What about your lot? Mirabel was it, the pretty one?'

'Marina, William and Annabel,' Lydia said. 'They're OK. Marina's husband lectures at the University of the West of England. She's an actuary, seems to be all right.'

'No babies?' Richard was checking his pulse again.

Lydia shrugged. 'Not so far.' She didn't talk about her own children much. She got sick of excited parents boasting about their offsprings' successes.

'William's just qualified as a solicitor, been taken on by Beavis and Beavis as an assistant. Annie's at art school.' They had talked about Annie during those mad three weeks. Would he remember how worried she had been about Annie's dyslexia, her air of not quite belonging in the family?

'Good for Annie,' he said, but his smile was vague. He found it difficult to think of anything but his own despair for more than a moment.

'This house is up for sale,' Lydia said.

'Where will you go?' Richard was looking at her now.

She shrugged. 'Somewhere else now motherhood is over.' Her fingers made inverted commas in the air round 'motherhood'. 'And the children have gone.'

'And your job?'

'I finish at the end of this term.'

'What you going to do?' Richard asked. She had caught his attention now. If he felt some kind of belated responsibility it was irritating rather than anything else. What was she going to do? She had had no answers so far from the publishers she had written to.

'Well . . .' It wasn't that she was dedicated to translation, it was what she could do, what she had done for ten years after Marina and then William and Annie were born, fitting it round small children's needs. She turned back to it now; it didn't matter if she couldn't get work at once. She was teaching two French evening classes as well, including a GCSE one at Park Lodge, a college of further education in the centre of town. She could survive until the house was sold.

'Well . . . it rather depends . . .'

Richard leaned forward and his eyes were bright as steel. ' "Come live with me and be my love?" ' he said.

'What?'

'Why not? My flat's quite large and we used to get on.'

'What the hell do you think I am?' Lydia exploded, startling them both. 'Any port in a storm – is that it?'

'Certainly not,' he said with a touch of his old suavity. 'I mean we could get married if you like.'

'Oh yes? What for?'

'Why not?'

'Because there's nothing *between us*!' Lydia shouted suddenly. She was shaking all over. 'Because what we had is gone. Dead.' Dead like Alison, she thought. But why was she so angry? Because getting angry with Ed caused sulks which made everything worse? Were fifteen years of repressed anger festering inside her? Or was it because she had let Richard destroy her life? Suddenly she picked up her plate and flung it crashing against the house wall.

Richard jumped back, startled. Oh yes, she had his attention now.

'Because we've nothing to marry for.'

'I wouldn't say that,' Richard said, getting up. 'And I'm sorry if I upset you but I still think it's a good idea. Please *think* about it, Lydia? Life is so short. Alison died of breast cancer.' He pushed his chair into the table. 'Second biggest killer in this country after heart disease. I'd better be off while you've still got some crockery.' His cool smile was familiar at least. 'Take care.'

After he had gone Lydia picked up the broken bits, gathered plates and takeaway dishes to the kitchen, and walked about the garden listening to the wild jangle in her head.

What a wreck, what a cheek, how dare he ask her to be what – his cook, his nurse, push his bathchair round Eastbourne?

Presently it grew dark. Next door Margaret was swimming and

singing under the stars. Not a melody that Lydia knew, not a melody at all but a song of joyous love.

At least Margaret was enjoying the heatwave.

CHAPTER THREE

O<small>N MONDAY LYDIA</small> woke with a sense of unease. Was it the continuing heatwave, Annie not phoning, or Mother and poor James that had made a life of her own seemed so unattainable?

Was it Richard? But his unhappiness had nothing to do with her. He was hardly a friend – ex-lovers didn't automatically qualify as friends – and he was too self-absorbed for friendship now. Had he always been like that but somehow concealed it, casually wrecking her marriage and then disappearing?

She was responsible too, of course, *more* responsible since she believed women were intrinsically more responsible. She had been angry last night at his calm assumption that she had nothing better to do than devote her life to him. She wished she had been angrier still, erupted like Vesuvius, said all the things she had never said to anybody. It might have released them both.

What *was* she going to do with the rest of her life? As Lydia paused on the upstairs landing, an unfamiliar black car drove slowly along Cedar Avenue. It stopped outside. Through the wrought-iron gate she saw a light grey suit, and a moment later Ed's dark, well-clipped head. He glanced left and right, gazed towards the house a moment, returned to the car and drove away, accelerating fast.

The car was a BMW. Why hadn't the children told her that Ed had a new BMW? Evidently he had come to check the 'For Sale' notice was in place, it wasn't, and Belstones were about to get it in the neck. Lydia smiled to herself. Once she had been as bothered by Ed's exacting standards as he was by her lack of them. It had been important to avoid spats and arguments for the children's sake until she met Richard.

An hour later, dressed and breakfasted, Lydia drove to Stoke Bishop High, a pleasant, two-storey brick building with an asphalt car park in front and a wide green sweep of tree-edged playing field at the back. Girls in green gingham and dark green blazers wandered along the pavement and gathered at the several entrances in groups.

'*Bonjour, madame.*'

'*Bonjour, mes enfants. Bonjour, mesdemoiselles.*'

That morning the after-weekend smell of disinfectant and polish, which would later mingle with sweat and chewing gum, was already tinged with the nostalgia of her last weeks, last days. What nonsense, Lydia thought, as she made her way to the staffroom. She didn't want to teach, she had never wanted to teach. It was only due to another of Mother's sensible choices that she was qualified. Still, despite herself, she had moved from poor through middling to competent teacher in her ten years' experience there. But she was free now and it was the rational moment to stop, to change direction. She could type and word process and if she couldn't get translation work, she would just have to get an office job for the time being.

'Got your papers marked?' Izzy said, coming in behind her. Izzy had come to the school three years ago, an independent, lively woman who gave no quarter.

'If only . . .' Lydia said, gathering notes and books. Classes were tiresomely restless after exams but at least she had a free period later on. 'You?'

'Course,' Izzy said. Izzy had a talent for life, said what she liked, never reproached herself and was never hassled.

'See you later,' Lydia said, wondering, as she paused to collect the class register for Year Eight, if Annie would phone tonight.

It was after the morning's teaching – the lunchtime buzzer had already gone – when two girls came running along the corridor behind Lydia.

'*Madame*, Mrs Kemp . . . is it true you're leaving at the end of term?' Bethany cried, breathless and pink.

'Yes, it is, Beth,' Lydia said. Odd that this plump and annoying girl, now blinking rapidly, should be so upset.

Her friend, Sharon, groaned. 'We crossed our fingers, all of Year Eight crossed their fingers, hoped it was a rumour.'

'Afraid not. I shall miss you all, of course, but I . . . er, have . . . I have been teaching here ten years now, you know.'

'Not us, you haven't.' Bethany dissolved into tears. 'Not fair, you took my sister to GCSE, you've only had us a year.'

'Oh, come now,' Lydia said, moving on towards the staffroom.

'I'm sure you'll get along very well with Miss Bird.'

'Can't stand that knitted dress,' Bethany said. 'Or her bad breath.'

'That's no way to talk about a teacher or anybody else,' Lydia said. 'Off you go to lunch, please, girls.'

'Never allowed to say what we think,' Bethany snuffled as Lydia pushed at the staffroom door. 'It's only because we like you so much, Mrs Kemp.'

'*Love* you, she means . . .' Sharon muttered as, collapsing into giggles, they ran away down the corridor.

By tomorrow news of her imminent departure would be all round the school, Lydia thought ruefully. She had kept it under wraps; she hated scenes, displays of adolescent tears.

'Youth!' she said, staring out at the playing field a few minutes later as she and Izzy ate their sandwiches in a corner of the staffroom. 'How do girls get to be so silly?'

'Tell me about it,' Izzy said. 'It's the hot weather – look what happened to the Ancient Mariner – and female hormones and being all lumped in together. *Brats* – I thought that word was twentieth-century but apparently Daniel Defoe used it. Fancy a gin half-four my place?'

'Shouldn't really,' Lydia said. 'I've still got half of Year Eight's papers to mark and—'

'Course you should,' Izzy said. 'Unwind, why don't you? Don't let the buggers get you down, *et cetera*.'

At ten past four Lydia dropped her briefcase into the Fiesta and scrambled in after it. The school was already almost quiet and the car park half empty. Bethany stood forlornly by the gate. Had Marina had crushes? Lydia wondered. Her adolescence had been uneventful except for the Kevin business. Annie's teenage headaches, which prevented her helping with the washing-up, had eventually been diagnosed as migraine.

Cool but kind, Lydia nodded to Bethany as she passed through the gate and turned to follow Izzy's precious scarlet MG. It darted along the back lanes and short cuts which Izzy currently claimed was the quickest route to Westbury-on-Trym village and her mews flat. She had been married for a short time in her twenties and showed no inclination to repeat the experience in her thirties but had somehow contrived to retain the marital dwelling. Izzy was excellent at contrivance.

'You drive too fast,' Lydia said as she hobbled across the cobblestones and followed Izzy up the narrow stairs to the living room. It was carpeted in beige and sparsely furnished with black leather chairs that hinted 'Bauhaus', a single divan with an Indian spread, and a variety of colourful cushions. Bookshelves covered one wall and accommodated a tray of bottles and accumulated artefacts as well as books.

'So people keep telling me,' Izzy said, laconic. ' "Short life and a gay one" as they used to say. In the Aids era rather more appropriate now than then. Tonic, lime, what?'

'Tonic, please. Go steady on the gin, I've got to work tonight, don't forget,' Lydia said, settling herself in a leather chair that struck her once again as exceedingly uncomfortable. 'What's happened to your television?'

'Gone. It was Toby's actually,' Izzy said, pouring drinks.

'And Toby's gone too?'

'Oh, ages ago.' Izzy seemed to have an unending supply of live-in lovers. 'It had been on the slide for yonks. He even went so far as to ask me to marry him.'

'He did?' Lydia was startled by the coincidence. 'But you didn't fancy it?'

'Cheers.' Izzy gulped and swallowed. 'Well, he only asked because we'd reached the last tango and he couldn't face being on his own. It was well over yonks ago ... know what I mean? "The lingering glance across the room," ' glass in hand Izzy acted the cameos, ' "the will he, won't he?", "the extravagant rococo bit" ... Love is an art form, don't you think?'

'Well, but you can't expect—' Lydia began. Wasn't the colour of love always blue?

'I don't expect ...' Izzy said, taking a pull at her drink. 'I *know* it only lasts a month or two and if it's what you want you have to split and start again. Cheaper than changing the wallpaper.'

'Sounds exhausting,' Lydia said.

'Dead right,' Izzy said. 'I'm resting at the moment.'

'But surely you have to accept—' Lydia said.

'I do bloody accept . . .' Izzy said, lifting the gin bottle. 'Freshener?'

'No, thanks. Don't you miss people, yearn afterwards?'

'I do rather miss the telly.' Izzy's shrug was a shade too elaborate. 'Just haven't got round to getting another one. Did I tell you I'm thinking of starting an after-school dance club? Anyway, what are you looking so peaky about?'

'Didn't know I was,' Lydia frowned. 'I worry about Annie.'

'What's new? Must be undermining to have your mother worrying about you all the time.'

'But she hasn't been in touch for ages and Ed wants to sell the house and I suppose I'm a bit thrown about where I'm going and what to do,' Lydia said in a rush.

'What, no brilliant offer from Gallimard begging you to translate a previously undiscovered Colette novel?'

Lydia sipped. It was not that she thought of translation as creative, unlike the other translators she met. *Creative* was making something where nothing was before.

'It's my life you're being so amusing about, Izz.'

'Sorry,' Izzy said. 'It's the hot weather. Sign on again here. Grapevine says they haven't appointed anybody yet.'

Lydia shook her head. 'No, thanks.'

'Why not?' Izzy sat down in the chair facing her. 'You've taught successfully for ten years. To be realistic, it's not that easy to change horses mid-stream at your age.'

'Whose side are you on?'

'Yours, of course, but it's stupid to pretend. People *become* what they do. The longer they do it, the better they get at it, *ipso facto*. Meanwhile they're *not* getting better at anything else.'

'What about Gauguin?' Lydia said suddenly.

'Gauguin was a *man* and a very considerable painter.' Izzy clapped her hand to her brow. 'Oh my God, don't tell me you're joining the droves of middle-aged ladies who paint? Clifton Arts Club has a waiting list long as an orang-utan's arm.'

'Well, it's *my time* now and I want to paint,' Lydia said. She had never said as much to anybody before, hardly admitted it to herself. She was not even sure she had sufficient talent, let alone the courage and dedication to let it evolve. 'Lots of middle-aged women paint well. If I could get some translation work for now and buy a cottage—'

'Cornwall? Lamorna Cove, don't tell me,' Izzy said. 'You're in fantasy land, kid. It's too late. Anyway you *don't* paint. When did you spend all day painting, for instance?'

'Actually, I've done an evening class in painting for years but I just don't talk about it.'

'You dark horse, you.'

'I wanted to go to art school, but Mother said a language degree and teaching was more secure.'

'Violin time for poor frustrated Lydia,' Izzy said. 'How is the dragon lady, by the way?'

'Stop it,' Lydia said, smiling despite herself. The title did fit Mother's hot-air style rather well. 'I'll have you know my mother is nobody's fool. She's back at The Cottage actually. I must go, Izz . . . Year Eight's papers.'

'What happened to your weekend? Making whoopee?' Izzy said, though her tone suggested she considered this unlikely.

'Had a visit from an old flame. He asked me to marry him,' Lydia said, and immediately wished she hadn't.

'No wonder you didn't get your marking done.' Izzy's eyes widened. 'Hard luck, Year Eight. Did you say yes?'

'Of course not. He didn't really mean it, it's just his wife's died and he's all confused, retired GP with heart trouble.' She decided not to mention the plate. 'Keeps taking his pulse.'

'Face it, you've more experience as a wife than a painter.'

'Never was much good at it, though,' Lydia said.

'Me neither,' Izzy said, and for a moment her mouth drooped. 'Still, practice makes perfect. Don't you need to be needed?'

'Not three meals a day needed.' Lydia got up.

'Might be your last chance,' Izzy said.

'Do you have to be so forthright?' Lydia asked. 'You get married if you're so keen on it.'

'That's telling her.' Izzy rolled her eyes.

'Anyway, look at Margaret next door, she's getting married tomorrow at seventy-four. Thanks for the drink. See you.'

What would happen to Izzy eventually? Lydia wondered, as she drove home. But then what happened to everybody eventually, Mother and James, for instance . . .?

Belstones' 'For Sale' notice floated high above the front gate against the relentless blue sky. Lydia let the car glide down the slope into the familiar garage, and wondered, as the garage door clanged down, how many more times she would do so. The guinea pig hutch was still there; the guinea pigs had welcomed her home cheeping cheerily through cold midwinters. Didn't they eat them in Ecuador? She might not paint at the moment but her head was full of ideas for pictures. Annie thought in pictures too.

She opened the front door, switched off the alarm and switched on the kettle just as the phone rang. Would she take this call from Penzance, a Miss Annie Kemp, reversing the charges? the operator enquired.

'Ma?' Annie's voice was quavery but she had to do it.

'I was just thinking about you, darling. How're you doing?'

'OK. I reversed the charges,' Annie said.

'I know. Lovely to hear you. How's Penzance?'

'Bit hot.'

'Hot everywhere,' Lydia said. 'Right weather for "still life", if they do "still life" at art school nowadays.'

'What?' Annie said.

'You know . . . fruit in a bowl and stuff. You do some painting surely?'

'Not much,' Annie said. She didn't *want* to tell Ma lies.

'You getting on better with Mrs Trewartha?'

'What?'

'Your landlady, Mrs Trewartha?'

'Mm.' You couldn't call 'mm' a lie.

'Why don't you put the address on your postcards?'

'Oh . . . I'll put it on my next postcard because I'm not going to phone any more,' Annie said quickly.

'But, darling, why not? You can always reverse the charges.' Lydia was suddenly breathless.

'Well . . .' Annie said. Trouble was Ma could talk her into anything – elocution lessons, freezing swimming baths, it had always been like that. Good job Jarvis wasn't listening but, like he said, she did have a tongue of her own. 'I'll send you a postcard every month.'

'Why not once a week?' Lydia said, trying to keep cool, not to get angry.

'You know I hate writing.'

'That's why I suggested the phone,' Lydia said. 'Phone once a week and reverse the charges.'

'Can't,' Annie said. It was like she belonged to Ma, like she was her plaything. Like Jarvis said, she didn't need it.

'Annie, please?' But Annie had put the phone down.

Lydia made herself a cup of camomile tea, 'calming' the packet promised. What was it all about – Annie breaking free or was there a boyfriend she didn't know about?

The sun had already moved off the rose garden. She had better get the watering done before she settled. The butt was almost empty but she scooped deep and spattered what she could on the pale parched earth underneath the yellowy petals of Peace and crimson petals of Fragrant Cloud.

Next door there was deep silence, the curtains closed. Margaret had sung her song and gone off to marry Bertie at Rye. *Quel courage!* For the moment she was flying high on love but what would happen when she came down?

What was *between* Margaret and Bertie?

Lydia stared towards the house, suddenly bereft of her neighbour's affirming presence. She could phone William; good-natured, content with himself, he was a comfort if she felt low . . . but she couldn't be doing with Ruby.

Ten miles away at the cottage in Pill, Ruby examined herself in the mirror. She had tried out her sunbed yesterday. A tan was sexy but peeling wasn't.

'What's wrong with getting married? Why you against it?'

'Nothing,' William said. 'I'm crazy about it, crazy about you, Ruby darling. It's just we have to be sure, both of us.'

'You think I'm not good enough, don't you?'

'Course I don't,' William said with emphasis. 'I mean it's great between us now but marriage has to last a long time . . . well, for ever in my book.'

'Like your mum and dad, for instance?'

'Quite,' William said. 'Like me to get the supper?'

* * *

In the house the phone rang. 'Been trying to get you all day.' Mother sounded hysterical. 'I can't put up with it.'

'Put up with what, dear?' Lydia said, projecting calm.

'James. He's back at The Cottage.'

'But how did he know you were there?'

'Phoned the ward, *with it* when it suits him. I explained to Sister that *nobody* was to say I'd gone, but there you are . . . The Lilacs phoned, said James was missing and he won't go back. It's me has to fetch his stuff . . .'

'Perhaps they could send—'

'It's me should be waited on. He'll be wanting cups of tea all day and then he wets his bed. Like Dr Hardy said, "Let your husband wait on himself, Mrs Price, or you'll be back in hospital." Know what the home help said?'

'Tell me,' Lydia said. Poor James, she thought, poor Mum.

'Said I should get a divorce. "You want to get a divorce, dear," that's what she said. "Get a divorce." '

'But James is eighty-eight, Mother,' Lydia said. 'Have a heart.'

CHAPTER FOUR

THE HEATWAVE WENT on, Tuesday another hot day, the sky pale blue with wisps of cloud delicate as butterfly wings, the garden earth the colour of sand. Lydia had read that the British Isles had been south of the equator once and now found it easy to believe. The world was changing, alternately drowning or running out of water, species which couldn't adapt dying out. Kangaroos had been predators once.

She was having breakfast when the phone rang. Annie or Mother? she wondered, and was startled to hear Marina.

'Jeremy's in Leeds.' Marina's voice was diffident. 'Giving a paper, "Who Needs History?" I thought of dropping in, Ma.'

'Lovely, darling. Come for supper. I'll get something to have cold with salad and we'll eat outside. This weather's amazing – exhausting though. If only it would rain. Grandma's back at The Cottage; so is James unfortunately. Have you heard from Annie?' Marina's spare style always pushed Lydia into excess loquacity. 'Had a postcard or anything?'

'You're the person she keeps in touch with,' Marina said.

'But you're all right?'

'Quite,' Marina said. Ed said *quite* by itself like that; William too. 'See you later then, Ma.'

'Tonight,' Lydia said, putting down the phone. She looked at the garden with Marina's fastidious eyes: delphiniums, collapsed in exhausted heaps like dead peacocks. She would water round the roots and stake them upright tonight. Years ago she had planted little ferny plants from St Nicholas' market. 'If you must put herbaceous plants in what is meant to be a shrubbery,' Ed had said, 'why not get red-hot pokers, which at least stay upright?'

He was right, of course; Ed was always right, Marina very much his daughter. But what was she going to do about Annie? And Mother and James come to that? And Richard? Perhaps she should apologise for throwing that plate. It wasn't his style or hers.

By now school had resumed its normal post-exam routine, the noise level reduced by a number of pupils on work experience and a Year Ten group which had gone to Sweden.

'The Swedes get everything right,' Izzy said at breaktime. 'Did you know that ninety-six per cent of them belong to their libraries, whereas about thirty-five per cent belong here? Their borrowing per person is mega too.'

'Could be the long dark evenings,' Lydia suggested.

'Philistines rule OK,' Izzy said gloomily. 'If we can't be first in football, at least we can lead the world back to the Dark Ages.' Izzy pushed at her hair impatiently. 'Sorry I came on a bit strong yesterday, Lyddy. Distrust unsolicited advice. Giving it is addictive and you never know where it's coming from nor where it's been,' she added. 'Having had ten years teaching French *imposed* on you and bringing up three kids on your own *imposed* on you, I reckon you're entitled to paint your socks off if it's what you want.'

'You did seem rather sure of what was for my own good.'

'I'm a witch, I get these insights,' Izzy said in a quavery sing song. 'Life's a slippery plank over dark water.'

'Well, I do have to eat and live somewhere and the money from the house won't last for ever,' Lydia said. Was it the heatwave made decisions so difficult?

'Roll on the end of term,' Izzy said. 'Did I tell you I've fixed a visit to The Globe next week? Years Nine and Ten in two coaches, *Two Gents of Verona*, takes all day, of course.'

'That should hold off the Dark Ages another week,' Lydia said.

'I shall miss you,' Izzy said. 'But I shan't get to Cornwall "in the deep midwinter when frosty winds make moan," so be warned.'

After school Lydia drove out to Waitrose instead of the usual Spar nearer home, pushing the trolley quickly, buying ham, salami, lettuce, mango, cantaloupe melon and a miniature Cointreau. It was after she got home that she saw the note scrawled in green ink and tucked under her windscreen wiper.

'*Chere Madame*,' she read. '*Tu es tres belle et tres bonne. Je suis desirant que tu est ma grande amie et ma grande soeur. Comment allez vous?*'

Bethany. She crumpled the unsigned note and pushed it into her pocket. Still, her French had improved.

She ran cold water into the sink. 'Never *cut* lettuce leaves,' Mother, disciple of Mrs Beeton, intoned in her head. Lydia broke lettuce into the sink and washed it with care. Marina did domestic tasks from the book too, a counterformation just as she was a counterformation to Mother, though nowadays she was aware of moving reluctantly towards her mother's pattern.

Of course, half Marina's genes came from Ed-the-punctilious, Lydia thought, slicing melon and mango together, adding Cointreau. She wiped pinkish dust like pollen from the white table outside and laid it with glasses and napkins.

If only it would rain.

The whole house needed dusting but Marina was unlikely to go upstairs. She hadn't had the chance to dust for Richard either. She ought to phone and suggest bereavement counselling. He didn't think of himself as needy. Doctors disliked role reversal, which was why they made bad patients.

Presently the bell rang. Marina stood on the doorstep, stylish in a long black shift sparsely dotted with small blue flowers, her straight dark hair loose around her shoulders. She had small features and blue-grey eyes, black-lashed.

'Hello, darling, you look nice,' Lydia said, kissing her cheek. 'Like a Botticelli *Venus*, anybody ever tell you?'

'Only you, Ma,' Marina said.

'But you look a bit pale. Weather's OTT, isn't it?'

'Mm,' Marina faintly smiled.

'White wine or would you rather have a soft drink?'

'White wine, please,' Marina said. If things had been different, she thought, she would have asked for orange juice.

'Sit down, I'll get it,' Lydia said, collecting the bottle from the fridge. 'Here you are.'

'I see the house is officially up for sale at last,' Marina remarked, sitting at the white table.

'Afraid so. Bit sad but, well, it's a family house.' Lydia glanced across the garden. The delphiniums had perked up quite a bit. 'And now you're all grown up . . .'

'Where will you go?'

'Not sure yet. I'll fetch the food.' Lydia had once supposed decision-making got easier. But words like *choice* and *freedom*,

glamorous when you first whisked them through your head, seemed
to become more diminishing every day.

'It's lovely to see you on your own for once,' she said, setting the
tray of food down. Did that sound possessive? 'Leeds, you said? Help
yourself, darling. How is Jeremy?'

'Fine,' Marina said. 'Managed to get hold of some real old
flagstones for the garden. What's this about Grandma?'

'Well, she's home,' Lydia said. 'Unfortunately James is home too.
She was hoping he'd stay at The Lilacs. I'm going over there when
I can but we've only just had exams . . .'

'We could go if you'd like?' Marina said. A biddable child, she
had always been her grandmother's favourite.

'Well, I'm sure she'd love to see you when she's stronger,' Lydia
said. Was she determined *not* to be usurped as *supportive daughter*?

'This looks good,' Marina said, helping herself to very small
portions. 'Could be your hostess skills are improving, Ma.'

'That's quite enough of that,' Lydia said. 'When *you* have a family
and a full-time job, you'll get a bit slapdash.'

'Perhaps,' Marina said, her smile wilting. She twirled watercress
between pearl-lacquered fingers. Disappointment was better shared,
Jeremy said. He assumed she confided in her mother, discussed
intimate details just as his sisters and mother did. She had told him
it wasn't like that but quite a lot she said to Jeremy, cast in a different
mould, never really took root.

Lydia allowed the silence, embraced the moment. Something
was wrong but she didn't know what. Fallen blossoms of pink and
white fuchsia lay in a circle round the drooping plant.

'Bit more ham or have you finished?' she asked eventually.

'Oh, no more, thanks.'

'Sit still.' Lydia cleared the plates, coming back with slices of
white melon covered in orange slices of mango. The intensity of
Marina's gaze made her nervous.

'I thought it would be easier to eat this with small knives and
forks,' she said. 'Melon in swaddling clothes, swaddled in mango
and Cointreau.'

'I like everything,' Marina said softly. 'Swaddling' was
unfortunate. 'Last week I thought I was pregnant.'

'But you're not?' Lydia said. Marina shook her head.

'I'm so sorry, darling, perhaps . . . perhaps you should see somebody,' Lydia said. 'I mean there are tests . . .'

'See somebody?' Marina cried, her voice rising. 'I've been *seeing somebody*, as you put it, for years and years, Ma. I just didn't want to talk about it, that's all.'

'I see,' Lydia said, trying not feel hurt. 'Perhaps we should talk about it now, though. It might be a help.'

'How?' Marina said softly, and a shiver went through her slight body. 'I can't bear everybody whispering. A woman without a child isn't complete . . .'

'Well . . .' Lydia said. Was this the post-feminist view? 'I don't accept that. Lots of remarkable women are childless,' she added, unable for the moment to think of any except Jeanne d'Arc and Elizabeth Tudor; neither seemed appropriate.

'We're getting to the end of the road with Metrodin and Pregnyl and sperm counts and taking my temperature,' Marina said. 'It feels like we're making love in a chemistry lab. I mean, it's been hideous for Jeremy . . .'

Jeremy had been a rowing Blue.

'Tough for you too, love. I wish you'd told me.'

'I couldn't.' A shadow crossed Marina's face. 'They're talking about IVF now but the success rate is quite low and each time it costs two thousand pounds. It isn't fair. Everybody has a baby but we've got to *buy* ours . . .' She blinked pink eyelids. Was she going to say it? She wasn't sure she could. Even if she could, should she? Better out than in, Jeremy always said, but was he right?

'You told them about the abortion?' Lydia said. 'Do they think it's to do with that?'

'Of course,' Marina said, deadpan. 'I was fifteen.'

'I'm not blaming you,' Lydia said.

'Well, I *am* blaming *you*,' Marina said, her eyes glistening blue like wet ink, her heart thudding in her chest.

'Blaming me? But . . . it wasn't as if you were ignorant, Marina. I told you all I could about safe sex and being careful and *not* getting pregnant. We talked about everything . . .'

Marina stared at her empty plate. 'I saw you in Weston. Me and Kevin, we saw you in Weston that weekend. You said you were visiting Grandma, had to go early Friday to miss the weekend traffic. Kevin and I got the bus to Weston, but you didn't go to Grandma's, did you?'

'Yes, I did . . .' Lydia said, breathless.

'I saw you in Weston that Friday night, Ma. I saw you with that Richard person. We followed you to a hotel.' Lydia said nothing. 'The risk . . . I mean what if Dad had phoned Grandma?'

'I phoned Dad from a Weston callbox,' Lydia said in a low voice. 'Said I'd arrived but Grandma's phone was out of order.'

If Marina heard she took no notice.

'What do you think it felt like? As if it didn't matter what happened to the family. I couldn't get myself together, we missed the last bus . . . spent the night under the pier . . . and it happened. If you didn't care, why should I?'

'And Dad?' Was that how Ed discovered? Lydia wondered.

'I phoned Will, told him I was staying over with Rosie.'

'You poor little girl, why didn't you tell me?'

'Why should I? You betrayed us, Ma, threw us away for a one-night stand. At fifteen I didn't know people like mothers did things like that. If you hadn't been there, I wouldn't have got pregnant and had to have an abortion. I'd have two or three babies by now.'

'Is that what the consultant says?'

'It's what he thinks.'

'I'm sorry,' Lydia said. Was it the conflict of roles, mother, wife, lover, made the situation so bizarre? 'But it was a long time ago.'

'That makes it all right?' Marina flicked at her hair. 'I'm sorry too. Sorry I may never ever have a baby.'

'Does Annie know about this?'

'What's Annie got to do with it? Always Annie with you, isn't it? Annie and her wonderful painting . . .'

'What do you want me to say, Marina?'

'Try "Life is tough and then you die",' Marina said, getting up. 'I'm going home.'

Late that night Lydia lay in bed sleepless, remembering the night in Weston, cold salmon in the dining room, tinned Russian salad, a cracked mirror in the wardrobe door of a cheap hotel, headlights crossing the bedroom ceiling, the wonder of a love so urgent, so hungry, she wanted to die, swallow Juliet's poison . . . extend the short moment into eternity.

Ten years on, Richard, flattened by bereavement and a worn-out heart, offering her marriage. The irony of it. Marina suddenly accusing her of being responsible for the abortion and her infertility . . . Talk about chickens coming home to roost.

But Marina, at fifteen, had been older than Juliet. Was the mishap, the pregnancy, all Lydia's fault? Anything wrong in your child's life made you feel guilty; *guilt* was part of 'Homo sapiens' survival kit', wasn't it?

It was true that for a few weeks her passion for Richard had taken over, put every ordinary consideration out of her head, lifted the constraints by which she, and most people in the affluent civilised world, lived.

Outside it started to rain. First a shower and then a steady downpour that grew in volume as she listened. Cleansing rain that battered the roof and streamed along the gutters like tropical rain, as if the whole world was weeping.

Lydia wept.

'It's raining,' Ruby said into the darkness after love. 'Rains a lot in Singapore. I went to the agency today.'

'You did?' William said, flat on his back, his arm still under her neck. Silence except for the rain.

'Anyway, there's this job with people called the Sandersons. Millionaires. They travel round the world all the time with two kids and three nannies.'

'Not church mice then?' William said coolly.

'Millionaires, billionaires, shouldn't wonder. What's that noise?'

'What?' William said. But Ruby had stepped to the window, her long hair swinging like a horsetail, her body slim and marble white in the streetlamp.

Suppose she went, William thought, suppose he never had her again? How could he bear it?

'You've gone and left my sunbed out, and it's all wet and spoiled . . .' Ruby said. 'You dickhead, you.'

PART TWO

Happenstance

CHAPTER FIVE

Driving home after school a fortnight later, Lydia let the car slide down to the garage where the electric mower was on charge. The lawn, like all the lawns in Cedar Avenue, was brown as coconut matting, spiked with bits of green since the rain. The garden had sprung a second spring. The magenta cistus had never been so brilliant; the hydrangea such a deep Victorian pink, each floret centred on a tiny blue eye; foxgloves invaded from the wild wood. Her 'mature garden' as Belstones described it, was certainly giving her a good send-off. Lydia was uncertain whether she was pleased.

She had shown two couples, the Sampsons and the Jacks, round last weekend but neither had shown much enthusiasm. 'Rather a labour-intensive garden,' Mr Sampson had remarked. Lydia juggled with relief and disappointment.

The eventual investigation of her bank statements had revealed a lower balance than in any previous statement on file. She had one more salary cheque to come. She dispatched two more letters to publishers and one to a university friend who appeared to survive on translation work. She still belonged to the Translators' Association, which made her seem professional to herself at least and might lead to something.

For the moment painting was on hold. Was this due to Izzy's scorn or just the daunting financial situation? Izzy was certainly right about her lack of art experience and Lydia was intending to make enquiries about classes at the West of England Academy when she had time. What had she got to lose? Either way she ought to have kept her ideas to herself, she decided, unlocking the front door and stepping quickly across the hall to switch off the alarm. A postcard from Annie lay on the mat. 'Job down here all summer. See you. Love Annie.'

Lydia smiled with relief. At least they were back on terms. She knew Annie didn't care for the telephone. The picture of blue sea and yellow beach and nine words felt like stepping into a warm bath. Annie was 'all right', and working through the vacation was better than getting into debt like lots of students. No address, but Annie's forgetfulness was legendary.

Did she worry about Annie too much, *undermining* her as Izzy said? Well, the world was hazardous and Lydia knew better than anybody just how vulnerable Annie was. Female turtles kept their eggs inside their shells until they found a place to lay them safe from marauding gulls. Annie was no match for marauding gulls.

Lydia made herself a cup of tea and trundled the mower from the door at the back of the garage on to the lawn. Next door the curtains were drawn back, Margaret and Bertie home again.

'Hello!' Lydia called over the hedge. 'Congratulations!'

Bertie, engrossed in scooping leaves from the swimming pool with a child's fishing net, didn't seem to hear her. He looked pleased with himself, understandable, Lydia thought, for someone who had exchanged a poky flat in Vauxhall or Streatham for the comfort of Cedar Avenue and Margaret's loving arms.

'Here you are, Bertie dear,' Margaret said, bustling out to the terrace in her towelling wrap with a tray of tea. She settled herself, watching him indulgently like a proud mother. Lydia steered the mower down the lawn.

'Hello, we're back, Bertie and me,' Margaret called over to the hedge. 'Lovely to be home. Wonderful time in Scotland, though. Bertie loved Scotland, didn't you, Bertie?' She looked from one to the other, distributing bountiful smiles like confetti. Bertie nodded and continued with his leaves.

'He doesn't hear very well, you have to speak up,' Margaret stage-whispered. 'He's getting the pool ready for my dip. Says we ought to build something over the pool, so we could heat it properly and swim all winter. Don't you, Bertie?' she added, raising her voice.

'What's that, dear?'

'I was telling Lydia, you want to enclose the swimming pool.'

'Wouldn't you have to get planning permission?' Lydia said. How would building next door affect the house sale? She felt herself blush as Bertie's blue eyes fixed on her. 'Are you keen on swimming too?'

'Bertie's not *as* keen but he knows all about planning

permission,' Margaret said. 'It'd be glass mostly, my own glass igloo.'

'Nice to have you back looking so bonny,' Lydia said. 'Congratulations! You're a good advert for married life.'

'It's being happy, haven't felt so happy for years,' Margaret confided. 'Well, never really. I mean with Frank . . . Still, that's all in the past. Come and say hello to Lydia, Bertie,' she called, raising her voice and extending her arm. 'Come along, my darling.'

Bertie put down his net and walked obediently round the pool. He was slightly built and moved more easily than Margaret and looked rather younger.

'We met at Margaret's Christmas party, didn't we?' Lydia said, putting her hand over the hedge.

'Of course,' he said, clutching the ends of her fingers in his. His eyes *were* a particularly bright blue, speedwell blue, and not just his eyes; his face, especially his chin, had a blueish tinge. Bluebeard, Lydia thought, seeing severed heads in a row. Why did she have to fantasise so nastily?

'But you're not so keen on swimming?' Lydia said loudly.

'Not in this country,' he said. 'North Africa in the war, swimming was OK there. If we build over the pool we can heat it properly.'

'Bertie has such wonderful ideas,' Margaret said, enclosing the hand which had touched Lydia's between both of hers.

'Isn't that your telephone, Mrs . . . er, Keep?' Bertie said.

'Oh . . . excuse me.'

'Lydia Kemp, *Kemp*, darling . . .' Margaret was saying as Lydia ran back to the house. Evidently he wasn't as deaf as all that.

'I've been trying to get you all day,' Mother said breathily. 'I can't put up with it, I can't . . .'

'Put up with what, dear?' Lydia said, taking a deep breath and trying to sound calm. Mother, being central to her own world, was inclined to assume Lydia had instant access.

'James. His daughters came round yesterday. The Ugly Sisters I call them, poking their noses in. You'd think The Cottage was going to *them* if anything happens to James. Hardly bother to talk to him, mind. "It's my time now," I told them, "and if James won't stop in The Lilacs I want a divorce . . ." '

Mother's voice flowed on, querulous but strong. It was best to let her talk, Lydia thought. Besides, she had no option.

'. . . waited on him hand and foot all these years, just rings his bell. Ding-dong, all day long. Know what Dr Hardy said? "Let your husband wait on himself, we don't want you back in hospital, Mrs Price." Know what the home help said?'

'Yes,' Lydia said.

' "You should get yourself a divorce," that's what she said.'

'But James is eighty-eight, Mother,' Lydia said, but people couldn't help being as they were, feeling as they felt.

'And I'm seventy-six. It's the age difference. I told my solicitor, "My husband, James, is too old for me." Twelve years is a big difference. I've been a good wife but men are so selfish. Only four years between your father and me.'

'Could you get extra home help?' Lydia said. She ought to know about all this kind of thing. 'Can't expect you to cope with all the extra washing.'

'But James expects . . . You've got to help me, Lydia. He might listen to you. Tell him he stops in The Lilacs or I get a divorce. I can't do with it, Lyddy, at my time of life with my arthritis. I can't put up with him . . .'

Mother was crying now – Mother who never cried, Mother who always knew what everybody else ought to do.

'Course, I'll come,' Lydia said, the firmness in her own voice unfamiliar. 'But it's term time, so I'll have to come at the weekend.' Right to Kent, she thought, all the way to Kent. 'Next weekend, all right?'

'Have to be, won't it? You will come, Lyddy, promise?'

'Yes, of course, Mother.'

Lydia put the phone down, walked out to the kitchen and poured herself a gin. Poor Mother, what a predicament. And as people lived longer now, the declining years must put an intolerable burden on the fitter partner. People talked all the time about the demise of the family, its caring function impaired by collapsing moral standards and a cash-strapped welfare state. By the millennium the divorce of the very old might well be commonplace.

A car paused on the road and then ran down the drive: William's battered Mini. Lydia opened the front door.

'William?'

'Hi, Ma. Just dropping in.'

44

'What a lovely surprise,' she said, stretching up to kiss his cheek. 'Mm. Like the aftershave!'

'Christmas present from a girl in the office. Phew!' He wrinkled his nose. 'You stink of gin.' He was tall, fair and looked what he was, a confident and good-natured young man.

'Want one?'

'No, thanks. Don't do gin.'

'Glad to hear it. But I've just had Grandma on the phone.'

'It figures.' He grinned and followed her to the kitchen.

'She wants to divorce James.'

William chuckled. 'What's the old devil been up to?'

'Getting too ancient, that's all,' Lydia said. 'Do you want to stay for supper, love? There's stuff in the freezer.'

'Great! I came to do the lawn actually.' He glanced towards the garden. 'Looks like an old brown dog!'

'I was just starting it,' Lydia said. 'What about Ruby?'

'Gone,' William said.

'You've split up?' Lydia tried not to sound relieved.

William shrugged. 'Suppose. She wanted us to get married, all that.'

'And you didn't? Much better wait if you're not sure.'

'Try telling that to Ruby.'

'Only child, isn't she? Used to having her own way?'

William's face was wooden. 'Ruby's got a sister actually, and we all *like* having our own way, Ma. Anyway, why do people get married?'

Lydia shrugged. 'To see what it's like? Children are the best bit.'

'Yeah? I'd better get on with the lawn,' William said.

'Haddock, salad, oven chips do you? Cherries for afters?'

'Sounds great.'

In the kitchen Lydia turned on the oven, took a double packet of haddock and chips out of the freezer, washed salad. She had never cared for Ruby but she had *tried* when it looked as if she might become her daughter-in-law. A pretty girl with red hair was likely to be spirited and Ruby was, but did she have to be so bossy, so critical of Will? She couldn't grieve for Ruby gone. Besides, getting over a broken heart was a rite of passage as well as an inoculation. If she opened a bottle of wine, would William interpret it as a celebration?

45

It was warm enough to eat outside. She put the fish and chips in the oven and carried a tray out. The garden was quiet, part of the lawn already shorn, striped light and dark brown. William stood by the hedge, talking to Bertie.

Half an hour later, lawn done and table laid, Lydia carried out the food and they settled at the table.

'How did you get on with Bertie?'

'Seems a nice enough old bloke,' William said, applying himself to his meal. 'Getting married at their age is a bit naff. I mean good luck to them but what's the point?'

'You might be surprised,' Lydia said, lowering her voice. 'They're very much in love, at least Margaret is. I do wonder if Bertie just has an eye to the main chance.'

'The mind boggles,' William muttered, shovelling chips. 'Did you ever think of getting married again, Ma?'

'Once you've got kids, suitors don't exactly queue at the front door,' Lydia said. She had married Ed because he was handsome, keen, professionally qualified and Mother liked him.

'What about that Richard bloke?'

'He was married already,' Lydia said.

'Married?' William's quick glance was surprised, even startled. Pendulums swung; you could end up with your children going trendily judgemental about transgressions of marital fidelity, Lydia thought. Actually it had happened already between her and Marina.

'Yes,' she said testily. Richard hadn't phoned. She required him to be reliable, but flying at him like that had she forfeited the right to have requirements? 'Anyway, how's work?'

William shrugged. 'Old Beavis takes the interesting stuff, us assistants are office fodder.'

'Still, you are learning, Will?'

He stared out over the garden. 'I miss her so, can't concentrate on anything.'

'Poor old boy.' She patted his hand. 'It'll get better, love. First time is the worst. You'll meet somebody else. What about the girl who gave you the aftershave?'

'Can't get interested in anybody else,' William said. 'Just miss Ruby all the bloody time.'

'Give yourself a chance. Anyway, where is she?'

'Singapore. People called the Sandersons, millionaires with two kids and a full set of nannies, all spinning round the world with Mum and Dad.'

'I had a postcard from Annie today,' Lydia said.

'Bet it said, "Job down here all summer. See you. Love Annie." Postmark Penzance.'

'Snap. Never tells you anything. Have you got her address? Gather she's left Mrs Trewartha.'

'Sorry,' William said with a sideways glance. Hadn't he promised not to give Annie's address to Ma? He phoned her sometimes; he and Annie had always been close. 'Scatty, our Annie, two sandwiches short of a picnic.'

'Do you think she'll come home at all this vac?'

'Doesn't sound like it,' William said. 'You do realise she's got some bloke?'

'Well, I sort of guessed . . .' Lydia said, wondering why confirmation chilled her so. 'Long as it doesn't interfere with her work. Anyway, why didn't she tell me?'

'She thinks you wouldn't approve. I gather he's not quite "out of the hanky-drawer".'

'What a ghastly expression.'

' "Fully paid-up member of the proletariat", that better?'

'Long as he suits Annie,' Lydia said heavily. 'By the way, I've got to drive over and see Grandma and James this weekend. Don't know what I'm going to say.'

'No problem. Let Grandma do the talking. Hell of a way to drive, why don't you go by train?'

'Expense,' Lydia said. 'No money coming in until the house sells; Cedar Avenue is F band for council tax . . .'

'I could drive you to Kent,' William said.

Lydia paused. 'Would you, Will? Sure you want to? You'll have to sleep on the Put-u-up . . .'

'Deal!' William said. 'Only let's get off early on Friday, miss the worst of the weekend traffic.'

'I *am* blaming *you*.' The words had rung in Lydia's head many times since Marina came to supper. Two weeks had passed but the reliable daughter who always phoned on Friday evening hadn't phoned since.

CHAPTER SIX

'WHICH WAY WE going?' Lydia asked, happy to relinquish the driving to William on Friday afternoon.

'M4, M25, A21,' he said, shifting the seat to accommodate his legs. Lydia said nothing. On her own she always took a scenic route, Winchester and Petersfield or right through Savernake Forest, enhancing the journey and the passing moment. She had always loved the forest; perhaps she would end up painting only trees? A compensation of the single life was the freedom to do things *your way* and you did get used to it. William did things his way but you had to be young to enjoy three-lane traffic, Lydia reflected, as they swooped down Falcondale Road towards the motorway.

She ought to have phoned Marina on Thursday, explained they were going to Grandma's for the weekend, just as if nothing had happened. Estrangements couldn't thrive if you ignored them. The thought of the phone ringing in the empty house seemed like a metaphor for Marina's empty body. She could imagine the damp darkness under Weston pier but she didn't want to think about it.

'Have you seen Marina lately?' she asked.

'Not since Christmas. She and Ruby don't exactly click.'

'I see,' Lydia said. Had he used the *present* tense by accident? William wasn't usually subtle in his use of words. Did he think and hope he and Ruby would get back together? Lydia sighed. Odd the way her children descended in sequence from Marina so brilliant to William very adequate to Annie so wayward and with less obvious gifts. Was it a genetic throw of the dice, or did it reflect the deterioration of the marriage?

As they entered the motorway her attention fixed on the noise of the Fiesta struggling to reach speed in the middle lane.

'It is ten years old, poor thing,' she said, as cars roared past.

'Don't be so pathetic, Ma,' William said.

They had left behind the hypermarkets round Cribbs Causeway, pioneer colonies of willowherb straggling up gravel embankments. Now Lydia gazed at fields of grazing cattle, yellow rape seed, yellow-green wheat, orchards; Satchmo's 'wonderful world', she thought. Was it landscapes she wanted to paint?

'Marina says I gave too much attention to Annie,' she said suddenly. 'Do you think that's true?'

'Dunno.' William didn't care for personal speculation, especially where no definite conclusion was likely to be reached. His eyes narrowed as he moved into the fast lane. He didn't want to talk, just to drive and think about Ruby. Ruby wrapped in her long red hair, Ruby so excitable, so inventive in bed. He had never met a girl like her, the way she knew just what he wanted, understood his body and hers.

What was he going to do? All he wanted to do was to put his head on the steering wheel, right there on the motorway, and sob like a baby. He had got off early from the office, special permission from Mr Beavis. 'My grandma's not well,' he had said. 'How many sick grandmas you got, young Kemp?' 'Only the one, sir,' William smiled politely. 'Let's keep it that way, shall we?' Mr Beavis said.

Midnight last night he had phoned the Raffles Hotel in Singapore. Sounds like the sea and chattering in foreign tongues but the Sanderson contingent had already moved on. 'Where to?' he had asked. 'Very sorry, sir, not at liberty to disclose that information,' the girl at reception had said in Cantonese-accented English.

'I don't know what I'm going to say to Mother,' Lydia said.

'Don't have to say anything. Just listen . . .'

'But suppose she insists on divorcing James?' The tip of James's tongue invaded her head, the way he licked his lips.

William shrugged. 'It's *her* life.'

'But poor old James . . . he really isn't up to all this.'

'Who is?' William said heavily. 'All snakes and no ladders, I mean . . .' Words spun in his head like lottery balls. Ruby, where are you? The Peninsular Hotel, Hong Kong was worth a try.

It was dusk when they reached The Cottage. Thirty years ago, anticipating his retirement, James had bought a seventeenth-century farmhouse – white walls and a steep brown roof – set in a square of garden with lawns, an old mulberry tree and a cowshed converted to a garage.

The light in the porch was on. Grandma, clad in a dressing gown with a scarf round her head, opened the front door as William drove in.

'Hush!' she whispered, fluttering round them like a large moth. 'He's asleep. I made sure of that, laced his cocoa.'

'Whisky or sleeping pills?' Lydia whispered.

'Never you mind.' Mother turned abruptly to William. 'Come in the kitchen, Will dear, I've made you some nice ham sandwiches.'

'Brilliant, Grandma.'

'What a handsome young man!' she said, her eyes wide, her smile flirtatious.

'I wish . . .' William said.

'I had to give the spare bedroom to Lydia, darling, so you've got the Put-u-up. We don't use the upstairs now.'

'Suits me.' William stretched his aching neck. 'Five hours, not bad going considering the traffic.' What would he give to have Ruby with him now – all his worldly goods, his eyes? No, not his eyes; he'd be useless to Ruby without his eyes.

'Put-u-up's brilliant, Grandma,' he added.

'How are you, dear? How's the new job?'

'Been there a year now.'

'Whatever you do, don't wake Granddad in the morning. I give him his breakfast in bed, shortens the day.' She winked.

Jeremy lay extended on the sofa reading the *Week*.

'Friday night. You going to phone your mother?' he murmured, suspecting a mood.

'Will's driving her to Grandma's,' Marina said, sipping camomile tea. 'I gather Ruby's taken off for Singapore.'

'Good riddance,' Jeremy said.

It was an hour before they got to bed, then cars chased and roared through Lydia's head all night. She dreamed of pink worms curling like tongues but woke to a bright Saturday morning and sounds of movement in the kitchen.

'Always give James breakfast in bed.' Mother was laying a tray.

'Shortens the day. Had a p.c. from Annie yesterday. Cup of tea, Lyddy?'

'Thanks,' Lydia said, tightening her dressing gown round her. 'Does James know I'm here? Shall I take his tray in?'

'Well, I'd better see to him first because of you-know-what. I got him his own toilet unit, looks like a space capsule, lavatory and wash basin, fitted *en suite* in his bedroom, so there's really no excuse . . .'

'Well, I dare say he can't—'

'Can if he wants to.' Mother's eyes were meaningfully round as she knocked on the bedroom door and went in. Voices, a lavatory flushed, she reappeared a few moments later.

'Dry today for once,' she said. 'Where's his tray?'

Annie leaned on the rail of the early morning Jersey ferry, watching Weymouth recede to a floating crust. The sea was something else, she thought, turquoise, sky blue, grey blue – ceanothus blue Ma would call it. Ma's head was full of words like 'ceanothus'.

Ferry did her head in first time, sick as a dog going. 'Morning sickness,' Dr Rinde-Smith said, 'part of being pregnant', him and the silverything, but she had morning sickness afternoons as well and what with the sea all rough that time and wondering if she might have to do it with Mr Spenser, help the speckything to grow or something, but Jarvis said 'No' because Mr Spenser had done it already but Jarvis didn't know everything. Both the Spensers had blue eyes and Annie and Ma had blue eyes too.

'Paint what's in your head,' Ma always said, but Annie's head was always bare as old Mother Hubbard's cupboard. Speckything was in the cupboard now with pinhead eyes of ceanothus blue . . . making her sick . . .

Lydia negotiated the door. James was sitting up in bed, an ancient pullover over his striped pyjamas, his thin hair on end, his jaw blotched with grey stubble like lichen.

'Edie?' he said huskily. A foetid smell hung over his bed.

'No, Lydia, James. I'm Lydia, your stepdaughter.'

He peered suspiciously. 'Where she put my glasses?'

'On the bedside table,' Lydia pointed. James picked them up and slid them into position.

'Lydia?' he said.

'Brought your breakfast.' She smiled encouragingly and put his cup of tea on the table, sliding the tray on to his knees.

'What she give me?' he said, staring down at it.

'Boiled egg and toast.'

'Always the same. I want sausage . . . dip in my egg.'

'Sorry. No sausage.'

'Morning.' William's tousled head came round the door.

'Do I know you, young man?'

'Course you do, Granddad,' William said.

'My son, William, we're here for the weekend.'

'Never tells me anything,' James said. 'Want my breakfast in peace.'

After breakfast Lydia washed up, William dried and Grandma made a fresh pot of tea.

'Let's take this to the sitting room, be a bit civilised.'

'Think I'll go out.' William glanced at the window.

'All right, dear,' Grandma said. 'Lovely county, Kent, the garden of England.' She waved as William's feet crunched down the gravel drive. 'Nice boy, my grandson. Mrs Gibbs has got three grandsons already, mind you.'

'You've got four granddaughters, Mother,' Lydia said.

'You two girls haven't done so bad. Have to get his lordship up in a minute, can't dress himself . . .' Mother squared her shoulders. 'I can't go on like this . . .'

'Did you see the solicitor?' Lydia said, carrying the tray.

'Course I did – Mr Adams, in Ashford. Told James I was going shopping, tell a lot of white lies nowadays.' She sighed at this duplicity after a lifetime of calling a spade a spade. 'Said to Mr Adams straight out – Mr T. J. Adams he is, T is for "Theodore", means gift of God, "William" means gift of God too. I told him straight out, "I want to divorce my husband, James Price, aged eighty-eight." He wasn't shocked or anything. "Lots of older folk are getting divorced nowadays," he said. "We all expect to get more out of life."'

'Hush!' she said suddenly. 'I can hear him now, James, trying to get himself up.' She lowered her voice to a whisper. 'He'll call me in a minute, you wait. "Course, you may have to sell The Cottage," Mr Adams said. I told him straight that wasn't right when I'd done such a lot to the garden. The mulberry tree's been here years but I planted the apple trees and all the roses. But it's getting too big for us, we don't use the upstairs now. James hasn't been up in years.'

There was a tapping sound in the passage.

'What's he up to now?' she whispered. Her face was pale, stricken. 'Never know what to expect. I'd be better off in a little retirement flat on my own with just the one bedroom. I can't go on like this . . .'

'I hear what you're saying, Mother,' Lydia said. She made her voice sound reasonable but she didn't *want* to hear all this; she had enough going on in her own life.

'We have to talk it through, think of the consequences. A divorce is going to upset James terribly, upset you both and where are *you* going to go? Have you looked at retirement flats or anything yet?'

Mother opened her handbag. 'I cut this out the local paper. Bay Tree Retirement Flats on the outskirts of town. I went round the show flat after I'd seen Mr Adams . . .'

'What show flat?' James stood in the sitting-room doorway leaning on his stick. He was fully dressed in blue shirt, white cotton jacket and speckly tweed trousers. A striped tie swung from his hand. 'What you going on about now, woman?'

'What you want to get all dressed up for?' she said shrilly, just as William came in the front door.

'Because . . . we are going out to luncheon,' James said with dignity. 'If somebody would very kindly tie my tie . . . ? And you, young man, would very kindly phone the King's Arms and book a table for luncheon?'

'Certainly, Granddad, if that's what everybody wants.'

'I think we'd all rather stay here, James,' Lydia said.

'I've got a cold chicken for lunch,' her mother said.

'Hate cold chicken,' James shouted hoarsely. 'One moment she says I don't take her anywhere, next moment she's going to divorce me but I don't listen.' He was struggling to pull his hearing aid from his ear. It pinged against the doorjamb as he swivelled back to the passage, slamming the sitting-room door behind him. His stick tapped back towards his bedroom.

'Phew!' William said. 'Does he really want me to phone?'

'Don't worry,' Grandma said, enlivened by the encounter, a

bright pink patch on each cheek. 'He won't remember. Doesn't remember a thing from one minute to the next . . .'

CHAPTER SEVEN

For the rest of the morning James stayed in his room. William read through *Country Life* and then went for another walk. Lydia got out the vacuum cleaner, *acting* the dutiful daughter, she thought wryly. Despite the increased frequency of visits, the home help's cleaning did not seem very thorough.

'Very good of you, dear,' Mother said. 'Doesn't keep it like I did – well, you can't expect it when it's not *her* home. Marina phoned, I told her you were coming, told her Mrs Gibbs' granddaughter was expecting too.' She pottered after Lydia with a duster, adding bits to the already familiar story of her encounter with Theodore Adams, the divorce, Bay Tree Retirement Flats and what everybody thought about it.

'Shall I have a go upstairs while I'm about it?' Lydia said, picking up the vacuum and preparing to mount the staircase. 'Won't take me a minute.'

'No, thank you,' Mother said sharply. 'Upstairs isn't safe, didn't I tell you?'

'What do you mean, *isn't safe?*'

'Dry rot in the floorboards,' Mother said, and added with an odd laugh, 'You can put your foot right through some places. Had to get Mr Stagg to look at it only last week.'

'Mr Stagg?'

'Local builder. Betty swears by him. Course, he *is* her cousin. He's putting in new floorboards soon as he can find the time.' Mother's face was flushed.

'Lot of cowboys about,' Lydia said, going up two steps. 'I'll have a look. Whereabouts is the dry rot?'

'You're not to go up there,' Mother said, echoing the angry-mummy voice of childhood. 'Come down at once. I don't go poking my nose round every corner of your house, do I?'

'Only trying to help.' Lydia came slowly down. Why was Mother so agitated, eyes darting like frightened mice?

'Course you were, dear, but I'd never forgive myself if you did yourself an injury. Let's have a nice cup of coffee.'

Waiting. William was tired of waiting. In the King's Arms he changed a five-pound note for coins at the bar and made for the call box. Tapped 153 for International Enquiries. Time was seven hours later, morning in England, evening in Hong Kong.

'What country?'

'Hong Kong. The number of the Peninsula Hotel, Hong Kong.'

Waiting. A computerised voice gave him the number.

'Thank you,' he said, and his heart leaped as he tapped it in. Ruby's voice, just to hear Ruby's voice.

'Hello?' A man's voice, accented and staccato. 'Peninsula Hotel. Can I help you?'

'I want to speak to Miss Ruby Field, please.'

'Room number, sir?' Another coin.

'Don't know,' William's voice rose. 'She's with the Sandersons.'

'Staying Peninsular Hotel?'

'Yes, with the Sandersons.'

'Wait . . . I look . . .' Waiting and waiting. Another coin. 'We have Mr and Mrs Sanderson here. What name you say?'

'Ruby Field. She's one of the Sandersons' nannies.'

'Nannies?' Another wait, another coin.

'Nanny for children?'

'Yes.' Waiting.

'Think she go out,' the voice said.

'What?'

'Take children out.' The voice was more confident now.

'Are you sure?'

'Sure I'm sure.' The voice had changed – Americanized, shades of Clint Eastwood, evidently a film fan. 'Try later. OK?'

'No,' William shouted. 'Wait. Please . . .'

But the phone had already gone down.

That afternoon Lydia spread her rug under the mulberry tree where James lay in his deckchair with his panama tipped towards his nose. He had stayed in his room for the rest on the morning, picked at his cold chicken salad in silence and afterwards retired to the garden.

Lydia waited. What was she going to say when he woke? The relationship between step-parent and child was never easy, especially in a culture where people cut their teeth on 'Snow White'. James had suddenly appeared from nowhere, or so it had seemed to thirteen-year-old Lydia.

In the all-female household she and Mother were already embattled, Mother declaring boundaries, Lydia attacking them. James had been an intruder. At first he had seemed to prefer Unity, sixteen and pretty, but on the day of her fourteenth birthday, he had come into Lydia's bedroom.

'Happy birthday,' he had said, eyes bird-bright as his arm snaked round her shoulders and he kissed her full on the lips, his tongue probing into her mouth where no tongue but her own had ever been, setting her heart thudding with excitement and revulsion. 'Get off,' she whispered, breaking free with the room reeling round her. 'Go away.' 'Little birthday kiss, no harm done? Better not tell your mother,' he muttered as Unity opened the door. 'What's up, Lyddy, you're white as a sheet?' 'Bit faint?' Mother said, coming in as James slid out. 'The usual, is it, on your birthday? What a shame, Lyddy darling.'

Lydia had never mentioned it, didn't think of it in the daytime unless she saw James. But the tip of his tongue licking his lips was like the pink worm of her dreams. If she spoke of it now to James would it exorcise the experience?

Would he remember? It was unlikely to have traumatised him. He had never kissed her again, never referred to it. Was it why he'd adopted the role of champion, interceding with Mother, playing buffer between her and Lydia just as Lydia herself was playing buffer between the two of them now? James already seemed to sleep much of the day. Suppose she did try to talk about it, a last chance to fumigate her dreams? But was *talking* the universal cure-all it was cracked up to be? Besides, she was supposed to be talking about The Lilacs and Mother not being strong enough to cope and all that.

A bird fluttered in the mulberry tree above and James stirred, yawned and opened his eyes.

'Oh, it's you . . . Edie?' he dredged from somewhere.

'Lydia,' she said. 'Your stepdaughter. I think we ought to talk, James dear.'

'Your mother does the talking in this house,' he said, turning his face away.

'How did you get on at The Lilacs when Mother was in hospital?' she asked. 'Nice and quiet, was it? Peaceful?'

'I'm not going back there,' he said, turning back, his eyes dark with suspicion. 'What's she been saying?'

'Mother's not well. She had to go into hospital for a rest, didn't she? She finds looking after you too much . . . all the extra washing. You have to think of her, James.'

'I think of her all the time, do like she says, knock on her door for a cup of tea, like I'm a servant . . .'

'Perhaps you could get *yourself* a cup of tea sometimes?'

'But she's my wife, her *job* to look after me.' His eyes were wet now. 'I've been a good husband, brought up her girls like my own, and now she wants to divorce me . . . dump me in the rubbish bin . . .' Tears ran down his cheeks.

'Reckon she's got a fancy man upstairs. Goes up in the afternoons when I'm asleep. Can't get up there any more.'

'Oh, James . . . there's nobody upstairs, just dry rot in the floor. Mother isn't strong enough to look after you; you're neither of you strong and it's not going to get any better. She wants you to stay at The Lilacs because she can't manage you and The Cottage and everything to see to . . .'

'Put me down like an old dog,' he said, pulling a red and white spotted handkerchief from his pocket and dabbing at his eyes. 'Talk, talk, talk, all day long. Wants to get The Cottage for herself and her fancy man, that's what she wants, but I won't put up with it. I won't . . .' His voice, fuelled with indignation, was quite strong. 'Thinks she can divorce me behind my back, get everything. Greedy, that's what she is. Well, I'm stopping here. The Cottage is mine, bought it and paid for it, I did.'

'The property is in both your names, James.'

A bird flew up from the mulberry tree squawking, and caught his attention. He stared up at the green leaves, his eyes picking out half-hidden berries, coral pink through crimson red to damson black, his silent lips counting . . .

'Fifty,' he said suddenly, and grinned. 'Always wants her own way, does Joan. Wouldn't let you go to art school, would she? You know why?' He smiled like a mischievous child. 'Because she couldn't get in herself, not good enough.'

'That's ridiculous, James. Her family were hard up, six children, they couldn't possibly have afforded . . .'

He laid a brown-speckled hand on her arm. 'You young folk think you know it all but you don't. In the WAAF, wasn't she? Anyone in the forces could get a "further education grant" afterwards. Joan tried art schools all over the shop, took her portfolio round, couldn't get a place. Talking, that's what she's good at, talk the hind legs off a donkey.'

'She told you this?' Lydia asked.

'Course she did. Before we married . . . but don't let on I told you or she might divorce me.' He chuckled and closed his eyes. 'Might divorce me . . .'

'If you won't go into The Lilacs, I think Mother *will* divorce you,' Lydia said.

'Can't. She's my wife. Talk, talk, talk . . .'

'James?' she said, and for a moment his eyelids quivered but his breathing deepened into sleep.

A few minutes later Mother came out with a tray of tea. Lydia carried it to the teak seat.

'Did he say anything?'

'Not really,' Lydia said.

Nothing had changed. Sometime perhaps she would ask Mother about the WAAF and not getting into art school but not now. It might not be true. She didn't remember Mother ever painting or even talking about painting but James would hardly have made it up. Was it the reason Mother had been so against Lydia going to art school, that she couldn't bear her to succeed where she had failed?

'He won't go into The Lilacs. Maybe you could try somewhere else?' Lydia said as William came in the gate.

'Only be the same thing.' Mother glanced across the lawn at James asleep in his deckchair and smiled wanly. 'Poor old man, he'll have to go to The Lilacs if I divorce him. The Ugly Sisters don't want him, The Cottage will be sold and I'll buy myself a flat at the Bay Tree. I'll ring my solicitor Monday . . . Theodore Adams.'

'Selling The Cottage may take a long time,' Lydia said as William joined them. 'Perhaps you should wait a bit.'

'I'm not getting any younger . . .'

'Things may sort themselves out, Grandma,' William said.

'But it's my time now,' she said. 'You don't want to put yourselves out because I'm old. Go on like this, James'll see me out in my box first and that's a fact.'

'Oh Mother, it's not like that,' Lydia said, and wondered if it was. 'We don't want you to do something you'll regret.'

Mother turned her back ostentatiously. 'Would you like a pizza for your supper, William dear?'

'Smashing, Grandma. If you can spare it.'

'Got it for you, didn't I? I'll make some fresh tea. Had a nice walk?'

'Great. Everything's so green here,' he said, stretching his long arms above his head with a sigh, smelling of beer and cigarette smoke, his head still full of the Peninsular Hotel, Hong Kong.

'I think we should get off early tomorrow, Will,' Lydia said. 'I've got a load of marking, and lessons Monday morning.'

'OK, Ma,' William said.

They left the following morning, turning into winding lanes, past fruit farms where chalked notices, faded or new, invited them to pick raspberries, strawberries, cherries in season.

'Shouldn't I be driving?' Lydia said.

'Take much longer,' William said with a winning smile. 'Anyway, mission accomplished? Did you do any good?'

'Not really,' Lydia sighed. 'Appeased the guilt feelings a bit. Thanks for coming, Will. I'd be exhausted tomorrow if you hadn't.'

'Don't put yourself down,' William said. 'Listening to people *releases* them, helps them make up their minds. Pity they live so far away . . .'

'A mercy, if you ask me,' Lydia muttered. 'If I become frail – elderly . . . just put me in a home. OK?'

'OK, Ma,' William said. 'No problem.'

From the evening ferry Annie watched the outline of Jersey recede. It was almost dusk when the rain started, fine drizzle falling on her hair and face like wet petals. Annie stayed where she was. Loads of presents the Spensers had given her, just on account of the specky-thing: a weekend bag – real pigskin – and two full nighties and a

wrapround skirt and matching flowery shirts for her and Jarvis.
Pity they wore only black.

When they reached Cedar Avenue that evening the phone was already ringing. Lydia jumped from the car and ran in.

'Where the hell have you been?' Ed said. 'Belstones arrived with new clients, the Holroyds, unlocked the front door and set off the alarm and of course the police turned up . . . I mean, what is it with you, Lydia?'

CHAPTER EIGHT

THE LAST DAY of term was always fraught but Lydia, waking early, had hoped for a surge of joy at the prospect of freedom ahead, vistas of trees and hills, the world her oyster. But her psyche failed to register, reminding her instead that Annie wasn't coming home for the summer vacation, William was miserable, she had fallen out with Marina and upset Ed by failing to tell Belstones she was away for the weekend.

Happy families.

Margaret and Bertie had disappeared too. Preliminary enquiries about enclosing the pool had elicited unofficial opinion that planning permission would be refused. The newly married Stringers had driven off in the Bentley to get over the disappointment.

What she had to construct now was a viable and autonomous life, Lydia thought, getting ready for school for the last time. She had to plan for after the house was sold, the furniture divided between them or sent to the auction rooms. Her plan must include solitude for when she was working but also have potential for meeting people, making new friendships, the relationships for which she had never had time.

She was going to paint eventually, but paints themselves were expensive and then there were brushes, canvases, hardboard or whatever. It didn't seem the moment for extra expenditure with the accumulation of unpaid and unpayable bills. She had never bothered about bills before. Her salary and Ed's standing order covered them, and she only had time for essential shopping but now the bills were piling up.

Lydia filed the unpaid ones on a bill spike discovered in Ed's uncollected desk. They made a thick white cluster like an Elizabethan ruff with a hint of menacing red here and there. She planted the spike on the oak chest, so she saw it as soon as she opened the front door but the sightings had not so far suggested a solution. The Holroyds had been back several times since their unfortunate first visit, Mrs Holroyd remarking on the nice big kitchen and asking, 'Is the big freezer to be left?' Lydia said sadly that it was.

On the up side she had been asked to translate six poems by Guy Maze, a significant, if not yet established, Left Bank poet, into English for a small magazine, *New Expectations*, and Richard had phoned, sounded better, and was taking her out to dinner next week before he went off on holiday.

Girls in green blazers gathered round the entrances of Stoke Bishop High and stepped back as she approached.

'Your last day, Mrs Kemp?' one of them said and several smiled encouragingly. '*Bonjour, madame, et bientôt au revoir.*'

'*Plutôt adieu.*'

'That's right,' she said, smiling too, and disappearing into the building. 'See you later.'

The door of the headmistress's room stood open and Mrs Busby herself look harassed, dwarfed by a large gift-wrapped package on the desk in front of her.

'Your last day, Lydia ... er, Mrs Kemp,' she amended as the buzzer went and pupils began to flood into the corridors. 'See you in assembly.'

'Yes,' Lydia said. Mrs Busby had traditional views about most things including the importance of regular Christian assemblies. There was always a special one at the end of the morning on the last day of term, followed in the summer by an open afternoon in which parents were invited to see displays of work and have strawberry teas on the lawn afterwards.

The staffroom was already full – discreet cups of coffee, chat about holidays, moans about next year's timetable which hardly concerned Lydia. Eyes glanced at her and away; already she didn't belong, her departure viewed as desertion or a wise career move, both an implicit criticism of the less adventurous.

'How's that friend of yours with heart problems?' Miss Tucker barked, offering further grounds for speculation. 'Still going strong?'

'He's well ... far as I know,' Lydia said. Odd to think of Richard harboured for so long in Miss Tucker's head.

A tapping on the staffroom door. 'Somebody wants Mrs Kemp,' Mrs Banks called over her shoulder. Lydia stepped forward.

'Oh Beth . . .'

'For you,' Bethany whispered, thrusting a small pink-wrapped parcel at her. 'Can I . . . can I come and see you sometimes?'

'Please do,' Lydia said in a less than encouraging tone.

'Your address?' Bethany opened her rough notebook at the back page. 'Could you write it here?'

'' 'Fraid I've got to rush. Thanks for the present, Beth. My address is in the phone book,' Lydia said, turning back to collect her register. Entertaining Bethany was certainly not part of the new agenda.

Last day of term zinged restless in the ether. A semblance of lessons was *de rigueur* until breaktime, after that textbooks had to be collected and stacked in the cupboard, exercise books baled with string ready to carry to next year's classroom. Meanwhile several small parcels appeared surreptitiously on the flaps of Lydia's desk.

'I may not get the chance to see you all together again,' she said as assembly time approached. 'So good luck, Year Eight. You've been a really nice year. *Très bien, jeunes filles, vous avez été excellentes . . . parfaites. Bonne chance, très bonne chance . . .*'

'So have you,' somebody muttered, and round the classroom eyes shone, wet and blinking. Lydia's own eyes pricked. Why was leaving, even when you wanted to leave, so difficult?

'Into line for assembly now, everybody,' she shouted briskly.

'Bet they give you a present, Mrs Kemp,' Bethany said as they filed out.

'What they going to give her?' Sharon said.

'How should I know?' Bethany said sulkily.

Lydia followed to the main hall, which took several minutes to fill with its six hundred pupils. The large gift-wrapped package was now standing on Mrs Busby's table.

Last times should be different, Lydia thought, but 'Lord dismiss us with thy blessing' followed by the headgirl reading Corinthians chapter 13 was conspicuously the same.

' "For now we see through a glass, darkly; then face to face:" ' – Lydia had puzzled about that 'glass, darkly' as a schoolchild, seeing now as then ancient glass blackened with smoke. The Romans had small glass receptacles but who had glass windows in biblical times?

' "And now abideth faith, hope, charity, these three; but the greatest of these is charity." '

Who has charity? she wondered. Margaret certainly, Izzy now and then, William sometimes, Ed never . . . but Richard was strong on charity.

Mrs Busby was speaking now. '. . . who has been with us for ten years . . .' Heads flicking round, short hair bouncing, long hair swinging, quick smiles, pink cheeks round as buns.

Lydia stepped out and walked forward.

'This looks so lovely, I really hate to spoil it!' she said, tearing nevertheless at the silver-patterned paper. 'What can it be?'

'Don't tell her,' Mrs Busby whispered, roguish.

The huge box inside contained peach-coloured bathroom accessories: towels in several sizes, a toothbrush rack, two tooth mugs and a scallop-shell soapdish, all peach.

'How absolutely lovely,' Lydia said. 'With all these beautiful towels to remind me, I shall think of you . . . *Je penserai à vous toutes les fois que je prends un bain.*' Bright eyes all round, gentle tittering. 'I am going to miss you all.' She was beginning to blink. 'Thank you so much. Goodbye and good luck. *Bonne chance pour votre avenir à toutes. J'espère que tout finera très bien. Adieu, adieu.*'

'We'll let Mrs Kemp go out first, shall we, girls?' Mrs Busby said, and Lydia picked up the box and carried it out through the door held open by a prefect.

'I wonder who chose it?' Izzy said, helping Lydia carry the package out to her car later that afternoon. 'Just the thing for your bottom drawer. What are all the little parcels?'

'Talc mostly, enough talc to last a lifetime.'

'Looks like somebody loves you.'

'Does it?' Lydia said. 'Last drinks at my house?'

'Good idea,' Izzy said with a quick glance. 'But it doesn't have to be the last until you sell it?'

'*Bonne chance, madame,*' a girl said, passing.

'Thank you, Marian, *et à toi aussi,*' Lydia smiled, and turned back to Izzy.

'Several people have been round but no offers so far. Ed's quite sure the Holroyds, the couple who tried to go round when I was away for the weekend and Belstones set the alarm off, were serious buyers. Trust me to muck things up.'

'Poor you, poor old Ed,' Izzy said.

'I had two lots round last weekend – Sneeds and Walls, Walls were very tight-lipped when they saw Annie's mural.'

'Obviously the wrong sort,' Izzy said. 'See you.'

Ten minutes later Lydia slid down into the garage. Izzy parked on the drive behind her.

'What's that?' she said, nodding at the bill spike when Lydia had opened the front door.

'Bills. Council tax, electric, gas . . . I'm a bit fussed actually. My last salary cheque's just gone in . . .'

'Then you should be OK?'

'Well, in the long run, when we sell the house,' Lydia said. 'But that may be ages and evening classes don't start until the end of September. Red wine, or I've got lager?'

'Red wine, thanks,' Izzy said, following Lydia into the sitting room. 'You could get foreign students in. I did that the summer I bought the MG. Bristol's full of language schools and they all have accommodation problems this time of year. How many bedrooms?'

'Five,' Lydia said. 'But I sleep in one and William's old room is my study and Annie's stuff's still everywhere in hers. But it's an idea. Suppose I'd have to feed them?'

'Course, hearty eaters that age too, but not *haute cuisine*, and they do get their lunch out weekdays. It's how people in Bristol pay their mortgages, didn't you know?'

'How much do students pay?'

'Goes up each year. Ring up and ask. OISE, that's Oxford Intensive School of English, or SHSE, School of High Speed English, lots of others. They tend to be a bit disorganised, temporary staff and that . . .'

'But what about my work?' Lydia murmured. Did she really want teenagers lumbering about? 'I've been asked to translate six poems by Guy Maze.'

'Good. Who for?'

'Small magazine called *New Expectations*.'

'Small magazines pay peanuts.'

'Well yes, I'm afraid . . .'

'So what are your options? Feeding language students or begging Ed for a handout?' Izzy was addicted to instant solutions.

'No way,' Lydia said. 'Do you have to be so bossy?'

'You're such a blinking ostrich. What're you going to do when the house goes and you're teaching here in Bristol two evenings a week?'

'Rent a flat or go and stay with one of the children.'

'Would that be such a good idea? You're welcome to camp at my place. You and your suitor.'

'He's got his own flat, but thanks, Izz. More wine?'

'No, I'd better get off. Did I tell you Chris turned up and we're off to Turkey in a week's time? I'll leave you my spare key. I mean the house could go quickly.'

'Exchange of contracts takes months,' Lydia said, following her out to the car. 'Anyway, who's Chris?'

'Used to be a good mate years ago. Not sure what he is now,' Izzy said, turning her head to back the scarlet car. 'But six weeks eyeball to eyeball in a camper van, I'll find out.'

'Take care then.'

Lydia walked up to close the wrought-iron gate as Izzy roared away. Bethany was standing on the pavement outside.

'What are you doing here?'

'Nothing,' Bethany said. 'Looked you up in the telephone book like you said. Nice place you got.'

'Until I sell it. Thanks for the ... er, lovely present. But you'd better go home, your mum'll wonder where you are.'

'She goes to the bridge club every afternoon.'

'But you've got a key?' Bethany nodded sulkily. 'Anyway I expect she'll be home by now.'

'No, she won't. Never gets back before six o'clock.'

'Well, there's no point hanging about here,' Lydia said, looking down the road for inspiration. Schoolgirls and their delinquent mothers were not her problem any more.

'Not exactly friendly, are you? I spent two weeks' pocket money on that soap and stuff.'

'Yes, well, you'd better have a cup of tea now you're here,' Lydia said, relenting. The tiresome child was a human being. 'After that you must go straight home.'

'*Merci beaucoup beaucoup, madame,*' Bethany said, following her down the path with polka skips.

Lydia switched on the kettle and planted the biscuit tin on the kitchen table. 'What are you planning to do this summer holiday?'

'Nothing,' Bethany said, helping herself to a bourbon.

'No holiday tasks?' Lydia said, pouring boiling water into two mugs. 'Do you take sugar?'

'Three, please,' Bethany said. 'Mrs Black said to read *Catcher in the Rye* and Miss Tucker said to read up about Charles Darwin and his beagle but I'm ever such a slow reader and I don't like stuffing inside.'

'You could sit in the garden . . . if you have a garden?'

'Our garden's really small, not like yours,' Bethany said.

'A garden this size is a lot of work, and I've lots of clearing up with the house being sold.'

'I could help you,' Bethany said. 'I'm ever so good at clearing up.'

'After twenty years it's the sort of clearing up I have to do myself,' Lydia said. 'But thanks anyway. Saying goodbye is never easy,' she added, stacking the mugs in the dishwasher. 'But you have to let people go . . .'

'Can I have another bourbon?' Bethany said, getting up.

'Please do and take one with you,' Lydia said, moving towards the front door. 'Bye, Bethany, the soap is lovely.'

'Wasn't just soap, it was talc and everything . . .'

'Yes, all lovely. Good luck, *bonne chance,*' Lydia said firmly, and shut the front door.

Beginning and endings . . . she was free now and couldn't take responsibility for Bethany. Wasn't as if she liked the child. Besides, worrying about her own daughters was quite draining enough. She had a lot to work out – the money problem, and Izzy's advice to be followed up or not, for instance.

Lydia's eyes went back to the bill stack. She picked up the telephone directory. The telephone at the Oxford School of Intensive English was engaged. She tried the other option.

'School of High Speed English,' a young woman answered against a background of shouting. 'Julia speaking, can I help you?'

'It's about accommodation for foreign students.'

'Where do you live, er, Mrs . . .' The shouting crescendoed.

'Kemp . . . Lydia Kemp. I live off Parry's Lane.'

'Where's that then?'

'Other side of the Downs . . . What on earth's going on?'

'Had a lot of staff changes at SHSE, only been here a week myself.' Julia attempted a casual laugh. 'How many bedrooms?'

'Well, two to spare, I mean I could take two students.'

'You have references?'

'References?'

'Good character. We have to be careful with young people.'

'Yes, I suppose . . . How much do you pay?'

'Ninety pounds a week but all our students are accommodated at the moment. Our principal, Mr Blake, isn't here but he'll want a word. I'll make a note of your address and send you an application form, shall I?'

'Well, all right then . . .' Lydia said, deflated.

Bethany leaned against the wall of 3 Cedar Avenue. She loved madame, Mrs Kemp, enormously but Mrs Kemp didn't care ten p for her even though she spent two weeks' pocket money on the pink box with bath cubes *and* soap *and* talc *and* moisturiser.

The pavement belonged to everybody; she could stay there as long as she wanted, all night if she wanted. Maybe she would . . .

CHAPTER NINE

IN HER FIRST week of freedom Lydia showed two couples, the Hansons and the Powells, round the house, but neither seemed keen. Otherwise she spent her mornings working on Guy Maze's poems and her afternoons in the garden, a labour of love debased now to a courting of prospective buyers. It typified the nineties, everybody trying to sell something to somebody else. But there were compensations: she had a painting day school booked for September, and the roses were still gorgeous at the end of July. Chinatown had been a mistake, the catalogue omitting to explain that the canary-yellow flowers bloomed and faded the same day. Now it was holidays, would children come and play again in the wild wood?

Lydia sighed and began to clear twenty years of family detritus, thrusting old toys – William's wooden Noah's ark which she remembered buying – together with discarded children's clothing into plastic bags. She pushed well down a blue party dress she had made for Annie, aged four, and delivered the bags to the Oxfam shop before she changed her mind. Annie, too busy with her secret love even to phone – what use was nostalgia?

The next afternoon she found a child's battered paintbox at the top of Marina's cupboard. Pennies from heaven via Marina, a benevolent symbol which had to be the start of her painting life. Should she phone Marina tonight, tell her about it as if nothing was wrong between them?

Now she no longer had any excuse to delay painting, a large piece of white cardboard propped on her desk proved too daunting, a polar landscape she couldn't defile. Instead she found an old exercise book and moved out to the garden; sketching outlines in pencil first, then working in water colour. The orchard, the Laxtons good this year, the rambling rose, American Pillar, clambering up the wall, the odd pale fruit of the strawberry tree. But *Annie at Four* was her first imaginative work, the frizzy gorse-bright hair that was mousy now. How she would love to cuddle the gorse-bloom Annie just for one minute. She thought of phoning Izzy, announcing her painting breakthrough, but Izzy would be getting ready for Turkey with Chris.

Izzy had a life.

Instead Lydia painted all weekend and would have painted all Monday but the secretary phoned from Park Lodge, saying the principal, Mr Sharpe, wanted to see her a.s.a.p.

'Tomorrow?' Lydia suggested, her voice husky with disuse, her eyes catching sight of the neglected lawn grown meadow-long. 'Tomorrow afternoon?'

'This afternoon at two fifteen,' the secretary said firmly. 'It's urgent.'

Lydia had met the principal at her interview, remembered his smile which switched on and off. Did he want to get rid of her at this late stage? The idea made her quivery. What about the bills on the bill spike?

'Well, all right then . . .' When she put down the phone, her fingers felt stiff as wood and she had to abandon painting.

Falling back to earth, had Icarus felt like this?

'Good to see you again, Lydia,' Mr Sharpe said, extending his hand across the desk. 'Holidays started yet?'

'Well . . .' Lydia flushed. Her PR was up to her now; should she pretend she was already planning classes for next term?

'Bit of a crisis here. You met Naomi Vincent, the pregnant girl, English specialist. Complications, I'm afraid. Bed rest, doctor's orders, resigned her tutorship, GCSE English literature quite out of the question.' His brown eyes stared out of the window, fixed on a pigeon on the adjacent roof but suddenly swung back. 'I thought of you at once as the best person to take it on.'

'Me?' Lydia stammered. 'Why me?'

'Offering courses which lead to a definite qualification has to have priority so we can qualify for the LEA grant, otherwise we're not viable. Hard times for adult education.'

'But my degree is in French,' Lydia said. If she refused could he, would he, sack her on the spot?

'A graduate is a graduate,' the principal said reverently. 'You'll do very well. I know a conscientious teacher when I see one . . .' His smile flashed on and off.

'But I've got two French classes already.' Lydia found herself looking at the back of his head as he rummaged in the bottom drawer of his desk. Wasn't *he* an English graduate? 'Isn't there somebody else, I mean *you*, for instance?'

'There set books here,' he said, his face reddened by the rummaging. Hadn't he heard or was he simply ignoring her? '*As You Like It, The Mill on the Floss* and a collection of poetry, *Contemporary Choice*. Have a browse tonight and let me know how you feel first thing.'

'But I've never even read *The Mill on the Floss*.'

'I wouldn't suggest it unless I knew you could handle it, a feisty young lady like yourself. Now, if you'll excuse me . . .?'

'Feisty?' Lydia muttered. She stopped off in the common room for a cup of coffee from the machine. Ridiculous git, she fumed, 'feisty young lady' indeed, flicking his papers to look busy and flashing his smile like an amorous firefly . . .

A young black man had come in after her and was having trouble with the coffee machine.

'Which button you press?'

'Third one down,' Lydia said pointing. 'Look, coffee with milk and sugar.'

'Thanks,' he said. He waited for his plastic cup to fill and carried it to her table. 'Mind if I sit 'ere?'

'Please do,' she said, still fighting in her thoughts.

'Rotten coffee, innit?' he said as he sat down. He was strikingly handsome, his features aquiline, his skin pale brown, his accent cockney-cum-West Indian, his hair African.

'Not too bad for a machine,' Lydia said, finishing hers.

He glanced at her books. 'You a tutor 'ere?'

'That's right. Lydia Kemp.'

'What thing you teachin' then?'

'French,' she said. 'And English literature.'

'Doing GCSE, me,' he said. 'Name's Jordan Mackay.'

'Well, nice to have met you, Jordan,' Lydia said, getting up and dropping her cup into the bin. ' 'Bye now.'

Was Jordan Mackay a typical Park Lodge student? she wondered making her way to Berkeley Square and her car. A parking space so close had seemed like a lucky break when she arrived; now she wasn't so sure. She felt exploited. Besides, she had a lot more reading to do as well as preparing totally unfamiliar lessons. When was she ever going to paint?

Bethany was keeping sullen vigil on the pavement outside the house. Poor kid, Lydia sighed, and tried to relax.

'Hello, going to help me with the garden?' she said cheerily.

'Don't mind,' Bethany said.

She mowed the back lawn that day and, rewarded with tea and biscuits, came back to do the front the next day. The day after she weeded the shrubbery. Meanwhile Lydia read her way through the GCSE literature texts.

'What's Sharon doing this holidays?' she asked, hoping to stimulate Bethany's social life in other directions. Hadn't she got enough trouble with her own daughters without taking on somebody else's?

'Dunno,' Bethany said. 'Anyway she's not my friend any more. She says my boobs are too big.' Bethany blushed crimson. 'Do you think they're too big, Mrs Kemp?'

'Course not,' Lydia said. 'You're just developing at thirteen. Lots of girls get overweight. *Puppyfat*, they call it, girls go through phases.' Was Annie going through a 'yob-boyfriend' phase, Marina an 'everything's-my-mother's-fault' phase, though both were in their twenties?

Annie leaned on the wall above the train station and pulled the postcard out of her pocket. She was standing on the same spot as the picture. Shining railway lines and blue sea and an island with a castle on top. St Michael's Mount.

'Working hard,' Annie wrote carefully but her eyes slid away along the rails. Like *she* could slide away, slide right back home. 'Clear that stuff off the tables,' Jarvis had snapped. As if that letter about the rent was her fault. She wasn't having it. She walked straight out of the scuzzy café into the yellow afternoon and the cool blue breeze.

'Standing on the spot in this postcard and looking at the island. Love from Annie.'

Never ever had a letter from Jarvis, except that reference he wrote. She knew it by heart: 'Annie Kemp has worked as a waitress here for three months. She is clean, honest and hardworking. Highly recommended. Jarvis Ryde.' He had written it for her and himself too, of course; he needed the money. Money meant a lot to Jarvis. But Personnel wouldn't take her as a waitress with no silver service experience, only as a chambermaid.

And that was how she met Drina Spenser and got taken to see Dr Rinde-Smith at the clinic.

Lucky break that was, especially for Jarvis.

'Can I come again tomorrow?' Bethany asked, smiling.

'Not tomorrow, Thursday, I'm going out,' Lydia said. Richard was taking her out to dinner. She needed the day to herself beforehand, sort out her head. She didn't exactly want him but she didn't want to lose him, and she couldn't help looking forward to Thursday evening.

'Come next week if you like. Lawns'll need doing again.'

'I might be busy next week,' Bethany said frostily.

By Thursday Lydia had managed a first draft of the Guy Maze poems in English.

A postcard had suddenly arrived from Mrs Trewartha informing her that her daughter Annie had gone without leaving an address before Christmas and had never fetched the two bags left for safekeeping, which was causing great inconvenience to the Trewartha family. Lydia sighed. Why did Annie have to be so tiresome?

That evening, she dressed with care. Whatever her feelings at the time, her behaviour at the last meeting had been OTT, letting fly a packet of resentment she hadn't even known was there. Should she apologise? It seemed rather a waste when Richard was always imperturbably good-natured.

As for the plate, didn't Picasso throw plates?

She selected a violet and blue silk blouse and a white linen skirt. Her fingernails, blackened and broken from the garden, did rather spoil the effect. She patted Chanel No. 5, which Marina had given her at Christmas, behind her ears, traditional like Richard – part of his charm and part of her problem.

From the landing window she watched his car trickle on to the drive, a newish silver-coloured Astra. Richard himself looked better, slimmer, his hair newly cut, a dark green jacket suggesting a change of image.

'Great to see you!' she said, finding it was, but as she stepped forward to kiss him, he stepped back in alarm – teasing or what?

'Sorry about last time,' Lydia said, forgetting her decision. 'Don't worry. I hardly ever chuck plates.'

'Glad to hear it,' Richard said. 'I wanted to see you before I went off tomorrow. Southsea, a sailing holiday.'

'Didn't know you were keen on sailing.'

'Quite a lot about me you don't know, Lydia,' he said. 'Never sailed before actually. Garden's looking nice.'

'I've been tidying up, term's just finished.'

'Excellent,' Richard said, but he seemed guarded. Was it the plate? It was Ed who threw things. Ed who had driven off that morning soon as it was light, leaving her to sweep up shards of wedding-present glass. Would she ever forget?

'Like a drink? White wine or I've got gin?'

'White wine, thanks,' Richard said, glancing at his watch. 'Table's booked for half-seven.' He followed her into the kitchen. 'Have you thought about what I said?'

'Well, yes . . .' The Woolworth glasses clacked on the kitchen table. 'You're very nice, Richard, but I don't want to get into anything I can't get out of . . . and I don't want to spend the rest of my life cooking anybody's breakfast.' She paused. 'Don't know what I do want, mind. I just put myself down with the School of High Speed English.'

'Another teaching job?'

'Foreign students needing accommodation for August.'

'Don't you have to cook?'

'A month is nothing with a big freezer,' she said, nodding towards it. 'Until the house goes, I've a cash flow problem.'

'Ah!' Richard said. 'Would you consider *us* if I said I'd do half the cooking?'

Lydia laughed. 'Have to get it in writing.'

'Any time you like,' he said. 'I've never been upstairs here, mind if I look?'

'Feel free,' Lydia said, startled nevertheless. Was he going to try something? How much did she know about him? How much did

75

you really know about anybody? In her head a bewigged judge banged the table with his gavel. 'Rape?' he said, his eyebrows rising further than seemed possible. 'When the defendant invited the accused, with whom she has admitted she had sexual intercourse on numerous occasions . . .' But Richard wasn't like that and besides she was middle-aged and plump in the wrong places.

'You thinking of buying it?'

'Bit big for me, wouldn't you say?' Richard said as he followed her up the stairs. If she turned now would she catch him looking at her legs or her bottom?

'That's my bedroom,' she said, opening the door but not going in. Fortunately her nightie was under the pillow.

'Tidy,' Richard said, staying beside her.

'And this is my study.'

'Not so tidy,' Richard said, stepping inside. 'Good view of the garden. Who's that?'

'Who's what?'

'Must have been a bird. I like the blue pool next door.'

'The neighbours are away in Wales,' she said, and wondered why she'd told him that. An oblique offer, *carte blanche*? What was she up to?

Further down the landing a small ceramic plaque said 'ANNIE'S ROOM', a yellowed page underneath was scribbled in a childish hand, 'KNOCK AND DON'T COME IN'.

'Friendly girl, your Annie,' Richard said. Lydia knocked from habit. Annie's room was still sacrosant. Smaller than the others' with posters edge to edge on one wall and a bed buried under stuffed animals, it felt claustrophobic.

'Annie and her stuffies,' Lydia said. 'Inherited from her brother and sister. Had to give them a good home.'

'But what about the mural?' Richard said.

'Annie's own unaided work.' Lydia stood back to consider what Annie had painted on the wall by her bed. A huge water lily appeared to rise from the pillow, climbing up beautiful and menacing, with green leaves which seemed alive, stems sprouting buds with faces like putti. 'Have you told Ma what you've done to your bedroom wall?' Marina had said at supper that night. 'Why should I?' Annie had replied. 'Who says you're the big prefect round here?' Lydia had had to be a bit cross, par for the course, but she was pleased too. The painting was evidence of a talent she alone believed in.

'Some picture,' Richard said, stepping close and then back. 'Pity you can't take it with you.' He turned to smile at her.

'Ages since I've seen Annie,' she said.

'Off with a boyfriend?' Richard asked. 'Not easy, children and their relationships. I could have murdered Fen's first chap in his dirty jeans and dreadlocks.'

'It's not like that,' Lydia said, and wondered if it was.

'Well, anyway . . . my offer still stands,' he said. 'People our age need to be married. Think about it, Lydia.'

'But there's nothing *between us*,' Lydia said. 'I was crazy about you once but, well, it doesn't last . . . it's dead flowers.'

'We were very good friends . . .'

'We were never friends,' Lydia said. 'And I'm no good at marriage.'

'Could be you're out of practice.' His smoke-grey eyes had a calculating look. 'Perhaps I could stay tonight?'

'And what about your heart?' Lydia said. Suppose he had a heart attack? Suppose he died in her arms?

'Specialist did a good job,' Richard said, punching his chest carefully. 'Us medics get the best of the NHS.'

'Bet you do,' Lydia said. 'Hadn't we better go?'

'OK.' He was standing by the landing window. 'Who's that?'

'What?' Was Bethany still hanging round?

A taxi had pulled up outside the gate and two young men with a lot of luggage were getting out. A girl with long dark hair paid the driver.

'Ciao,' she said, waving as the taxi pulled away. The gate opened and the trio came down the path.

'What's going on?' Richard said.

'Search me,' Lydia muttered, running down to the door.

'Excuse please,' the girl said, smiling and sweeping back her long hair. 'Signora Kemp, yes? You feed students?'

'Well, yes, but I wasn't expecting—'

'School of High Speed English, she send me, Carmel,' Carmel said, holding out an addressed envelope. 'She say she phone.'

Behind her the young men were bright-eyed but silent.

'Well, she hasn't phoned,' Lydia said. The dinner with Richard seemed to fade, grow transparent before her eyes, like a mirage in the desert. 'We were just going out . . .'

'Me hungry,' the taller young man said in an injured tone.

'You phone School of High Speed English?' Carmel said.

'Well . . .' Lydia said.

'I'm afraid you've arrived earlier than Mrs Kemp expected,' Richard said smoothly.

'Not eat, two weeks,' the tall young man said.

'He mean two days,' Carmel suggested.

'Far too long,' Richard said, deciding to take charge. 'You'd better come in. I'm sure we can find you something.' He glanced at Lydia and picked up the phone.

'I'll cancel the table,' he whispered. 'You want to phone the language school?'

'But I said two students and we *were* going out to dinner.'

'A mix-up,' Richard said. 'It happens. Dare say the boys can double up if you've got a camp-bed?'

'Quite. Everybody wait here a minute, please.'

She walked out to the kitchen and switched on the oven, crossed to the freezer, took out fish pie and a packet of peas. If she was disappointed at least she could be efficient. She slit open the letter Carmel had given her. It invited her to complete the enclosed form and supply two references as to her good character. Lydia banged the fish pie into the oven.

'But you speak such good English already, Carmel,' Richard was saying, his eyes shining. Did he flirt to conceal how boring he was? Lydia wondered irritably.

'No, no, me Italian,' Carmel was saying. 'English small – small. Boys from Albania. Sacha and Joseph.'

'You are Sacha?' Richard shook the hand of the taller Albanian.

'Me Joseph,' he said. 'Me hungry.'

'I'll show you where to put your things,' Lydia said, indicating the luggage spread round the hall. The great hilarity as they dragged their bags upstairs suggested the three saw it as victory by cheek, which did not augur well.

Richard found a camp-bed in Marina's cupboard. The smell of fish pie drifted through the house. The telephone rang.

'You don't know what I'm going through.' Mother's voice was dangerously high-pitched. 'Theodore Adams, my solicitor, said James should have a solicitor too. I told him and he swore horrible words, very embarrassing with the home help here, and locked himself in the toilet capsule I had had fitted in his bedroom specially, and refuses to come out and—'

'I hear you, Mother,' Lydia said with a calm authority she didn't know she possessed. 'But three foreign students have just arrived here. I'll ring you back later. OK?'

SHSE's phone was continuously engaged but somehow Lydia got the beds made up, the meal on the table. Once fed the students quietened and settled, disappearing upstairs, the two young men to Marina's room with the camp-bed, Carmel into Annie's room.

'Thanks for everything, Richard,' Lydia said. In the front garden white phlox loomed in the darkness like snow. There was a faint chemical smell. 'What would I have done without you?'

'You don't have to do without me,' he said. Chatting up Carmel while Lydia organised the meal had improved his mood but done nothing for hers. 'If you let me stay tonight . . .'

'How can I?' Lydia said. 'Think of the letters home. Kids'll think they've landed in a bordello.'

'Young Europeans are more grown up about these things,' Richard said. He loved women, liked being married, always had, a safe house from which to venture. Alison understood, refrained from weepy scenes, kept busy with the children, house, let him get on with it. 'Nice to come home to' would be on her headstone if headstones were in fashion.

Lydia switched on the porch light, turning the snow back to white phlox. The silver Astra gleamed but its wheels were bright blue. The chemical smell was paint.

'Who the hell . . . ?' Richard said.

'It . . . it could be the girl who helps with the garden,' Lydia stammered.

'Tell me about it,' Richard said, leaning to touch the paint with a fingertip. 'Still tacky. Quick, get detergent, paper towels, bath cleaner, anything. Hurry . . . quick, quick, quick.'

CHAPTER TEN

THE FOLLOWING MORNING Lydia knocked at the door of Marina's old bedroom at seven o'clock and then at the door of Annie's room. It was best to establish a routine; SHSE classes were said to start at nine. Her students were not going to be late on their first day if she could help it. Besides, she had a lot to do.

She ought to phone Mother, hear 'the James and the toilet capsule saga' in full. It would be sensible to get to Sainsbury's, slightly cheaper than Waitrose, before the rush. Last night Carmel, Sacha and Joseph had appeared to possess gargantuan appetites. But a comforting chorus, *ninety-pounds-a week-each*, sang in her head. Some problems did have solutions.

What time was Richard leaving for Southsea? She imagined him leaping to the phone, tousled and in his pyjamas . . .

After a second knock five minutes later there were sounds of stirring, footsteps on the landing. What did Albanians eat for breakfast, she wondered, croissants? She put cornflakes and orange juice in the middle of the table, distributing knives, spoons, bowls, making toast. A cooked evening meal would have to suffice as demonstration of British hospitality.

'*Buongiorno, signora*,' her charges said, coming downstairs.

'Breakfast at eight,' she said pointing to her watch.

'Eight for weekend too?' Carmel said.

'Today, Friday, breakfast at eight. Tomorrow, Saturday, and Sunday, breakfast nine o'clock,' Lydia conceded. Would they lounge round the house all weekend? But she managed to get them through the gate and pointed them towards the bus stop by half-past eight.

'Get off at Seafield Road bus stop,' she said for the umpteenth time.

'*Dove?*' Carmel said, and all three looked so puzzled that Lydia led them to the stop at the corner of Cedar Avenue.

'You wait here, right?'

'*Sì, sì*,' Carmel said.

'I'll expect you back about five o'clock.' Lydia held up four fingers and a thumb. She might phone Richard and apologise for the lost dinner and the blue wheels, which had not proved quite the disaster they had seemed. Detergent, turps and fifteen minutes' hard graft had got them clean again last night but they mightn't look so pristine in the bright of day.

A crisp packet and blue spots on the garage floor confirmed Lydia's suspicion of Bethany. On the up side the silly child probably wouldn't have the nerve to come back again. Richard had been good about it all, considering. Had he asked to stay the night again she might well . . . but all he said was, 'See you when I see you, Lydia,' and drove off along Cedar Avenue rather fast.

The phone was ringing as she got back.

'Hello?' Lydia said.

'Guess who this is.'

'Jordan Mackay?' she said, startled. 'How did you get my number?'

'Aksin' about coachin' for me GCSE in the office, wasn't I? She say maybe Mrs Kemp give us coachin' in French and English lit. Them things is me GCSE subjects, but we didn't do no French at my school.'

'Sorry, Jordan, I don't do any coaching, the office got it wrong,' Lydia said firmly. 'I'm just off shopping. 'Bye.'

Were his subjects coincidence or some kind of wind-up? she wondered. She gathered her baskets and backed the car up the drive just as her three students came in the garden gate.

'Bus no come. Bus no good,' Carmel said, fixing the car with her dark eyes. 'You have car, *signora*? Car very good.'

'Right. I'll drive you today but after this you take the bus or you walk,' Lydia said with untypical firmness, and drove them to Seafield Road pointing out the bus stops on the way to the large Victorian house which was SHSE.

Students stood in groups round the hall, talking in their own languages. It was after nine o'clock by now but the door labelled 'OFFICE' was still closed. How long would SHSE survive if it went on like this?

'You have to wait,' she said, smiling encouragingly. 'The staff will be here in a minute. See you later.'

They looked at her doubtfully, Sacha and Joseph flopped on to the window seat. Carmel smiled her way into a group.

Annie stared down at the quay. Jersey was all right but doing what the Spensers wanted all the time did her head in. They bought her loads of gear, of course – talk about paying the piper and calling the flipping tune. It was like she belonged to them, Alexandrina's toy and poodle.

'Call me Drina, Annie, please.'

Drina sent her money every month, same wages as the hotel paid plus extra for fares to London and Jersey.

The ferry bumped gently against the quayside, people waved and shouted and the gangway clanged down. Annie patted the fat wallet in the bumbag over her jeans. Fat cat, that's what she was.

'Better put it in the bank,' Jarvis said.

'No way.'

Annie liked the fat cat feel of it. She loved Jarvis to bits but she didn't have to do everything he said.

As she walked down the gangway, she couldn't see Drina.

'Excuse me, miss. You come to Jersey for business or pleasure?' A customs man in a dark uniform.

'What?' Annie said, blushing lobster pink.

'Are you in Jersey for business or pleasure, miss?' he said speaking slowly. Right one here, he thought, but his smile stayed reassuring. 'Staying with friends?'

'Yes,' Annie stammered. 'No.'

'Can I have their name and address?' His eyes watched her.

'Sorry.' Annie panicked easily. 'Discretion, Annie,' Dr Rinde-Smith said in her head like he was always saying it. 'Your lips must be sealed.'

'My lips must be sealed,' Annie stammered.

'Would you mind stepping this way, please?' The customs officer's eyes were bright like a stoat's. 'Just a routine check.'

Annie went.

People passing glanced sideways, glad not to be the one suspected. The room where Annie found herself was fluorescent lit and windowless. A policewoman sat at a desk, plastic chairs backed against the walls.

'Fetch Judy,' the customs man said. The policewoman left. He read out a list of forbidden items. Annie's heart beat so loud she couldn't hear. He unzipped the pigskin bag like it was his own. 'Anything to declare?'

'Nothing,' she said.

'Have you any means of identification, miss?'

'Shit!' Annie muttered, taking the fat cat wallet from her bumbag.

'A UB40, name of Annabel Kemp, Penzance. Drawing your social security looks like.' Annie nodded. 'Six hundred pound, near enough,' he said, counting and smiling. Could be a tom, except she hadn't got the nous. 'How come a young lady on the dole has six hundred pounds in her wallet?'

'That's my business,' Annie said.

'And what exactly *is* your business, miss? See you came to Jersey last month too.' Annie opened her mouth and then shut it again. 'Let's have a look, shall we?' He dipped into the pigskin bag and took out items – the new nightie, matching dressing gown, new bra and pants. He undid the toothpaste.

'How d'you get all this stuff?' he said.

'Mind your own business,' Annie muttered.

'New bag too?' he said, unperturbed. But there was an air of excitement as the policewoman came back with a woman customs officer and two customs men. Five pairs of eyes stared at their quarry, hunting hearts thudding.

'What's it to you?' Annie cried. 'I don't do drugs.'

'Funny you should say that,' he said. 'We can search you now or you can wait while we apply to the magistrates' court.'

'Search me now,' Annie said. 'You won't find anything.' He nodded and left. The other men followed.

'Excuse me, miss.' The woman customs officer stood behind Annie. Hands moved quickly and expertly down her body.

'Take your coat off and put it on the table, please.' Annie did so. The customs officer searched the pockets. 'Take your jeans off and put them on the table . . .'

Annie stood stripped naked, waiting and shivering. The policewoman stared steadily at the opposite wall.

'Bend over and touch your toes, please.'

Annie leaned forward and for a moment the fury, fighting with the fright inside her, won.

'In your face,' she shouted as her fingers touched cold toes. This little piggy went to market. 'I'm pregnant, you know.'

'Aren't we all?' said the customs officer. 'Nice try.'

Lydia drove to Sainbury's. Despite the disappointment of the previous evening, a hectic gaiety seemed to have replaced the despondency of the previous week as she piled packets of frozen cod, fishcakes and lamb burgers into her trolley and drove home to pile them in the freezer.

It was like the old days, the single-parent days – three children and a full-time teaching job – when she knew what she had to do today, tomorrow, and the next day just to keep going, a situation which freed her from the burden of choice.

She got through to SHSE. Julia apologised profusely for not being there when she phoned and not letting her know three students were coming the evening before. Their applications got put in the wrong file, which wasn't her fault, and anyway the school wasn't expecting students to arrive until Saturday. SHSE was a bit chaotic but she hoped to get the first cheques out to all the host families today. Yes, Carmel was younger than some students, her father had phoned late, family crisis, and Carmel did have very nice manners.

'Well, yes,' Lydia agreed, wondering whether a landlady would ever describe Annie in such terms. Certainly not Mrs Trewartha.

The Bentley was standing on the drive next door with its boot wide open. Evidently Margaret and Bertie were home.

'It's me,' Lydia called into the front door. 'Can I come in?'

'Of course, dear,' Margaret said, coming forward, a floaty blue wrap over her swimming costume, folding Lydia in her plump embrace. 'Let's have some coffee, shall we? Bertie makes the most gorgeous cappuccino.'

'Cappuccino it is,' Bertie said. He appeared to fall in happily with anything Margaret suggested.

'Have you had a good time?'

'Marvellous,' Margaret said. 'We drove all down the west coast and then stayed just outside Tenby for a few days, a little hotel right by the sea. Midnight picnic on the beach, just Bertie and me. I actually got him into the water.'

'I like swimming in the sea,' Bertie said.

'He's a good swimmer, stylish,' Margaret said. 'Does everything well, my Bertie, wonderful with his hands . . .'

'I'm sure,' Lydia said, avoiding Bertie's eye.

'He made this barbecue thing with bits of metal left on the beach and cooked chipolaties,' Margaret went on.

'Learned that in Benghazi,' Bertie said. 'Cooked rats.'

'Poor little gerbils, I dare say,' Margaret said. 'I had my first midnight picnic. We keep having these *firsts*, Bertie and me.' Bertie cleared his throat. 'We made love on the beach!'

'Wonderful,' Lydia murmured.

'Yes,' Margaret agreed. 'First time ever. But I still saw the chipolaties were properly cooked. You can get parasites from underdone pork. We got back to the hotel very late.'

'Covered in sand,' Bertie said.

'You would be,' Lydia said, not sure she wanted the image of the two of them entangled on the beach in her head for ever.

'We got in the bath together. I hope we didn't wake anybody, Bertie. The notice in the passage said "No Baths After Midnight".' Margaret's brow furrowed but the anxiety which had once been so visible had disappeared.

'What about our cappuccinos, Bertie?'

'Coming up, milady.'

'Isn't he sweet?' Margaret whispered as Bertie went out to the kitchen. 'Such a happy temperament. The Stringers were all like that according to Bertie, his mother and grandmother. I must show you the family album . . . But how are things with you, dear?'

'I've got three foreign students at the moment,' Lydia said. 'Thought I ought to warn you.'

'Three foreign students?' Margaret said. 'Why?'

'Well, we haven't sold the house and the bills keep coming, it seemed like a good idea,' Lydia said, recognising a half-truth. Wasn't it also because she couldn't face the empty house and the necessity to make a serious start with her painting once she had finished the final draft of the Guy Maze's poems?

'Doesn't seem right you having all this trouble when Bertie and

I—' Her face widened into a smile at the sight of Bertie trundling down the passage with an old tea trolley. 'Loves the trolley. A tray would have done just as well,' she added in a whisper. 'Thank you, darling.'

'Cappuccinos,' Bertie said.

The phone was already ringing as Lydia approached her front door ten minutes later. The receiver felt warm already in her hand.

'Wherever did you get to this time in the morning?' Mother's voice was strident. 'I got through to Unity straight away over thousands of miles of Atlantic ocean.'

'I was having coffee with Margaret next door,' Lydia said. 'Is something wrong?'

'James has had a stroke and I have had the most *terrible* shock,' Mother separated each word, staccato. 'Collapsed inside his toilet capsule. The home help had to get a hammer and break the door down and there he was, all bunched up in the shower, unconscious. I put a cushion under his head, like they tell you in First Aid, and dialled 999 straight away. The ambulance took him off to hospital. I shall never forget how he looked lying there . . .'

'How is he?' Lydia said.

'*Comfortable* is all they say. I'm visiting this afternoon. Thought you might like to come and support your mother.'

'Well, it's a bit difficult with three foreign students staying here. I mean we haven't sold the house and—'

'You should never have left Ed.' Mother's voice rose alarmingly. 'Ed was a *good provider*. No woman with common sense would leave a good provider.'

'I did not *leave* Ed,' Lydia said. How many times had she said it already? 'Ed left me, but that's by-the-by. If you want me to come, I expect I can fix something.'

'Good of you, dear,' Mother said, suddenly quieter. 'I'm not quite myself, the shock . . . One has to hope for the best but James may not last long. He was so fond of you, Lyddy . . .'

'I'll work something out and phone later,' Lydia said. As she rang off she was startled by sounds on the landing above. Carmel came down the stairs. 'What are you doing here?'

'SHSE not good school for me. I phone Mama, I go home.'

86

'But she'll be very disappointed, Carmel. I mean your parents will have paid the fees already and . . .'

'No worry,' Carmel said. 'Mama want happy daughter.'

'But it's always difficult at a new school. I really think you should try again. Monday might be better.'

Carmel shrugged. 'Maybe I go school one more time.'

'I'm responsible for you when you're here. *In loco parentis*,' Lydia went on. It was like having Annie home again. Annie gave up at the least difficulty. 'I want you to be happy, Carmel. Let's have lunch. Cheese and salad OK?'

'I like,' Carmel said without enthusiasm.

'Monday you'll get on better,' Lydia said, laying the table, dropping salad into the sink. 'How old are you, Carmel?'

'Eighteen years.' Her English comprehension seemed very good, perhaps that was the trouble?

'You look so young,' Lydia said.

'Always I look young,' Carmel said, smiling again. 'Grandmama say this lucky.'

'Grandmama is right,' Lydia said, shaking out lettuce. If only Izzy was around to step in for the weekend. 'Can you cook, Carmel?'

'Cook? Why I cook?' Carmel frowned.

'My mother just phoned,' Lydia said, putting bread and cheese on the table. 'My stepfather is in hospital. I want to visit but I have to look after you and Sacha and Joseph.'

Carmel smiled suddenly. 'I cook very good, cook for four brothers. When you go to Mama's house?'

'Tomorrow,' Lydia said. 'I'll come back quick as I can. Away just one or maybe two nights. I'll show you what to cook for the evening meal and . . . er, while I'm away you should lock your bedroom door at night.'

'Lock already.' Carmel wrinkled her nose. 'Albanian boys all peasants. Italy take country Albania any time she like.'

CHAPTER ELEVEN

THAT EVENING LYDIA explained the problem to Sacha and Joseph as best she could over the lamb burgers, peas and potatoes followed by a choice of an apple or banana. Carmel helped, interjecting explanations in Italian and enjoying her new role. The two young men grinned and muttered and seemed quite pleased with the arrangements. Lydia had already phoned Belstones. She explained the situation to Carmel, who agreed to show prospective buyers round the house and see that it was always tidy.

'Sì, sì,' Carmel smiled. 'Carmel sell house for you.'

Lydia also phoned William, asked him to keep an eye on things. 'Got a date,' he said. 'Try the Newtons, why don't you? You worry too much, Ma.'

Probably true, Lydia thought, pleased by Will's date, and because it was Friday, exalted by her enterprise, she phoned Marina, told her about James's stroke, her weekend away and her three students just as if nothing was wrong between them. Marina was monosyllabic but then Marina was often monosyllabic.

'How are things with you two?' Lydia finally ventured.

'All right,' Marina said flatly. 'Thank you for asking.'

'Er . . . no developments babywise?' Silence at the other end impelled her to rush on. 'I'm sorry if I'm to blame . . . but I really don't know what I can do.'

'Nothing,' Marina said.

'I suppose I could pay for your IVF treatment when the house is sold.' Was she making things better or worse?

'You're such a yo-yo, Ma. Now it's the martyr bit.'

'Martyr? Who's talking?' Lydia said, and wished she hadn't as Marina put the phone down.

On Saturday morning, the Newtons went out early. Lydia put a note through their door. She was letting the rush hour pass, when the phone rang.

'Me again, Jordan Mackay . . .' His chuckle was nervous and

jokey. 'About this coachin' . . . can I come and see you?'

'Jordan, I don't *do* coaching, not ever, never,' she said sharply. 'Please don't phone again.'

Ten minutes later she set off on the A4 route through Savernake Forest. She had to go, didn't she? The word *duty* might be unfashionable but you couldn't ignore the conditioning had you received it. The arrangements she had made for the students were precarious; possible disasters buzzed in her head like anxious bees. No wonder SHSE required character references. What would Carmel's mama, not to mention papa, think about their certainly precious and probably virgin fledgeling, left all night with two young males and no adult supervision?

Had she imagined the excitement in Sacha's eyes?

But she ought to be thinking about James. That afternoon at The Cottage he had confided more about Mother than a loyal husband should. Was it true that she had tried and failed to get into art school? Was Lydia flying across the country for Mother's sake or for James's, who had frightened and disgusted her once but befriended her later, enmeshing her for ever in an uncomfortable ambivalence about James and perhaps about all men?

Would his death finally set her free?

Poor old Granddad, William thought, too young to find the prospect of death interesting, sliding the letter from Ruby into his breast pocket as he heard the front door of the office suite open and close.

'On your toes in five minutes, if you please, young Kemp,' old Mr Beavis said, crossing to his inner sanctum.

'Right, sir,' William said, retrieving the letter as the door closed. Australian stamp . . . what the hell was Ruby doing in Adelaide? The letter didn't really say. Usual crap about how she missed him, then on about the Sanderson kids, Tarquin and Sophie, who were spoiled to bits. But then half a page about *a gorgeous hunk* from Hong Kong who had suddenly turned up in Adelaide, 'a totally amazing coincidence'. They were going out tonight to celebrate how totally amazing it was.

What was going on? William ground his teeth. Ruby wanted him to grind his teeth, Ruby was devilish. Quite likely she had made it up; quite likely they were fucking right now.

Ruby and the gorgeous hunk . . . going going gone.

How could he bear it?

'How is he?' Lydia asked, arriving at The Cottage in the late afternoon. Mother opened the front door, apparently calm and neatly dressed, hair newly set. It was two days since James had collapsed and some twenty hours since she had phoned.

'No change.' Mother presented her cheek. 'I've got veal and ham pie for tonight but I've just switched the kettle on. Expect you'd like a cup of tea now?'

'Please. I'll just sit and get my breath, then go straight to the hospital. Would you like to come?'

'No need for that,' Mother said. 'I went this morning, told Sister you'd be in tomorrow. She's expecting you, though.'

'Oh well . . .' It was annoying but typical, Mother arranging her programme in detail, but it didn't seem the moment to argue. 'Anyway, are you all right, you sounded . . . not quite yourself.'

'Oh, I'm fine now,' Mother said. 'The shock knocked the stuffing out of me for the moment . . . James lying there. But I'm not going to let things get on top of me.'

'Good,' Lydia said, circling her neck and shrugging her shoulders like they did in yoga class. How would Carmel cope with cod, chips and beans for three? She could have asked Marina to look in.

'I'd like you to have a look at the car,' Mother said brightening. 'See if you can get it started. I haven't driven for some time but if I have to keep visiting James, I can't afford taxis.'

'I'm not good at cars,' Lydia said. 'Expect the battery's flat. You'd better get a chap from the garage. Is the tax up to date?'

'Of course. James wanted to sell the Austin when the doctor said he mustn't drive with his blood pressure but I didn't let him. Men are so selfish . . .'

'What did the specialist say?'

'Didn't tell me anything I didn't know.' Her expression softened. 'Paralysed down one side, poor old boy. When I think of all there's been between us . . . so many years . . .'

'People do recover from strokes,' Lydia said.

'Nobody knows except God, do they?' Mother said. 'Ward Three, level Two, I'll write it down for you. How are the children?'

'All right, more or less,' Lydia said. 'William's missing Ruby . . . Annie's got a job in Penzance all summer.'

'And my Marina?' Mother smiled. 'Any sign of a baby?'

'Not yet,' Lydia said. Her voice sounded odd and she cleared her throat. 'Far as I know.'

'Tell her from me she ought to get on with it. Girls leave it too late. Mrs Gibbs' daughter had her first at thirty-six, had to have a Caesarean. Just shows you.'

The same evening Dr Rinde-Smith sat on the veranda of his Sussex house with his wife beside him. Down the garden the boys knocked up on the tennis court. He could hear voices, shouts of laughter, occasionally a ball soared white against green leaves.

'All four at home together,' Hermione said. 'Red-letter day. When was the last time?'

'All right, are they?' he said. Two boys at public school, and one at Oxford, one at Cambridge, merited respectful glances. 'Don't know how you can do it, Julian,' they said. Neither did he. There were seven more years before he could retire. Hermione was keen on France.

'Course they're all right, why shouldn't they be?' Hermione said. 'More coffee?'

'No, thanks.' Hermione poured herself a second cup and wandered down the garden, leaving him to brood. He didn't sleep too well, woke in the night and thought about Annie Kemp. Primigravida was unusual for surrogacy but with her innocent blue eyes and fair hair she had seemed so appropriate to accommodate the foetus and heir of the blue-eyed and fair-haired Spensers.

It was a month later she smilingly admitted she had a boyfriend, had been living with him for months, she said, quite unabashed.

How was he supposed to know she was a natural-born liar?

If liars were forced to carry bells and shout 'Unclean' like medieval lepers it would save people like himself a lot of trouble. Uncertainty was the difficulty. Suppose the child was black or Chinese, that would at least be something definite, something which could be negotiated.

* * *

On Sunday morning Lydia drove to the hospital and stared a moment at the square glass and metal building.

'Ward Three, level Two,' she murmured to herself, crossing the car park to the swing doors, studying the signposts inside.

'Mr Price? He's just over here,' a nurse said, flicking back the flowered curtains drawn round James's bed.

He lay cradled in an nest of gadgetry, an oxygen mask half-covered his face, a white plastic-covered wire stretched from a heart monitor beside the bed and disappeared into his pyjama coat, a drip was attached to his arm.

'Are you feeding him?'

'Not yet,' the nurse said. 'Watching his fluid balance. He's not conscious at all.'

'Do they think he'll come round?' Lydia said.

'Hard to say, you never know, not with strokes.'

'Can he hear us?'

'Unlikely,' the nurse said. 'Your father is he, Mr Price?'

'Stepfather,' Lydia said, her voice sounding odd, husky.

'Looks peaceful,' the nurse smiled. 'Twitchy at first, sedated now.'

'Twitchy?' Lydia murmured. Better if he dies, poor old man. Better for him, better for everybody.

The nurse shifted uneasily. 'Would you like a chair?'

'Thanks.'

Lydia sat down. Her hand crept across the blanket and touched James's speckled one. It felt cold, the arthritic fingers were curled. James, could you call it James, this old battered body lying insentient like a felled tree. How long should she stay? What did custom and good behaviour require? As she looked at him, the kiss, the colour of his tongue probing her mouth, flooded her head with a brilliant swollen pink which gradually faded into pale insignificance.

Why hadn't she said something that afternoon in the garden, cleared the air for them both? Had James headed her off or had he forgotten? Mothers, fathers, stepmothers, stepfathers, brothers, sisters, cousins, no slate was ever absolutely clean. You had to forgive. It was no good not forgiving, that corroded the spirit inside which some people called the soul.

Outside the world was turning; she belonged in the turning

world. 'Goodbye, James, time . . . to let go?'

One eyelid quivered or was it her imagination? Lydia pushed out through the flowered curtains. Last time, she thought, last time.

'How was he?' Mother asked at The Cottage half an hour later. 'What did Sister say?'

'Sister wasn't there,' Lydia said. 'It's hard to tell how someone is when they're unconscious.'

'I can tell . . .' Mother said, complaisant. 'A wife can always tell. I'll make some coffee. Charlie from the garage is coming to look at the car.'

A few minutes later she slid the tray on to the sitting-room table. 'There's Charlie now, d'you think he'd like a cup? Wherever did I put those keys?'

She bustled away. Lydia sipped her coffee as Mother and Charlie crossed to the garage, unlocked and pulled back the heavy doors. She got up then and walked upstairs.

Five doors led off a long straight passage, four of them stood open. Most of the furniture had been brought downstairs. Dust-sheets shrouded the abandoned pieces, turning them into bony white ghosts of themselves. Lydia tiptoed to the closed door.

A smell of turpentine – an easel stood in the middle of the room, a palette and tubes of paint lay on a table beside it. Mother's studio. Half a dozen oil paintings hung on the walls, each one predominantly green: the garden in summer, the mulberry tree, the village pub, orchards in blossom, the river, each picture neatly framed, adequate, recognisable but empty.

More were stacked along the skirting, uninspired, toy stages after the play is over and the audience gone. That much was evident even to Lydia's untutored eye and would certainly be evident to art schools or anybody else. Was that why they had had to be hidden away, concealed . . . like an idiot child?

Mother had always laid such emphasis on telling the truth, whipped her with a riding crop for telling a lie so small and white it was almost invisible. But a thicket of lies lay between them now, a thicket Mother had planted and cultivated.

Lydia closed the door and went quickly downstairs.

'He's charging the battery overnight,' Mother said, flushed with excitement. 'He'll take the car in for service tomorrow and then we'll see . . .'

'Will you be able to drive just like that?' Lydia said.

'You don't lose a skill once you've got it,' Mother said. 'Charlie's going to take me round the lanes if I'm nervous.'

'Good idea,' Lydia said, glad to be relieved of the task. 'I'd like to get back if you're sure you're all right?' A phone call to Cedar Avenue had revealed a background of eighties pop, the tapes the children had left behind.

'Of course, dear,' Mother said, composed. 'The shock upset me but I've got to get on with things myself now, haven't I?'

'You're very brave,' Lydia said, thinking a compliment was expected. But wasn't bravery partly an absence of feeling and wasn't living for years with a confused partner enough to atrophy all feeling? If James died now the divorce would probably never be mentioned again.

Lydia set off after lunch, anxious to avoid the build-up of Sunday picnic traffic. Her back was still stiff from the previous day. How much of herself had been scolded and moulded into shape by Mother's private needs? she wondered, following green-hedged lanes towards the A4. Was all family life like this?

She stopped for supper at The Old Coach just after Savernake Forest. She had done her best for Mother and by chance discovered the paintings. Seeing Mother's paintings for the first time threw light upon her own malaise, her lack of confidence, her timidity, her wanting to paint but not allowing herself to do it because Mother had forbidden it. She could conjure each picture hanging there clear in her head, feel their lifelessness, feel her mother's disappointment. Lydia knew she would remember the pictures all her life. Feeding foreign students was a stopgap, an absurdity, but at least some money was coming in and August would give her the chance to clear up the rest of the house, and after that she would paint.

The light was fading as she turned into Cedar Avenue. Loud music flooded from the house. Bill Newton from next door hovered on the front path.

'What's going on? Bedlam, and nobody answers the door, kids can't get to sleep. Sarah's trying to get hold of Ed . . .'

'Didn't you get my note?'

94

'What note?'

'Sorry, Bill. It's OK now,' Lydia said, inserting her latchkey. 'You get off home, I'll see to it.'

'Sure you'll be all right . . ?'

'Quite sure. Hello, Carmel!'

Carmel put the phone down quickly, shouting above the music. '*Signora* home, *Signora* Mrs Kemp back home.' She turned to Lydia. 'But you say away two nights?'

'One *or* two,' Lydia shouted automatically.

'I phone Mama, I get what you say . . . sick-home?'

'Homesick,' Lydia shouted. She walked on into the sitting room, switched off the tape and gazed round her.

Sacha lay on the sofa with his feet on the arm and a can of beer balanced on his chest, apparently asleep. Joseph and a strange girl lay sprawled in one armchair, two more young men lay on the floor. Beer cans and crisp packets spread across the carpet like the detritus left by a receding tide. There was a strong smell of gin.

'What's going on?' Lydia said loudly and Sacha woke. She didn't want to look, didn't want to recognise the chaos of her sitting room, the violation of her home, her life, she didn't want to know.

'You beautiful womans . . .' he muttered thickly.

'Shut up and go to bed,' Lydia ordered, stepping back to the hall. 'Carmel, where are you?'

Footsteps retreated up the stairs, the door of Annie's room closed, the key turned in the lock. Behind the sofa somebody moaned. Lydia turned back to the sitting room. Thirteen-year-old Bethany lay behind the sofa with her eyes closed; Lydia's bottle of gin lay on its side, empty. Even adults die overdosing on spirits, she thought distracted. Hadn't Dylan Thomas died of twenty-four whiskies? Was this the worst experience of her life?

'Beth?' she said, patting the pale but still-warm face. 'Bethany? Wake up.' She would remember this moment for ever.

'Wha?' Bethany muttered, turning her head away. 'Wha?'

A black BMW slid on to the drive. Lydia ran to the front door, locked it with the mortice key and threw both bolts. A moment later Ed rang the bell, then rang again, and again, each ring held longer than the last, banging on the door with the flat of his hand, shouting through the letter slot, 'Open up, Lydia, I want to talk.'

He moved round towards the terrace. Fortunately she got there first and locked the side gate. Ed shook it violently, shouted imprecations. Finally he left.

'*Déjà vu*,' she murmured as the black BMW backed up the drive, just as the grey Citroën had ten years ago. She had known then that life would be different and it had been, but not different enough.

Clearing up beer cans was a doddle compared to shards of broken glass from the wedding-present glasses . . . and Bethany was trying to sit up.

PART THREE

Fresh Start

CHAPTER TWELVE

W HEN THE ALARM woke Lydia the following morning, she got
up and went to the landing window. Dew shone on the front
lawn, which needed cutting again, but at least there were no bodies.
After Ed had left she'd got the semi-somnolent, and from her
viewpoint *uninvited*, guests on their feet and out of the front door
with help from Sacha. They were all SHSE students from various
European countries. Bethany, who had told her mother she was
staying over at Sharon's, had slept on a mattress on Ed's study floor.

Lydia walked down the passage, knocking on doors and calling
out. 'Monday morning, seven o'clock.'

Was this the future she had chosen? Lydia wondered, repeating
the procedure five minutes later. Was it to become a neccessary daily
ritual? But did she really *want* to live with overgrown kids who gave
drunken parties in her sitting room? She did not. She needed the
solace of adult conversation, Izzy was in Turkey, Richard in Southsea
learning to sail, making a fresh start.

She really must make a fresh start too, think it out.

Behind the house at Frenchay the violas were still flourishing.
Marina was good like that, Jeremy thought, standing at the window
with his breakfast coffee, never forgot to water plants, never forgot
to water him come to that.

'We ought to ask your mother over to see the garden.'

'Not yet,' Marina said. 'Not quite yet.' Mothers and daughters,
she thought, a complicated web of love, hate, jealousy and poisoned
apples. Today was ovulation day.

Downstairs the phone was ringing.

'Hello?' Lydia said.

'I'm coming to see you,' Ed said heavily.

'When?' She looked at the deconstructed sitting room and
thought of saying *please don't* but Ed had already hung up.

Would it be best to bring the wheelie-bin straight round to the terrace? The delphiniums were done for but the crimson roses, Fragrant Cloud, were perfect as were the African daisies, mauve-grey petals opening each morning brilliant white.

Lydia gazed for a moment and started on breakfast, standing a bottle of aspirin in the middle of the table in addition to the usual array. The young men appeared, Sacha's eyes downcast, Joseph's face greenish pale as he shambled to the table.

'*Buongiorno*.' Carmel was her usual smiling self.

'Last night,' Sacha muttered huskily. 'Very bad.'

'Sorry, sorry,' Joseph added, sheepish. 'Very sorry.'

'So I should think!' Lydia said.

'*Signora* say *two* nights away,' Carmel said, petulant.

'I said one *or* two,' Lydia said in a *fresh start* voice. She would need to toughen up to get through August. 'You behaved very badly. Please eat your breakfast and go to SHSE. Bus stop Seafield Road.'

'Very sorry, very sorry,' Joseph and Sacha chorused meekly.

After they left Lydia stacked the dishwasher and pushed the wheelie-bin round. Bethany emerged yawning from Ed's study.

'Wicked headache!'

'Drinking gin is bad for girls your age,' Lydia said. 'It's also illegal. You'd better take two aspirins and go straight home. What were you doing here anyway?'

'Sharon asked me to stopover Saturday night at her place, but she forgot and went out, so I came round here and this party was going on,' Bethany said, swallowing aspirin. 'Can I mow the lawn?'

'You'd better phone your mother first.'

'She won't be up yet, goes ballistic if I wake her.'

'Shall we talk about *blue paint*?' Lydia said.

'What you on about?' Bethany said, blushing bright pink.

'I'm talking about you spraying the wheels of my friend's Astra bright blue.'

'Who says?' Bethany's eyes were defiant.

'You'd better go straight home then,' Lydia said.

Bethany dropped her gaze to her Doc Martens. 'Can't you take a joke?'

'It isn't a joke, it's criminal damage and it's silly.'

'So I'm a crim?' Bethany seemed to find the idea gratifying. 'Twice times a crim, drinking all your gin.'

'Fortunately there wasn't much left.'

'Mr Walker doesn't think I'm silly. He says I'm the best-developed girl he's ever set eyes on. Brings me tea in bed.'

Lydia didn't want to hear this. 'Does your mother know?'

'Course not, she'd go ballistic. Used to have the attic to myself but then she made this top flat and the Walkers moved in and I got this manky room at the back and we can't go on holiday because Mum berserks if she doesn't get to bridge.'

'Lots of people don't go away for holidays, Bethany. Where does your sister, er, Judy, sleep?'

'Nurses' home at the BRI.'

'And your dad?'

'Moved out, Christmas before last.' Bethany followed Lydia to the sitting room. 'Cor . . . stinks in here!'

'You had an orgy, remember?' Lydia said, picking cushions from the floor. Grandmother's kneehole desk had a line of white rings on top from wet beer cans. 'I want to get to the supermarket early.'

'Can I come?' Bethany said.

'I suppose . . . if you behave yourself.'

'That Carmel girl, she was on your phone to her boyfriend, lovey-dovey stuff all evening.'

'What boyfriend?'

'Fabrizio. Lives in Naples. Just thought you'd like to know,' Bethany said, going out to the car.

The supermarket car park was already full, everybody evidently deciding to get there before the morning rush.

'I'll push the trolley,' Bethany said.

'Two cornflakes . . . two sliced browns . . .' Lydia held her list in one hand and pulled items off the shelves with the other. The two of them was like shopping with Annie again.

'Tesco's cheaper,' Bethany said. 'Kwiksave's *much* cheaper.'

'Oh well . . .' Lydia said. 'I'm used to this place and it's near and very convenient.'

'Kwik Save's nearer *and* more convenient,' Bethany said.

'I'm not a good shopper,' Lydia said. 'Always too much to think about, three children and a job . . .'

Behind the piled-up trolley, Bethany grabbed a chocolate bar.

'Put that back,' Lydia said.

'It's on the list.'

'Not on my list. Put it back, please,' Lydia said firmly. 'I'm *not* paying for it.' Their eyes met and locked like antlers. Had she imagined she was cut out for this sort of thing? You had to be qualified for buddying problem schoolgirls; she was only qualified for teaching French. Bethany bit the chocolate bar and crunched noisily.

'You can pay for it yourself then.'

'Haven't got any money.'

'Then you're shoplifting.' Lydia's voice rose.

'That's nice,' Bethany announced loudly to a passer-by, who moved quickly away. 'Shoplifting, mega-nice, that is.'

'Thank you very much, Bethany,' Lydia said through clenched teeth as she piled shopping on the counter and the assistant clicked it over the scanner. Bethany crammed the rest of the chocolate bar in her mouth, pushed the empty trolley through and began to reload it, smacking full red lips.

'It's stealing,' Lydia said furiously as Bethany pushed the trolley back to the car.

'Big deal!' Bethany said.

'You are going straight home.'

'But you said I could do the lawn,' Bethany slumped down in her seat. 'You promised. You promised. You must never break a promise or you'll have bad luck for the rest of your life. A promise is sacred.'

'I promised before you stole that chocolate bar.'

'People steal because nobody loves them,' Bethany said.

'Well, you'd better do the lawn and then go home,' Lydia said, thinking the tiresome girl might be right.

She heard Carmel's excited voice before she opened the front door and the phone slammed down.

'What are you doing here?' she said. 'You're not supposed to be back till five o'clock.'

'Sick-home. I phone Mama,' Carmel said. Her face was still pink but her smile had faded to wan.

'Home sick, we say home sick. And please do *not* use my phone. Phoning Italy is expensive, you understand?'

'But you say—' Carmel began.

'I said you could phone Mama *once* to say you had arrived. If you want to phone again, please use the SHSE pay phone. Anyway you should be at school now.'

'No like. Class no good,' Carmel muttered. 'Here I like.'

Lydia sighed. Two problem teenagers was too much. She took a deep breath and forced her voice to a lower key.

'Let's unpack the car.'

'I'll tidy the sitting room,' Bethany said, keen to establish herself as part of the scene. 'Yucketty yuck! Somebody's been sick under this chair.'

'No like sick . . .' Carmel said, disappearing upstairs.

'Thought I could smell something,' Lydia said, fetching hot water and disinfectant. She was scrubbing at the carpet when the front door bell rang, and she leaned over to look through the window. A familiar black BMW stood on the drive.

'Ed,' Lydia said, sitting on her heels. 'My ex-husband.'

'What's he want?' Bethany frowned.

'An argument mostly,' Lydia whispered, breathing deeply and wondering why she felt like a cornered rabbit. She wasn't exactly frightened of Ed, it was just that whenever he came near her heart started to thud.

'Is he going to hit you?' Bethany said as the bell rang again.

'Course not,' Lydia said. What a world when a thirteen-year-old automatically expected violence! Not that she and Ed were exactly models of post-divorce harmony.

'What shall I do?' Bethany said.

'Go to the kitchen and wash the salad for lunch.'

'Oh, it's you, Ed,' she said, opening the front door. Why was his hair cut so short? Had she missed the latest fashion?

'That's right!' Ed stepped into the house and stood in the doorway of the sitting room. 'Jesus wept.'

'As well he might, especially if he had been required to clear it all up single-handed,' Lydia said perkily.

'Just look at the kneehole desk.'

'I have.'

Ed pushed the sofa and armchairs into the positions they had occupied ten years before. The castors clanked against further beer cans.

'What are you playing at, Lydia?' he said, depositing them on the mantelpiece with a clack.

'I've got three foreign students staying here for August,' she said. 'One Italian, two Albanian.'

'Is this a deliberate attempt to sabotage the house sale?'

'Course not,' she said. 'James had a stroke and I had to go to Kent. Last night was just unfortunate . . .'

'You left the house in charge of three foreign juveniles?'

'They're not barbarians, just high-spirited young people.'

'Belstones brought the Powells round again yesterday. They were going to up their offer . . . now they've withdrawn.'

'Well, I'm sorry but—'

'Sorry isn't good enough, Lydia. Just get your bloody students out of here.'

'I can't. They pay ninety pounds a week each. How else am I supposed to eat and pay council tax?'

'You should have thought of that before you gave up your job.'

'And you might have told me before you cancelled the standing order,' Lydia said.

'No law in this land requires me to support an ex-wife who cheated on me, Mrs Kemp—'

'Cheated on you? Because I fell in love with somebody else ten years ago?' Lydia cried, and suddenly her voice was soaring like a bird in the eye of a storm. 'Thank God, I did. How else could I have found out about *love*? Not from you, you robot, you. Get out of here, get out of my life.'

'You heard what she said,' Bethany screamed, suddenly at the door with a kitchen knife in her hand. 'Get lost, you.'

Ed moved quickly to the front door.

'What do you think you're doing, Bethany?' Lydia said as it slammed behind him. 'I hate people messing about with knives.'

'I wasn't *messing*, I was doing the salad like you said. But you don't like *me*, do you? Doesn't matter, Mr Walker does.'

'Of course I like you, Beth . . . This Mr Walker . . . er, does he touch you?'

Bethany hesitated. 'Sometimes . . .'

'You don't have to let him, you know,' Lydia said.

'He got me this box of chocs for my birthday and Sharon comes faffing round every breaktime. 'What's he do, what's he do?' she says all the time because her boyfriend, Josh, is fifteen and doesn't do anythink.'

'Listen, Bethany,' Lydia said, resolute. An adult had responsibilities after all. 'Mr Walker coming into your bedroom has to stop. You must tell your mother about it . . .'

'Can't,' Bethany said. 'His rent pays my school fees.'

'But the flat can be let to somebody else.'

Bethany considered this. 'Who says I want it to stop? Anyway, how d'you know I'm not making it up? All that stuff you said about girls my age and phases and puppyfat, I got this making-things-up phase, Mrs Kemp. Made it all up about Mr Walker. Honest . . .'

After lunch Bethany went home, Carmel lay outside in the sun and Lydia applied brown shoe polish to the white rings on the kneehole desk. After that she retired to her study and wondered why she hadn't heard from the editor of *New Expectations* and whether Richard was enjoying his sailing holiday and why he was away for so long. It was perplexing, even perverse to decline all his various proposals and then find herself thinking about him all the time.

Downstairs the front door bell rang.

'It's only me,' said Jordan Mackay, smiling widely but swaying nervously from one foot to the other. 'Droppin' in, know what I mean? Nice place you got 'ere, real style. You aksin' me to come in?'

'Well . . . I suppose so,' Lydia said, stepping back, irritated by his cheek but moved by his persistence at the same time. 'Long as you don't start about coaching again, Jordan.' His eyelids, delicate as seashells and thickly lashed, quivered. He was beautiful despite his fractured English.

'Fancy a cup of tea if you was aksin'?' he said. 'It's the biz, this place you got, innit, plenty-plenty rooms, fetch a good price, 'ouse like this, know what I mean?'

'I'll put the kettle on,' Lydia said. Jordan followed her into the kitchen. How would Richard handle this? He was good with people, insightful, sympathetic but shrewd.

'I'se got ambitions, man, thass why I'se doin' this GCSE, black man wiv ambitions, innit? Thass why I needin' coachin'. Didn't do no French in Brixton, man. Never ever done no French yet, thass why I needin' coachin'. Exam's December, innit?'

'But I told you I don't do coaching, Jordan,' Lydia said, pouring boiling water on teabags in two large mugs. Did he think she was a soft touch or what? How could he possibly get his French up from scratch in four months?

'I've got French tapes you could borrow. I used them when I taught French in school. Where did you live before Bristol?'

'Railton Road, Brixton, but I was in care, see, ten years old I couldn't read and wettin' the bed, stepfather beatin' me with his wild cane, put in care up to fifteen. Housemaster give me ideas, ambitions, man. Say you can choose what you want, white or black, you can choose. But I'se washin' up this late night café city centre, see, very small room, very noisy, not quiet like 'ere. Tapes is all right if you got a player, innit, but I ain't got no player, man.' He heaped three spoonfuls of sugar into his mug, stirred vigorously and gulped the syrupy tea. 'Thass better . . .'

'I've got three foreign students staying here for August,' she said.

'White boys, yes, you's coachin' white boys?'

'No. They're learning English at a language school all August.' If he was trying to make her feel guilty was he succeeding? 'September you could come here and use the tapes if you like.'

'Cool,' Jordan said, cool.

'Anyway, why do you want to do French?'

'My dad, 'e come from Mali.'

That evening Jeremy listened to *Newsnight* with Marina at his feet. His arm enfolded her neck as she leaned back against him; she knew a subservient posture turned him on. He'd been miffed earlier, she couldn't afford to throw the chance away.

Jeremy was such an innocent. It was like being married to a teddy bear, a thinking, thoughtful teddy bear. Better not to confide and turn love into a duty. She was so tired of hoping and waiting, thermometers, pills . . .

'I phoned Ma from work. She's got foreign students all August . . .'

'Least you tried.' He kissed the top of her head. 'Good girl. Lovely girl . . .'

She turned her mouth towards him.

It was going to be all right.

CHAPTER THIRTEEN

O N THE LAST day of August Lydia dusted her desk and arranged
her letters for filing. The students had already departed with
thanks and expressions of gratitude, and it was over now, cheques
banked, council tax and SWEB paid up to date.

A postcard had arrived from Annie: 'Penzance still ever so
crowded. Love Annie.' Better than nothing but not much. Why did
she never mention the art school, so much the stuff of Lydia's
dreams? She tried to imagine it, everybody talking and thinking
about art all the time, what it was and wasn't . . .

A fresh start was possible now – essential. Tomorrow was the
one-day painting workshop. After that she must start thinking about
the GCSE classes, some of the time at least.

Was Richard back yet? He hadn't phoned.

She had forgotten about the painting workshop when she'd
made her impulsive offer to Jordan and she hadn't heard from him
since. He would have to postpone starting because of her workshop,
and she had left a note at Park Lodge to that effect. Was the original
impulse born of generosity or guilt? If Jordan's mother was from
Ireland, his father from Mali, he wasn't exactly a survivor of the
slavery holocaust. Blacks often got a raw deal, but inviting him to
house-share during the day when she was trying to work might prove
to be an error, especially with someone as addicted to talk as Jordan.
Lydia sighed as she collected all the French tapes and simple French
texts she could find and put them in Ed's study together with the
tape-recorder.

As well as the SHSE money a small cheque had come from *New
Expectations* with a letter from the editor thanking her for her
excellent work on the Maze poems. Two publishers had written to
acknowledge her letter but regretted they had no translation work
to offer. Once she had had no trouble getting such work; had things
changed in ways she hadn't realised? In a market-orientated world
so many organisations seemed in continuous transition, which made

getting a foothold perilous. Would she be able to cope?

For the moment the house was quiet, the garden hung with billowing sheets, Michaelmas daisies mauve against the ornamental wall, the lawn spattered with tiny stars of white jasmin. Having failed to persuade Carmel to attend SHSE all the first week, Lydia had abandoned the attempt. Carmel had spent her mornings shopping and her afternoons sunbathing, splashing the grass with chic Italian gear in brilliant citrus colours, chattering with visiting friends or painting her toenails while Lydia clipped the hedge. In such an atmosphere it was difficult to prepare classes, impossible to paint. Besides, there was Bethany.

'Soon as you go out Carmel phones Fabi in Naples,' Bethany had said. 'Yes, you told me.' Lydia would rather not know. She had to go shopping herself and unplugging the phone was out of the question with James in hospital, and Mother, publishers, Belstones, Annie and even Richard might ring.

'Papa has forbidden her to see Fabi ever again. He sent her to England so she can't because she's only fifteen. Juliet was thirteen, same as me,' Bethany had finished, eyes shining with the romance of it all, forbidden fruits. But after insisting for several days that Mr Walker's early morning visits were her making-things-up phase, Bethany had suddenly stopped coming to Cedar Avenue.

What should she do? Lydia wondered. Bethany's predicament, imaginary or real, tapped in her head like a woodpecker. It was her responsibility to do something and, risking the ballistic rage of Bethany's mother, she phoned. 'What's she done now?' Mrs Greene sighed resignedly. 'Well, she talks about your lodger, a Mr Walker . . .' 'Oh him, he's gone, his firm moved him back to London last June.' A pause. 'Sometimes Beth throws herself at people, you know?' 'Misses her father perhaps?' Lydia suggested. 'That's what they say at the child guidance.' 'Could she write to him?' 'Could if we had his address, could do a lot of things if we had his address, couldn't we?' Mrs Greene said wearily.

If the child guidance clinic were aware of Bethany's problems, Lydia could give herself permission to forget them. What she wanted now was the house sold to somebody who would care for the garden. Then she could get somewhere to live where she could really start painting, even if she still didn't know how or what. She had bought herself oils – six fat virgin tubes at considerable expense – new brushes, a palette, a second-hand easel and pieces of hardboard treated with gesso to paint on. Hardboard was cheaper than canvas.

Belstones had phoned a week ago with an offer from the Sneeds.

'Sneeds?' Lydia tried to get a fix on half-forgotten faces. 'How much?'

'Low, I'm afraid. Hundred and sixty,' Mr Belstone said, but even a low offer turned the house to quicksand under Lydia's feet.

'You had better let Mr Kemp know.'

She remembered the Sneeds later. She had shown them round some weeks ago. Mr Sneed had gazed disapprovingly at Annie's mural and said he would expect the bedroom to be redecorated before any exchange of contracts. She had expected Ed to refuse the offer without consulting her, as indeed he had.

'Told Belstones they could stuff the Sneeds' offer.'

'Diplomatically, I hope.'

'And I hope your students have gone, especially that crazy fat one.'

'Bethany's not crazy, just attention-seeking, traumatised by her parents assaulting each other and then splitting up . . .'

'What do you mean *not crazy*? She came at me with a knife.'

'She didn't *come at you*. She's thirteen, she was chopping salad.'

'Always have to have the last word, don't you?' Ed said putting the phone down instantly.

Afterwards Lydia made herself a cup of coffee and wandered in the garden in search of tranquillity. Was it Ed had put her right off marriage?

Something was going on next door. The blue pool had a silver-coloured cover right across the end like an extra blanket.

Margaret had asked her to tea. Was it to explain this innovation?

Lydia wandered back to the house but wraiths of the children emerged to take over, voices hovering in the air: 'When you die, Mummy, I'll dig and dig and lie beside you.' 'You're the dog and you've got to say Woof or you can't play.' She remembered William's escaping hamster, Annie's kite stuck all day at the top of the strawberry tree, Marina's need for new pink ballet shoes every three weeks. Why now? Was it a delayed mourning for the stuff she had cleared so unceremoniously and scattered along the charity shops of Whiteladies Road?

She had forgotten the loft.

The trapdoor was above the landing. She fetched a chair and pulled down the expanding ladder from inside. Moments later she climbed up, sniffing dust and cobwebs as she reached for the light. There wasn't as much there as she had imagined – no treasure-trove, just a rusting mouse cage, a chair with a broken leg, a doll's pram and the dropside cot the children had slept in, packed flat and wrapped in clear plastic.

A particular excitement seized her as she carried it down, unwrapped and sorted it. Everything seemed to be there, the screws and metal bits tied up neatly in a separate plastic bag and carefully labelled. Typical Ed. It took her longer than she would have supposed to get it all together but finally it stood there, a light-wood cot, the colour of honey, a faded and stained blue mattress.

For a moment it was what she wanted to paint but almost at once familiar doubts and uncertainties came piling in. Why and how, and could she do it anyway? She gazed at the cot for a few moments, clicked her tongue just as Mother did and felt the excitement die away. 'You girls had a good education, made sure of that, didn't I?' How many times had Lydia heard it? Hundreds, thousands . . . it was engraved deep in the fissures of her brain. But it wasn't education or lack of it that prevented Mother getting into art school but lack of talent, six empty green pictures without point or feeling, hanging on the wall like six empty green bottles.

Teatime, Margaret's front door was open. 'Bertie's away for a few days; daughter's got husband trouble,' Margaret smiled cosily. 'Bertie'll sort it out and he loves driving the Bentley.'

'I should imagine most people would,' Lydia said, wondering if his paternal visit was a cover for something less innocent. 'What did he drive before?'

'A Ford, I think,' Margaret said. 'But he drove an armoured car during the war. Blown up two weeks after D-Day, in hospital for a year. Earl Grey, all right for you, dear?'

'Fine.'

'Expect you noticed Bertie's latest brainwave?' Margaret nodded towards the pool as she carried out the tray. 'He got those balloon people to make the cover to his design. It goes right over the pool. Hasn't worked out the electrics yet, he's putting wires either side, you press a button and the cover slides back. *Hey presto*, there's the pool, warm as mother underneath. Milk or lemon?'

'Lemon, please. Sounds wonderful,' Lydia said, but wasn't electricity so close to water dangerous, even lethal?

'It *is* wonderful,' Margaret said. 'Least it will be. I don't need it this weather but I soon will. Something I've been wanting to show you . . .' Margaret went inside and returned with a large photo album.

'Not the holiday snaps?' Lydia said.

'The Stringers, Bertie's family, three generations. Look, wasn't he a little angel?' Margaret pointed to a photo of a small fair-haired child in a sailor suit, surrounded by three formidable women dressed in black with skirts to the ground and wide-brimmed black hats.

'What a dear little boy!' Lydia said.

'Wasn't he a sweetheart? And three generations, mother, grand-mother Beatrice, and great-aunt Ethel, all good old-fashioned names, none of your Dawns and Kylies. Grandma kept a corner shop in Bethnal Green, thirteen children she had.'

'She looks strong, they all look strong,' Lydia murmured.

'Used to go down to Kent for the hop-picking every summer. The tales Bertie tells . . .' Margaret turned the page. 'Look, Grand-ma's funeral!' Lydia stared at the carriage and coach drawn by four black horses, each with black plumes on their heads.

'Thought the world of Grandma, the Stringers did. Hundreds lined the streets. If Bertie goes before me I shall try and give him a send off like this . . . black horses with plumes . . .'

'Could be a problem getting hold of four black horses?' Lydia suggested. 'I didn't know Bertie came from Bethnal Green.' Wasn't that where the Kray brothers came from?

'Bertie's quite a chameleon, fits in Buckingham Palace or the Old Kent Road. Loyal to his family, though. He'll be back tonight. I'm cooking him Lancashire hotpot, his favourite. Got the ingredi-ents but I'm not sure how long it takes to cook.'

Margaret always raised her spirits but as Lydia walked home through the late afternoon, she felt almost in a trance. Her legs seemed to carry her into the house and up the stairs of their own volition.

She would paint, of course she would paint.

The cot was waiting. She tucked a teacloth in the top of her skirt, propped a piece of hardboard on her desk and began, honey-coloured wood, a blue mattress, a flowered curtain green from the garden in the late afternoon light. She covered the hardboard from edge to edge without thinking. Almost without looking, she picked up another piece and started painting again, the same cot in a changing light.

Repetition and obsession, nothing wrong with that. How many times had Monet painted the lily pond? Once Lydia had started she couldn't stop . . . like the girl with red shoes. If she stopped she might never start again. Shadows lengthened across the garden as she began her third painting. The sun shining through the bars of the cot spread dark lines across the carpet like a grille across a prison window. But she had escaped from her prison, she was running away.

Downstairs the phone rang.

'Hello, Lydia. Listen, your place tomorrow, innit?' Jordan said cheerfully.

'Jordan, glad you phoned. I'm out all day tomorrow – got this painting workshop – but you can come the day after if that's all right?'

'After August, you said. September now, innit?'

'Yes but I forgot about this workshop tomorrow.'

'You don't want me comin', you just say, missus.'

'But I do want you to come, I forgot, that's all. See you the day after tomorrow? OK?'

She put the phone down and went back to the study but an argument ran on in her head.

Suppose Jordan didn't come the day after tomorrow?

Well, it was up to him, wasn't it?

She ought to have got his address from Park Lodge.

He didn't have to be so surly.

How would she feel if he didn't come?

Lydia sighed and went back to her painting. As the sun went down she switched on the light, banishing shadows, turning her world yellow. What was happening? Had she found a magic key?

Somebody said in her head, 'To copy objects in a still life is nothing. One must render the emotions they awaken.' Matisse, was it?

And she had and she was. She could have, would have gone on painting through the night but downstairs the phone was ringing again.

She felt a little giddy as she ran down.

'Phoned you this afternoon.' Mother's voice came out of the dark night croaky, rook-like. 'Bad news, I'm afraid. Your stepfather, James, died this morning without regaining consciousness. He was always so fond of you, Lydia.'

CHAPTER FOURTEEN

A T THE ONE-DAY workshop Lydia discovered acrylic, a man-
made paint much cheaper than oils, which dried quickly and
didn't fade or crack. Its colours were enticing, their names evocative:
cadmium yellow, bright as daffodils; *Payne's grey*, as blue-grey as
English eyes and skies; *viridian green*, a luscious bluish green like a
drake's head. Acrylic was a fresh start and a revelation too, so quick
to dry that painting had to be as fast as thought, or abandoned
altogether.

Lydia left early and bought all the acrylic she could afford. The
next day she painted all day, keeping the acrylic moist in a flat plastic
tray lined with thick damp paper, finding it difficult to work fast
but encouraged by the thought that she was *really* painting for the
first time. Moving from one piece to the next and back to the first
again, moving from her study into the house, painting as she went.

Jordan neither came nor phoned but she hardly noticed that. If
he had to sulk, it was up to him.

James's funeral was to be held in Kent a week after his death.
Lydia decided not to go. She couldn't mourn for James, freed at last
from the long years of fragility and confusion. She had expected to
dream about him but no dreams came. Instead she woke to find
traces of Richard hovering like mist in her head but the more she
tried to fix his image, wonder why and what she was feeling, the
more elusive it became. Should she try and paint Richard?

Two days after the workshop another postcard came from
Annie: 'Everything OK here. Very busy. Love, Annie.' Two postcards
so close was vaguely disturbing but then she had written to Annie
herself last week, sent it to Penzance Art School. Lydia stared at the
seven words, trying to expand the meaning of the spidery scribble.
Annie was usually truthful; the 'OK' presumably meant she wasn't
ill or desperately unhappy; she hoped 'very busy' might refer to some
aspect of art. Did students still cluster round a model for 'life
drawing' or did they do things with piles of washing powder and

dead sheep *à la* Damien Hirst as the popular press suggested?

The postcard was different too – the Morrab Gardens, a luxuriance of palms, yucca, bamboo, banana plant, making a green forest round a square white house. Everything growing in a strange place, transplanted like Annie to Penzance, an environment promising cultivation and opportunity for growth.

The Morrab Gardens appeared to be flourishing but what about Annie? And would a hundred years of sub-tropical plants survive global warming? Lydia imagined a manic yellow sun melting white icecaps, water rising everywhere and the encroaching sea.

Annie was working too hard, Dr Rinde-Smith had said quite sharply on her last visit to London. There was surely no need with Mrs Spenser paying her such a generous allowance? The Spensers' speckything had grown to a baby now – Annie had seen it on the scan. Not that she wanted to but Dr Rinde-Smith told her to look.

So now she only worked mornings in the café. Sitting in the Morrab Gardens or minding Clover's jewellery stall all afternoon. That was OK, but Sophie back working in the café afternoons and Jarvis cheerful even though trade had dropped off, that wasn't OK.

Did they turn the 'Open' card to 'Closed' and slip upstairs? Annie didn't want to think about it but Clover said you had to be firm with kids and blokes, same difference. Thing was, Annie and Jarvis didn't do it much now, though she wasn't that big.

But people knew; it was nudge-nudge all round the pub.

After the babything came out, what then?

After breakfast next day Lydia went up to the study and considered the previous day's work. What should she do today? Should she go back to the cot which had released her imagination, work on it some more, or go on with interiors, bits of the house or even the garden? She had done no work on the garden itself for over a week. The unmown lawn would be soft and plushy-wet under her feet but it was what she wanted. She carried the easel outside and settled near the strawberry tree. On the level space below, neglected roses scattered petals, crimson, white, apricot, covering brown earth. Beyond was the hedge and the wild wood.

Halfway through the morning the phone rang.

'James's funeral is the day after tomorrow,' Mother remarked. 'Are you thinking of coming?'

'You know I'm not, Mother,' Lydia said. 'I told you.'

'People can change their minds, can't they? I hoped you'd change yours and come. Marina and Jeremy would be happy to give you a lift . . . if you let them know . . .'

'Marina has offered but I *haven't* changed my mind.' At least she was back on terms with one daughter. Was it because she had offered to pay for the IVF? Lydia gazed out at the garden; her footsteps had made a dark path in the dewy grass. She was going to do what she wanted. Why was it Mother could never accept her decisions, as if Lydia had no mind of her own? It had always been like this.

'You know Unity's coming, your only sister, flying right over from the United States out of respect for James? She was *so* looking forward to seeing you, dear. It's been such a long time . . .'

'Ages,' Lydia said, exasperated. 'Years, but she knows where I live. Listen, I hate funerals and I'm not coming, Mother, I'm too busy . . . a lot on my plate.'

'I'm glad, my dear, James can't hear you say that,' Mother said in a softer tone. 'You were his favourite, you know that, don't you? William's coming. Why don't you come with Will?'

'Because I'm *too busy*.' Lydia's voice rose.

'What do you mean *too busy* when you're not even working?'

'Evening classes start in less than a fortnight,' Lydia said.

'That gives you plenty of time. Annie wrote me such a nice little letter of condolence. Well, a postcard actually . . .'

'Morrab Gardens?' Lydia said. So, someone knew Annie's address, had been in touch. Did Annie phone her grandmother, even though she no longer phoned her mother?

'How did you know? Course, there's such a lot to do. Undertakers and everything . . . Vera's been a great help but she's not family and I don't like to put on people.'

'Sorry, Mother, I'm not coming. 'Bye for now.'

Lydia went back to the strawberry tree. Why did people get so possessive about funerals? She hated the flummery of it all, the snuffling, the wan faces, the dreadful waste of cut flowers. If she had said she was busy painting, Mother would have contested her right.

Next day William dropped in at four o'clock.

'You could still come, you know,' he said as Lydia switched the kettle on. 'Grandma would be so pleased.'

' "*Et tu, Brute?*" ' Lydia murmured. 'I'm busy.'

'Just fetch your toothbrush and hop in. We'd be there by eight o'clock. A clan gathering, I've got my best suit.'

'Quite an inducement,' Lydia said. How pale and thin he looked. 'What's the point? I'm busy and I don't want to go.'

William shrugged. 'Got to see the old boy off the premises. Doesn't ritual help you to let people go?'

'I can let James go quite well from Stoke Bishop, thank you. Besides, Izzy just phoned and asked me over. Haven't seen her for weeks,' Lydia said, pouring tea. 'Anyway, doing things you don't want to do isn't good for people. Saps the vitality.'

'Since when? Know what old Mr Beavis said?' William shifted into falsetto. ' "How many grandfathers you got, young Kemp?" "Only the one, sir." "Glad to hear it, my boy." Don't think he believed me actually.'

'Still, he did let you leave early today?'

'Two hours, big deal. And he takes the day off tomorrow out of my annual holiday.'

'Mean old thing. Still, you have got a job and a home.'

'Point taken. Anyway, why don't you want to go?' William said. 'You got on OK with James.'

'I'm a free agent,' Lydia said. 'I don't *belong* to anybody but people seem to think I do. Mother, for instance.'

'So you're busy doing what?'

'Painting.'

'Oh . . . painting?' William said. 'Poor old Granddad. Still, he had a good innings. Grandma's had hundreds of letters. Nice hobby for wrinklies, studying the obits and writing off to the bereaved.' Bereaved, William thought, that's what he was. Ruby's being gone was worse than bereavement.

'Where's Ruby at the moment?' Lydia said.

'Sydney,' William said, swallowing tea. 'Gotta get off now, Ma. I'll drop in and do the lawn next week.'

'You could borrow the Fiesta if you like,' she called as he backed his battered Mini up the drive.

'Devil you know . . .' William called, and gave a thumbs up sign as he disappeared along Cedar Avenue.

That fellow who followed her to Adelaide, William accelerated, if that bloody prick turned up in Sydney . . . Tears rivered down his cheeks. William blotted them with his sleeve.

Lydia poured herself a second cup of tea and carried it out to the easel but she couldn't go on. Poor Will, but it would have been a disastrous marriage. Ought she to have gone to keep him company? If only young men were allowed to cry . . .

Tomorrow she must start preparing her classes. Teaching adults at Park Lodge was somewhat different from GCSE at Stoke Bishop High, a different exam board and besides, adults could and did vote with their feet.

She would tidy round the garden and then phone Richard again. 'How are you?' 'Had a good holiday?' – such routines were an obligation of friendship and Richard claimed they were friends. If he wasn't there she would just ring off, two messages left already on his answerphone were quite enough for any male ego.

She tapped the number, the phone lifted immediately.

'Richard Foy speaking.'

'Richard?' she said startled. 'So you're back?'

'Not exactly,' he said. 'You're lucky to have caught me, Lydia, matter of fact.'

'I am? Yes, I am,' she said. 'I phoned several times.'

'I got your messages but I'm only back for a flying visit, getting cleaned up, catching the mail and back to Southsea.'

'Whatever for?'

'Really into sailing, got the bug.' His voice was almost too enthusiastic. 'Done the beginners' course, going to do the inter-mediate . . . might do the advanced.'

'Sounds like you'll be away all autumn,' she said. She wanted to see him. Was he pushing himself to prove he was fit again? Men were so competitive, though she could hardly complain.

'What's so wonderful about sailing?' She wanted to talk to him, a really long talk.

'Hard to say,' Richard said. 'Something to do with the elements, wind in your hair, all that. Anyway, I haven't forgotten I owe you a dinner.'

'Well, give me a ring when you get back. Take care,' she added, but his phone had already gone down.

Lydia walked upstairs, flattened. Somehow his story, his sailing enthusiasm, wasn't quite convincing. He had played rugger in his youth but later seemed too dedicated to the pursuit of 'ladies' to play golf or cricket.

Was sailing compensation for his lost professional life?

Lydia rummaged for her teaching notes, laying them out in their faded cardboard files, Years 7, 8, 9, 10, GCSE, A level. She didn't *want* to look at them but it was an advantage to have old notes from which to compile new ones . . . tomorrow.

Tonight was Izzy.

Just before seven Lydia drove herself to Westbury and parked outside the mews flat, smiling at the sight of the familiar scarlet MG, Izzy's mascot and icon. At least she still had that.

'Hello, love.' Izzy flung out her arms and they hugged in the hall. 'You don't look too bad considering,' she added, releasing Lydia half a minute later. 'Come in the kitchen.'

'Considering what?' Lydia asked.

Izzy shrugged. 'Considering your advanced years, I suppose . . . or the burden of your chronic indecision.'

'Thanks a bunch,' Lydia said.

'Glass of red wine?'

'If you have it.'

'What's mine is yours,' Izzy said, pouring the last of the bottle into a glass and dropping the empty ostentatiously into the bin. She was drinking orange juice; she looked thin and brown and somehow chastened.

'You heard about the disaster?'

'What disaster?' Lydia said. The wine was vinegary.

'Our camper van was stolen.'

'How awful!' Lydia said. Evidently she had dropped right off the grapevine of Stoke Bishop High.

'Was a bit rough,' Izzy said. 'Had to wire Mrs Busby, we were going to be late back. I've done a vegetarian quiche.'

'Sounds great.' A new kelim was flung across the sitting-room sofa, quiche and salad sat on a table laid for two.

'Chris has gone then?' Lydia said, sitting down.

'Hunting camper vans. There's this police auction in London, where you can pick them up cheap. But there's some fuss about the insurance . . .' Izzy said, cutting quiche.

'Didn't put him off camper vans then, getting it stolen?'

'Course not. "Life is tough and then you die" but if you've got a camper van you're free!' Izzy flung her arms out wide. 'I mean you can go anywhere, you've got everything you need. Like a tortoise – well, more like a hare really – until it's stolen, of course. Help yourself to salad. Orange or fizzy water?'

'Orange, thanks.'

'Turkey has so much sky and whole fields of blue flax and these mountains, right in front of us.' Izzy's hands sketched the range. 'So we parked the van, locked it, of course, and walked, got back absolutely knackered and the van had gone. Bed, clothes, cooker, visas, passports, money . . . the lot.' Izzy's wide eyes relived the moment.

'So?'

'So we walked to the nearest police station. Miles. Just as well we had hats or we'd have got sunstroke. Police roared with laughter . . .'

'They understood English?'

'A bit. Lots of Turks come over, work as waiters, save up for a strip of land back home.'

'So what did you do?' Lydia asked.

'People in the villages were very kind. Gave us food, let us sleep in their barns, even gave us bits of money. At night everybody comes out to dance round a fire or even a pressure lamp, like they're grateful to be alive in this wonderful world. We danced too, classical Arabic, what you call belly dancing.' Izzy jumped up and began to chant, dancing in a slow circle to the beat, hips swaying but feet hardly moving. 'Got the school dance club off to a great start.'

'Good. Has Bethany joined, Bethany Greene?'

'Certainly has. Got a thing on *me* now, poor little sod.'

'So how did you get back then?'

'Hitched into Istanbul, embassy did the paperwork. Didn't seem surprised, epidemic of stealing camper vans at the moment.'

'And Chris?'

'Buggered his plans, poor bloke, and now this insurance hassle . . .' Izzy shook her head. 'It's a shame because he was all set to teach English . . . Trieste, Timbuctoo. Teaching half the year and spending the rest getting there. Proper nomad, Chris, doesn't give a toss about material things. Taught metalwork one time, fix anything, jack of all trades . . .'

'And you're back at school?'

'Bored out my head,' Izzy said, disconsolate. 'Boring without you, even more boring when Chris goes . . . Camper van, you got a different view every day.'

'Travelling mania, it's like the seventies over again,' Lydia said.

'Before my time,' Izzy said. 'Anyway, how's your Annie?'

'Wish I knew,' Lydia said. 'I think of going down there.'

'Leave her be, she's a grown woman.'

'Easy to say,' Lydia said.

'You'll find you improve with practice,' Izzy said, but she sounded sad. Izzy was the expert on letting people go but was she finding it hard with Chris? The biter finally bit, Lydia thought. Not so much a change as a metamorphosis.

CHAPTER FIFTEEN

L YDIA PAINTED ALL day for the rest of the week, stopping only to eat and drink. She painted as if her life depended on it – indeed she felt it did – finishing one picture and propping it against the study wall, going straight on with the next, falling into bed and dreamless sleep. 'A day without painting is melancholy and confused,' Cézanne had said, and, threatened by two such dismal emotions, how could Lydia stop? Besides, she had detached herself from the world and ordinary preoccupations, staggering like a toddler at first, but now floating happily in the warm September air and learning how to paint, just as Richard was floating on the Solent and learning how to sail.

Why did she keep thinking about Richard? she wondered. Was she falling in love with him again or was she just offering an obeisance to their dead and buried love, the one overwhelming feeling she had ever experienced?

The class notes lay unused but spattered with paint on her desk; her eyes tried to avoid them. She must get to them tomorrow or the day after or sometime soon.

One morning two items dropped on the doormat, a picture postcard of Michelangelo's frescoes in the Sistine Chapel, on which Carmel thanked *Signora* Kemp for all her kindness and hospitality, and a bill from BT for £255.54. It was five times bigger than usual. It had to be a mistake, a computer error, but further investigation revealed over a hundred pounds was calls to Naples.

Carmel. Bethany had warned her. If you didn't pay, they cut off your phone. What could she do? Lydia sighed and paid.

Later the same day Mr Sharpe phoned from Park Lodge to say all her classes were well subscribed, but the GCSE English literature had twenty-five students. He considered that the maximum and had reluctantly closed the register.

'So I should think,' Lydia said, imagining the small classroom with only one window that opened, canvas and metal chairs against every bit of wall space. 'What about the health and safety regulations?'

'I'll worry about health and safety regs for the time being, Lydia,' the principal said. Did his smile flash on and off as he spoke on the telephone? she wondered. 'When your class numbers drop below the statutory minimum this winter, you can worry.'

'I will,' Lydia said, reminding herself that both GCSE classes would involve written work requiring marking. Mr Sharpe might be right in suggesting it was difficult to hold the French conversation class numbers once the winter evenings set in, especially as the students were mostly elderly and female.

The following morning the front doorbell rang.

'Morning, Lydia, how y'doin'?' Jordan said jauntily. 'Got to get started, know what I mean?' A woollen cap, red, yellow and green contained his hair, a plastic bag swung from his hand. 'Got me books, cost all me sosh.'

'Your dole? I thought you had a job washing up at a late night café?'

'Can't live on that, man, no way,' Jordan said. 'What you take me for?' His smile was mischievous, childlike. Evidently he had got over being offended and didn't feel it necessary to explain the lost weeks between.

'Well, I'll show you the room, it's my ex-husband's study. The tapes are all there,' Lydia said.

'Nice place you got 'ere,' Jordan said as he followed her upstairs. 'Real style, flippin' bourgeois, know what I mean?'

'Shall I show you how it all works?' she said, pointing to the tape recorder.

'Ain't that ignorant,' he said, casting an experienced eye round him. 'Playing tapes since we was kids, man. Wouldn't say no to a cup of tea.'

'Well, all right,' Lydia said. Down in the kitchen, she switched on the kettle and showed him the whereabouts of teabags, milk and sugar. 'After this you make your own tea, Jordan, OK? I'm busy all day.'

'Sure,' he said, helping himself generously to sugar. 'What gets you so busy? You should relax, man.'

'I've got to get my classes together,' Lydia said, startled at the way his eyes shone, reflecting the light like black glass.

'Same 'ere,' Jordan said, taking a book from the plastic bag, which he'd left propped by the kitchen door. As he stared at the first page his expression shifted from mischief through puzzlement to deep gloom.

'Told me I 'ad to get this book, didn't she, *French Irregular Verbs*?' He read the title syllable by syllable. 'Can't read a single word, first page. What I need, Lydia, is a bit of coachin'.'

'And I told you I don't do coaching *ever*,' she said irritably, but somehow her voice lacked conviction even to herself. She didn't want to do it but courtesy of Mother, James and good fortune, she had had a good education. Didn't she owe it to Jordan, trying to pull himself up by his bootstraps, to help? He didn't seem exactly bright but it was hard to tell. Not everybody was up to studying Greek and Latin by candlelight like Patrick Brontë.

'Why don't you start with English literature? We'll be doing the first two scenes or so of some Shakespeare in the first class. Be good if you'd already read them,' she said, slipping inexorably into her teaching mode.

'*As You Like It*,' he read out the title and looked at the first page, blinking rapidly. 'Don't make no more sense to me than pigshit. Listen, I *got* to get on this Access course.'

'Well . . .' Lydia said, thinking guilt was a patchy motivator. 'Maybe the first page is a bit boring. I mean if you think about places like the Globe Theatre, where Shakespeare's plays were put on, people would be just arriving, talking, finding a place to stand, so the plays start sort of slowly. Suppose I tell you the main story . . .?'

'OK,' Jordan said, swallowing tea, but his eyes, gazing at the text, were bright with triumph.

'Annie dear, I do understand you don't want to come to Jersey again after what happened,' Drina said. 'So why don't we meet in London the day before the clinic and get you kitted out? You'll need warm clothes, maternity clothes that is, for the winter, won't you?' She gave an embarrassed little laugh. 'We'll stay the night at the Cumberland Hotel and have a really good talk. What do you say?'

'Cumberland Hotel?' Annie said. 'Where's that then?'

* * *

In the next few days Lydia managed to establish what was from her point of view a tolerable pattern: part-time coaching Jordan, though neither of them used that word, combined with minimising general conversation, essential with someone as extrovert as Jordan or her days would be swallowed entirely. She spent the first hour after his arrival on French, then left him with a list of exercises, tapes to listen to, verbs to learn for the rest of the morning. During this time he made himself several mugs of tea and the sounds of this in the distance as well as the French tapes requiring his responses was distracting but she had to start organising her classes and she did.

A snack lunch of cheese or ham and salad followed, his great need of sugar suggesting to Lydia, Mother Theresa of starving cats, that his diet was poor. In the afternoon they read one or other of the set books together and then she left him to read the piece again and answer a list of questions which hopefully would eventually build into something resembling the essay form required by exam questions.

Two weeks later the Park Lodge term began. Both GCSE classes covered a wider spectrum: eager school-leavers who had failed this particular subject, the middle-aged trying to remould career prospects, and a few retired people hoping to expand their social and leisure horizons.

At the first class Lydia smiled engagingly and went through a routine recommended at the Park Lodge reception by a more experienced tutor. First she might explain her name was Lydia Kemp and invite them to call her whatever she preferred, then she should carefully mark the register with what each student chose to be called in the class, then she could talk a bit about the aims and outline of the course and any additional books required, finally she might invite everybody to talk to, and then introduce to the whole class, the person next to them.

Several students came to both classes and a few like Jordan Mackay attended all three. His dark eyes stared at her with a solemn concentration that was unnerving. He still knew very little French and nothing about English literature, parrying all questions in class with, 'What you aksin' me for?'

Friday night at last, Lydia thought, exultant, driving home across the Downs. Friday night was freedom. All three classes were up and running. Now it was the weekend and her head was fizzing like a Catherine wheel. She was going to paint, she had surely earned the right.

She unlocked the front door, switched off the alarm and walked straight upstairs to the study, clearing class notes and texts from the desk into drawers in an impatient sweep.

She stood for a moment looking at the backs of the hardboard stacked against the wall. Suppose when she looked they were empty stages, like Mother's paintings? Lydia took a deep breath and lifted them up one by one, propping each on the easel and standing back, eyes searching the surface for evidence of feeling.

First the cot paintings, pale wood, faded blue mattress, garden-green light. Lydia smiled with relief. The cot itself might be empty but the cot paintings were suffused with life, alive in her head too, just as Van Gogh's yellow chair or the sunflowers were alive in her head as they had been in his and, with millions of prints and calendars on walls, were alive now in millions of heads.

Lydia turned to the next stack. Interiors of the house bereft, a house bought for children who had now abandoned it. Next the garden, neat at first but growing wilder in late summer, green already touched with yellow. Life was passing all the time, she thought, ecstatic, but what did it matter if you could catch and paint the moment as it passed?

Downstairs the phone was ringing. Mother hadn't called since the funeral.

'Wherever have you been?' she said testily. 'I've been ringing all evening. You all right, Lydia?'

'Fine. I teach a class on Friday evenings, I did tell you.'

'Whatever do you want to do that for?'

'Money, mostly . . .'

'You should never have left Ed . . . and you should have come to James's funeral. It went off so well, everyone was there and the flowers were lovely and Unity was so disappointed not to see you but her flight was booked straight back.'

'I was busy, Mother.'

'We are all busy . . . Unity's busy but she still found time to fly over from the States . . .' A pause. 'Anyway, what are you so busy about?'

'Painting,' Lydia said, wondering if this was the moment to jump right in.

'Painting? But you don't paint.'

'But I always wanted to paint, Mother,' Lydia said. 'I wanted to go to art school.'

'I don't remember that,' Mother said. 'Saw to it you girls had a good education, didn't I?'

'I did have a good education,' Lydia said. Feisty, Mr Sharpe had called her. 'And I am grateful but I wanted to go to art school just as you did after the WAAF.'

'Who told you that?' Mother said.

'James . . .'

'Poor old James, he got very muddled, been confused for years, came out with all sorts of nonsense. You don't want to believe anything James said.'

'But I do believe him,' Lydia said. 'I believe you tried for art school after the WAAF and didn't get in.'

'Did I?' Mother said doubtfully. 'It's such a long time ago.' Her voice was rising. 'I did my best for you girls. No sense living in the past, my age. I can't be expected to remember every little thing . . . every little hiccup.'

'Of course not, Mother,' Lydia said, holding the phone away from her ear and speaking quietly. 'But it's not a little thing. It's both of us wanting to paint, it's what's between us, and it's been buried, covered over with lies.'

'What lies? I don't tell lies. I don't know what you're talking about . . .'

'Think about it . . .'

Lydia put the phone down gently. Confronting Mother at last but was that bullying or was it feisty? Well, she had said her piece after all this time. Was she right to say it? More important, would it do any good, change anything, set her free?

Probably not but she had to try, she had a right to try.

Mother was old, not very fit, forgetful, disappointed by life, the long years of caring for James, disappointed perhaps by her own painting, her lack of talent.

Was it quite fair speaking out now, when it was too late to put things right? Was it abusive . . . daring to cast the first stone? People were not entirely responsible for how they were; nobody chose their DNA – or their parents or their children come to that.

She had spoken out but she would never do it again. Not to Mother, not to anybody. Couldn't. Because of the children ... Marina. You tried to do your best but did mothers ever get things right? But Annie was at art school, she had done her best for Annie. At least she had got that right.

CHAPTER SIXTEEN

W AS MOTHER AWAKE yet? Lydia wondered, when she woke on
Saturday morning intending to paint all day. Was she all right?
Well, she would certainly ring if she wasn't. As for Lydia, she
intended to paint all day and not to think about anything else. In an
odd way she owed that to Mother now.

William would mow the lawn some time next week, and anyway
the rate of growth was slowing into autumn. She was having
breakfast when Belstones phoned to say they had a couple, the
Wards, wanting to view the house.

'But I'm painting this morning,' Lydia said, surprised by her
own assertiveness.

'No problem, Mrs Kemp. Our Mr Burridge can easily take them
round.' Mr Belstone was always urbane.

'Well, all right then,' Lydia said after a pause. No doubt Ed would
interpret this as another attempt to delay the sale and extend her
residence at Cedar Road indefinitely.

Was Richard back yet?

The best thing about working again, even part-time teaching at
Park Lodge, was the intensity it gave to time spent otherwise – that
is, *not* teaching or preparing to teach, not steering Jordan through
what he saw as the impenetrable forests of French and English. Now
the first week of term was over she would be able to relax and spend
the weekends at least painting again.

Would Jordan come on Saturday or wouldn't he? She had never
intended that he should but he had been so offended by the painting
workshop débâcle that she hadn't actually established a five-day
week.

She tried to keep their conversation round his studies and
syllabus but Jordan was naturally talkative and she heard a lot about
his life as well. His student father had gone back to Mali before he
was born, his Catholic mother had married a West Indian and
continued to work full time as a nurse between her maternity

leaves, despite bearing seven more children.

Jordan had broken up with a long-standing girlfriend. He had come to Bristol to get away, and because he was offered a job but when he presented himself at the workplace, his employer looked at him and said the vacancy was filled. 'Blatant discrimination! You should have gone straight to the race relations people.' Lydia said indignantly, but Jordan was more philosophical. 'Nah, they don't want me, I don't want to work there, man.'

Saturday was greyish and, as Lydia had feared, it wasn't easy to start painting again immediately. She tried to settle in the study first and then carried the easel out to the garden but wherever she went the students from her classes paraded through her head.

What did they want, her attention, her approval, what? Why wouldn't they leave her alone? Arriving unknown and uptight at Park Lodge their first evening, some students had presented faces of blank anxiety, others smiled too widely or laughed too loud, but gradually each class had turned into individuals, people who wanted something, wanted to be called Tom, Dick, Alice, Daisy, wanted to tell you their story.

All the time Jordan's eyes, black night in the dusky evening of his skin, had watched her, listening with intense and nervous concentration. He wanted to tell her his story too but not right now. He wanted some GCSEs to get on an Access course as a road to a different future but if she asked him a question in class he still smiled and said, 'What you aksin' me for?'

Later that Saturday morning Lydia fetched the stepladder and set it up by the hedge and sat on top staring down at the wild wood. Silver birch, a thicket of blackberry and laurel, invaded by feral clematis and rhododendron from surrounding gardens.

She settled better there, her precarious perch focused her on the moment, as she peered into the dark green. She had wandered there sometimes but the children had known it better, their play protected with repeated warnings. 'Don't talk to anybody', 'Never get in a stranger's car. Not even if he says your mother's in hospital and he'll take you to her.' 'Suppose he says your father's in hospital?' Marina had asked.

Once started Lydia went on all that morning, looking up to nod and smile at the Wards being taken round by Mr Burridge, and painting on. Trees that were not just trees, hardly plants at all, an abstract of trees, growing with a strange and particular significance.

She was making herself a salad sandwich when the phone rang.

'That you, Lydia?' Jordan attempted a sportive tone. 'How you gettin' on?'

'Did you want something, Jordan? I'm busy at the moment.'

'All this busy-busy, you want to relax, loosen up,' he said. He seemed perpetually nervous, out of his element, Lydia thought. What had Karen Blixen said about Africans being at home in the world as a fish is at home in the sea? Perhaps a mixed-race man had special problems; was Jordan a nowhere man?

'Look, I'm busy right now. See you next week.'

She put the phone down. Had he been expecting to come on Saturday? Didn't sound like it. He was always polite but there was something tiresomely pushy about him too. She should have told him not to phone again. Why did people always think they could talk her into doing what they wanted?

Because they can, a voice in her head informed her.

Did she *have* to help him because his skin was brown?

Yes, because she was born out of *protestant ethic* by *politically correct*, the voice said, and Jordan knew a mug when he saw one.

But the never-ending millions of Africans dying of famine, or transported into slavery in past centuries, were not her fault, Lydia tried to say. Likewise the corrupt dictatorships and collapsed economies disfiguring so much of post-colonial Africa.

Having answered already, the voice was silent.

Suddenly Lydia wanted to see Richard. She tapped his number and listened as his voice informed her he couldn't come to the phone at the moment but if she left her number he would get back to her.

She couldn't go back to painting straight away. Was it Jordan's call or the visit of Mr Burridge and the Wards that had so violated her privacy that the house and garden didn't seem to belong to her? Lydia walked round the lawn twice, reclaiming it with her feet.

William lay in bed most of Saturday morning. He thought of phoning Sydney where, ten hours ahead, it would be about six o'clock in the evening or seven or eight . . .

What would he drop straight into the delicate seashell curl of

Ruby's ear? Would he tell her about his date with Lori last night? First date, nice girl, pretty girl, rabbiting on about her family, a Labrador called Sandy, her year at secretarial college in London.

So boring he couldn't even kiss her good night.

'How did the classes go?' Margaret called across the hedge. 'Come and tell me all about it.'

'OK.' Lydia made her way up and down the two front gardens. 'But next week I'll be marking a whole lot of essays as well as getting my classes together. Where's Bertie?' she added, suspecting another trip in the Bentley.

'Working upstairs,' Margaret said. 'The electrics for the pool cover. We've made the spare room into a workshop. You have to be very careful with electrics close to water. Bertie wants to get it all set up ready before we go away. Such a dear, my Bertie, nothing's too much trouble. When I think of Frank, so clumsy at first . . . well, he couldn't help that but I think he got to like hurting me, needed it like a sort of addiction . . .'

'When are you off on your Mediterranean cruise?' Lydia said quickly.

'Soon. Autumn's so sad, isn't it – the fall, as they say in America. We're cruising along the African coast. Bertie was in the Eighth Army fighting Rommel, you know. Do you remember all those towns . . . Tobruk and Benghazi and El Alamein?'

'I was born after the war,' Lydia said, wondering how Bertie managed to appear on so many dramatic fronts.

'I keep forgetting how old we are, Bertie and me,' Margaret said. 'He's fit as a fiddle, of course. He hates doctors but I give him vitamins and antioxidant pills every day and that queen bee stuff Barbara Cartland swears by. Marvellous for a woman her age, isn't she, though I don't really care for so much pink . . .'

'Your telephone, Lydia?' Bertie's head appeared at the spare room window.

'Isn't he marvellous, the way he hears everything?' Margaret was saying as Lydia hurried away.

She opened the front door and picked up the telephone.

'How y'doin'? It's me,' Jordan said in his jaunty tone.

'Yes?' Lydia frowned at the receiver. 'Did you want something, Jordan?'

'Yeah well, that question you give us. Read act one and write down the outline in not more than two pages?'

'What about it?' Lydia said.

'I can't read stuff like that by meself. Need 'elp, Lydia, know what I mean?' She did know only too well. 'If I was to come over your place . . .?'

A long pause. Lydia stared down the garden and felt the brightness of the afternoon slip away. Was she ever going to start saying and doing what she wanted? But her voice said flatly but clearly, 'You'd better come over, Jordan. We'll go through act one again together.'

'Brilliant,' Jordan said. 'You're the biz, Lydia.'

You poor silly cow, you, said the voice in her head.

Jordan arrived five minutes later; he had evidently phoned from the box on the Downs. He stood on the threshold rocking nervously from one foot to the other.

'What you sellin' this 'ouse for?' he said.

'Necessary, I'm afraid . . .' Lydia said.

'How much you aksin'? I might know somebody what's lookin' for an 'ouse.'

'Depends . . .' Lydia said vaguely. They would work through act one of *As You Like It* again, exploring every speech, every nuance, ten pages in her edition, twenty pages in his, rehashing much of what she had said in class as simply as possible.

Jordan was in his twenties, but he seemed to listen with his eyes rather than his ears, staring at her like a small child. Was he acting listening rather than actually listening? Was that why he absorbed or at any rate retained so little of what they had already done? But when he sat watching her and listening, she couldn't help noticing how singularly beautiful he was.

The act one session took longer than she would have thought possible. Once he was carefully persuaded through the text he proved perceptive and quickly grasped the human element. He was particularly pleased by the Elizabethan convention of boy actors playing female parts which then involved the 'girls' pretending to be men. But his concentration was short-lived, punctuated by restless fidgeting and frequent cups of sugared tea over which he told her about his chequered life.

From his years in care and his house-father, a widely travelled ex-merchant navy man, he had learned of the world's infinite possibilities. In particular he learned that you could go to different places, get along with different people, choose a different life, find your own niche.

Jordan's life had become a continuous experiment.

Though he never again used the word 'coaching', the weekday routine was already established and by Saturday evening it was perfectly clear to both that Saturday was also part of the pattern. Had there been a precise moment when she accepted this? Lydia wondered, but came to no conclusion. The extended lesson took all afternoon and much of the evening before Jordan had to leave for his work at the late night café.

'All right, miss . . .' the guard said opening the door of the sleeper as Annie negotiated her three different-sized parcels.

'Thanks,' she said, and closed the door. She opened the middle-sized one first, a pinafore dress like a wide black tent. 'Do you really want black?' Drina had said. 'I only ever wear black,' Annie said, and Drina sighed. She felt Annie belonged to her and she didn't care for black, never had. Now Annie undid the big parcel and put on the long black coat. Her hands in the pockets raised the sides like huge black wings. She didn't bother opening the small parcel, smocks in flowery colours.

Harrods didn't have a black smock.

The following morning, silent except for distant church bells, Lydia tried to finish painting the wild wood but Jordan's restless presence still seemed palpable, 'real style' and 'know what I mean?' hanging in the air like chandeliers, his Biro left on the kitchen table, an intimation that he would return.

How could she settle when at any minute he could phone?

At Park Lodge she had picked up a flyer advertising an exhibition of paintings at Bath. She had to get out of the house, and parking in Bath was at least *possible* on a Sunday.

An hour later Lydia wandered round the Pulteney Gallery.

Three artists were exhibiting, all innovative and significant, according to the programme. Rachel Briggs painted entirely in small squares of black and white. Hans Franken made collages from German memorabilia of the First World War, fragments of sepia photographs, flags and medal ribbons, despairing totems of their time. Finally there was Gretel Holt, a Hampstead painter somebody said, though a primavera rising against a fanciful sea of flowers was more obviously drawn from Greek mythology. Other paintings of nuptial couples were magical and comical too. Why did she like them so much? Lydia wondered. Was it the loving pairings, eyes looking into eyes, the endless cycle of creation, birth, growth, couplings, all comfortable and placid. If only I could paint like Gretel Holt, she thought ruefully, but I can only paint like me.

In the afternoon she drifted back into the outside world, dreamily following the tourist trail past the sumptuous shops of Milsom Street to the abbey and the click of cameras. She had coffee in an alley shop and branched away, making for the slopes of Lansdown. The outsides of buildings belonged to everybody, the creamy terraces arranged row behind row, façades plain but casually symmetrical, exuding their own peaceful composure. Apparently nobody built vulgarly in Bath.

Slowly but purposefully Lydia wandered towards Henrietta Park, her feet carrying her towards Sydney Gardens and finally to Albert Place where Richard lived. The houses here were nineteenth-century, tall and gaunt, black railings along the pavement, a basement below.

Lydia peered at the names beside a heavy front door. She rang a bell labelled 'Richard Foy'. Why had he selected Bath? His aesthetic sensibility was limited, his children lived in Luton and Golders Green.

A young man ran up behind her and unlocked the door.

'Who did you want?' he smiled. 'Richard Foy's been away for ages . . . unless he's back? Was he expecting you?'

'Not really.'

'Well, let's have a look? Come in,' he collected his mail from a pigeonhole by the door and walked down the hall to a second door. 'Richard?' he shouted through the letter slot and added, 'There's a load of junk on the floor there. Looks like you're out of luck. Want to leave a note?'

'No, no, I was just wandering,' she said, rendered shy by his cheerful but uninterested gaze. 'I must get back to my car.'

'He's been away most of the summer.' The young man followed her to the front door. 'Shame really, his flat gets the garden, lucky beggar. Complete waste with him away. 'Bye then.'

Lydia stood on the steps a moment and then followed the railings to the end of the building where they met the garden wall of the house next door. Between this and Albert Place was a narrow alley with trees at the other end, an overgrown lawn and what looked like a summerhouse.

She had no idea Richard had a garden and a summerhouse.

CHAPTER SEVENTEEN

IN THE MIDDLE of October the weather dipped suddenly into winter. Next door Bertie connected the silver cover to the electric rails, watching it slide up and down without a hitch, like a boy with a toy train.

Even Annie's postcard, Morrab Gardens again, green as spinach, admitted in its message, 'Cold here. Bought jersey in the market. Love Annie.' There was no mention of Lydia's letter. What sort of jersey, what colour, how come Annie, apprenticed to art, didn't know that detail would give her message life? Lydia wondered irritably.

Didn't she realise, or perhaps she did?

Mother hadn't phoned since the art school confrontation after James's funeral, a relief at first but gradually the scales tipped towards regret. A letter from the bank manager drew reproachful attention to her overdraft.

At least the Millennium Press had written inviting her to translate three poems by Eugene Gallant and three by Jules Vauclus for their new anthology of European poetry. Gallant was new to her, but Lydia had always admired Vauclus, obscure though he was. Peanuts moneywise but it had to compare favourably with the hours she was now teaching Jordan daily for no pay at all.

Lydia had allowed it to happen. Jordan was Jordan, his predicament unusual and his personality engaging; the more she understood his background, the more she felt obliged to help him. In the nineties putting children into care was seen as best avoided, often exposing them to worse perils. But for Jordan in the eighties, though his time in care might explain some of his nervous talk, his brashness, it had also enriched and opened up his life.

All the other GCSE students at Park Lodge were aiming to take their examinations next June but Jordan had already applied to take his in December. His total ignorance in both subjects was a challenge and an obligation. Could she and Jordan get his English literature and French together in what was now a matter of weeks?

Well, they could try.

Lydia had already looked out books and French tapes she had made herself from BBC programmes when her own children were doing GCSE, as well as for use by the pupils of Stoke Bishop High. But with every passing day the task became more daunting. She drew up for Jordan a rigorous daily programme of French listening, speaking, dictation and learning by heart as well as of reading, understanding and writing answers to questions on English literature. She had hoped he would get on with it but like a small child he needed constant encouragement and as well as constant interaction which used all her energy and most of her weekend.

Painting had to be on hold for the moment. Jordan was a priority; she had the rest of her life to paint and besides, she could only paint when she had swathes of uninterrupted free time ahead of her.

'You all right, Ma?' William said, arriving briefly one Saturday afternoon and looking at the half-clipped hedge.

'Course,' she said, conscious of only two chops for supper. 'You?'

'I've got a date actually, Lori from the office. I'll finish the hedge another time, OK?'

'Sure,' she said, kissing his cheek. He was looking better, the new girl perhaps? 'Go off and play then.'

'Only got the one life. Least it's a strong possibility,' he said, stretching long arms above his head. 'See you.'

Later she and Jordan ate two chops, tomatoes and sprouts, followed by jam tarts and coffee at the kitchen table. Jordan was quieter than usual, discouraged perhaps?

'At least you've got *être* in your head at last,' Lydia said cheerfully. It was already dark outside.

'Yeah,' Jordan said. 'Yeah, *être*. *Je suis* and all that, innit?' He stared at the kitchen table. '*Tu es mon père?*'

Would he ever get himself to Mali?

'Hadn't you better get off?' she said, catching his unease.

'Don't mind walkin', do I?' he said with a shrug, and suddenly looked up. 'Unless I was to stay,' he added softly but distinctly. 'You very nice lady, know what I mean?'

'Stay?' Lydia said, flustered. She had always thought of him as beautiful but as flowers or children are beautiful. It was what he was, a beautiful streetwise child, courtesy of Brixton and social services.

'I don't think that's a good idea.'

'I mean you been real good to me, Lydia, you got real style.' His gaze was steady and for a moment he seemed more mature and resolute than she was. 'Like me and my girlfriend just split, know what I mean? Maybe you and me, we could go upstairs? Whatcha say, make love?'

'I don't think so,' Lydia said, startled. 'I mean it's not *like* that, is it, you and me, not like that at all?'

'Why not?' he said. 'You cold or somethink, you don't like it? Think I got Aids or somethink? Well, I ain't got Aids nor HIV nor nothink.'

'It's not that, it's just there's nothing *between us*, Jordan, is there? Only Shakespeare and *être* and stuff. Otherwise we hardly know each other.' She was floundering now. 'I mean I'm your teacher and you're young enough to be my son.'

'And you're old enough to be my mum but I don't 'old that against you,' Jordan said sullenly. 'Whatcha mean, nothink between us? What you want then, loads of love crap? Pisses me off, people talkin' like that. Don't know nothink about nothink, you don't.'

'Sorry, Jordan, I just—'

But Jordan scooped his books into his plastic bag and disappeared into the night, the door slamming behind him.

Lydia slept badly. She had set the alarm, read for a while and gone to bed. Suppose Jordan came back, would she let him in or not? She had never thought of him like that. Not for a moment.

Sunday, her only painting day, was tomorrow, but already she knew she wouldn't be able to paint. The day was labelled 'Jordan' now, a day of waiting, a day of mourning because possibly he would never come back.

Two couples were due to look round the house, the Robsons and the Humphreys. The services of Mr Burridge had not been offered this time, indeed Mr Belstone had suggested that sales were likely to dip from now until Christmas and not pick up again until March. Contrary to his expectation, Lydia found this a relief.

Would Annie be home for Christmas?

After breakfast Lydia went outside. The grass was cold and crisp, a scatter of clippings lay beside the hedge. She gathered them into the compost bin. Next door the silver cover concealed the pool and the terrace curtains were closed. Had Margaret and Bertie departed already?

What was Jordan doing? Lying on his narrow bed in a crummy room at the late night café, staring at the ceiling? She could certainly see it. Perhaps it was something she could paint, but not today. Today she would work on the Eugene Gallant poems. Lydia wandered to her desk and read them through, polished, worldly, cynical. She could find the English words, but could she capture the Gallic tone?

The Robsons arrived at eleven and seemed keen as they toured the house, commenting politely on 'the spacious kitchen' and 'the sitting room like part of the garden', smiling silently at Annie's mural. In fairness Lydia marked them eight out of ten, but they didn't please her. Nobody buying her house and garden could do that. They left just as the phone rang.

'Lydia?'

'Richard, you're back at last?'

'For the moment,' he said. 'How are you?'

'Fine, thanks,' she said coolly. It had been so long, should her voice suggest he had forfeit the right to ask?

'Listen, I want to see you, Lydia. Are you free tonight?'

'Free as a bird,' she said, her spirits rising into blue air.

'I'd like to take you out to dinner then, pick you up about seven, all right?'

The Humphreys failed to arrive. Lydia went steadily on with the Gallant poems and in the afternoon made her way carefully through act two of *As You Like It*.

Richard's call, whatever it signified, had at least pushed Jordan out of her head. She hummed to herself as she showered and dressed in a white silk blouse, green jacket and plaid skirt, mid-calf, which swung charmingly in the wardrobe mirror as she moved. She added the glass droplet earrings.

'Long time no see,' Richard said, stepping into the house and kissing her enthusiastically. 'Shall we do that again?'

'Let's . . .' she said, breathless in his arms. It wasn't just that he looked better – tanned – he looked different too in a way she couldn't quite define – self-contained. Why should that surprise her? Richard had always been his own person.

'Haven't booked,' he said. 'Let's go or we shan't get a table.'

'It's good to see you,' she said, following him to the car. A certain excitement seemed to be emanating from him. 'It's been a long time.'

'Sex is a terrible tease,' he said as he backed up the drive. He had misled her back in the summer. His offer of marriage was tampering with her affections, he admitted it. That she had turned him down flat was rather to her credit. He hadn't been himself for a long time after Alison died. But now . . .

'Have you ever noticed that being *in love* makes you both attractive and attracted to everybody else?'

'Can't say I have,' Lydia said warily.

'Keep yourself on a tight rein, don't you?' he said with a smile. 'What I mean is, if you fall in love suddenly everybody else starts coming on to you.'

'Not sure I want that,' she said coolly. What was he trying to say? 'Anyway, I don't fall in love that often.'

She looked out at the brightly lit restaurants on Whiteladies Road. Somehow the evening had lost its momentum.

'Bit of luck!' he said, slipping neatly into a vacant meter space at the top of Park Street. 'What about the Fanfare over the road there? Looks all right.'

'Fine,' she said.

'You remember what I said last time?' He took her arm as they crossed the road.

'Which bit?' she said as they were shown to the only empty table in a corner by the window.

'Let's order first, shall we?' he said, picking up the menu as the waitress hovered. 'Chef's special sounds all right. Fried goat's cheese and salad for starters; main course, chicken in lemon sauce with *légumes* in season.'

'Me too,' Lydia said, happy to abdicate choice. 'Delicious.'

'And a bottle of medium dry house white.'

'Right, sir.'

The waitress was under twenty. Richard's eyes followed her legs to the bar. Lydia glanced round the restaurant: two well-heeled middle-aged couples at the next table, groups of young people beyond. The waitress returned with the opened bottle.

'Fine,' Richard said, waiting as she filled their glasses.

'Fruity and unassuming?' Lydia suggested.

'Bit like me,' Richard said and his eyes met hers. 'You remember what I said last time? About us getting married?'

'Course I remember.'

'I thought you might.' He paused as the starters arrived. 'Thank you.'

'Fact is, Lydia, I've fallen very much in love.'

'What?' she said, smiling because just for a moment it wasn't clear what he meant. But suddenly it was.

'Congratulations,' she said, forking up fried goat's cheese. A frozen hand clutched at her heart. 'Somebody at the sailing school?'

'Not exactly. But she lives near.' Richard sipped his wine and refilled both glasses, relaxed by his clean breast. It was what he had come for.

'She's married but it hasn't worked out. He's in the navy and away all the time.' His smile was tender. 'No sort of life for a girl like Yolande. Needs lots of attention. To tell the truth she was depressed when we first met, absolutely blooming now. Anyway, her husband's got Christmas leave, she's going to ask him for a divorce . . .'

'How old is this Yolande?' Lydia said.

'Twenty-nine,' Richard said with a certain diffidence but his eyes were boasting bright.

'But you're forty-nine,' Lydia said as the waitress removed their plates.

'Forty-eight, Lyddy dear. Please don't go all moralistic on me. It's not your style.'

'But what about your heart?' she said. Why should she feel so desolate? What gave her the right?

'Excellent,' he said, replenishing their glasses. 'Thank you for asking. Standing up to the not inconsiderable demands being made upon it at the moment.'

A pause as the plates of lemon chicken arrived, followed by two dishes of vegetables.

'This looks good,' Richard smiled at the waitress.

'*Bon appétit*, sir,' she said.

'What is it with you, Richard?' Lydia said as quietly as she could. The couples at the next table were already showing discreet interest.

Fortunately plate glass and Park Street flanked the other side. 'Do you need an audience or what? Is *talking* about your love life what really turns you on?' The couple at the next table stared at their plates.

'What makes you say that?'

'Evidence,' Lydia said. 'Why do you always get interested in women committed to somebody else? It's perverse. You never go for an available single woman.'

Eyes flashed wide towards them and looked away.

'Sorry, Lydia, you've lost me,' Richard said. 'You turned me down flat, what right have you to get angry now? Just say what you want and there's a good chance you'll get it. Now can we eat our dinner while it's still hot?'

'Carry on,' Lydia said, picking up her own knife and fork. 'Does this Yolande know what you're like?'

'I told her I'd asked an old friend to marry me, if that's what you mean?'

'I said "No", didn't I? I'm not talking about now, I mean the marriages you wrecked, the professional philanderer?'

'I've always loved ladies,' Richard admitted. 'But everyone's responsible for their own lives. You feminists can't fall back on helpless little me nowadays.'

'You came on to me ten years ago, you know you did.' A man she presumed was the manager was glancing uneasily in their direction. 'I was in love but then you just dumped me.'

'I didn't just dump you,' Richard said, and his eyes looked right at her for the first time. 'Please try to keep your voice down . . . I already told you, it got too serious. I had to break it off. You wanted my whole life, everything. I was beginning to want it too. I couldn't do that to Alison and the kids, not to mention the practice. I had to pull out.'

'Excuse me, sir . . . er, madam,' the manager put the bill in front of Richard. 'I'm afraid I shall have to ask you—'

'I'm going anyway,' Lydia said, getting up. 'Sorry, everybody,' she shouted into the body of the restaurant.

'Wait,' Richard called, planting a handful of notes on the plate. 'Lydia, wait. I'll drive you home.'

'Get lost.'

By the time he had collected the Astra, turned it and driven off towards Stoke Bishop, Lydia, cocooned inside a bus, was already halfway across the Downs.

PART FOUR

Decisions

A s a cold October moved into a bleak November, Lydia tried not to think of Richard. He had proposed to her twice in flight from his own grief and loneliness, but the second time he had considered her needs too and a partnership between them had seemed a real possibility.

But he had offered himself and she had refused him.

Now he was involved with somebody else, she could hardly blame him. It was nothing to do with her any more.

What had changed? Only the wisps of thought that drifted in her head, longings and dreams she couldn't admit, couldn't quite recognise. She didn't want to marry Richard, she didn't want to marry anybody.

She wanted to paint, she had always wanted to paint.

'Why do you have to be so angry?' Richard had said. He didn't like anger, considered it childish. When Bethany sprayed the wheels of his Astra bright blue, he simply scrubbed them clean a.s.a.p., an adult reaction.

Mrs Busby used to talk of justified anger in school assembly – Jesus throwing the moneylenders out of the temple . . . But it seemed to Lydia now that once you took charge of your own life, you relinquished the right to anger. If things went wrong it was your fault, you had miscalculated, failed to think them through.

Now she had to get on with selling the house, translating the French poems, preparing her teaching and pushing Jordan through his GCSE. Lydia sighed, the way ahead had a heaviness, a sadness she declined to examine. Everything seemed up for grabs but eventually it would all be finished and she could start painting again. But she had to stop thinking about Richard.

'What I said, Lydia,' Jordan offered a week after his suggestion that they should make love, 'it was out of order, way out of order.'

'Forget it.'

'Yeah . . . OK.'

But she hadn't been offended by his proposition, just surprised. He was so much younger than her, twenty-five years at least, a whole generation. She was conditioned to the idea that older men fancied younger women, a notion for which there was plenty of evidence. The reverse possibility – that young men might fancy older women – had never seemed to apply. Sexual mores were changing all the time, and where older women had their own careers and income, perhaps they were regarded as staging posts by young men not in a position to form long-term attachments. Supposing that anybody still thought about long-term attachments . . .

Working so long in the cloistered atmosphere of Stoke Bishop High had concealed changes of this kind from pupils and teachers alike. It was supposed to, wasn't that why parents bought it?

Jordan came every morning as usual but he had backed off, smiled less, stayed for longer periods alone in Ed's study and began to take more responsibility for organising his own time and applying himself to his studies. His behaviour was thus both more adult and more attractive. He stopped talking about his childhood, a deliberate change of tactic. People got tired of a sad tale. Besides, he was going places now, wasn't he? His head was full of *être* and *venir* and *comment allez-vous*? and questions like 'Why did Maggie Tulliver drown?' and 'What is poetry?'

Lydia had never felt so restless. Painting was on hold but there were still the poems of Vauclus and Gallant to be translated, classes to prepare and students' homework to be marked. Jordan was not just a student, he was a project and a responsibility; his background gave him a special pathos. Since his casual suggestion his dark eyes had invaded her imagination where he danced like some wayward faun. His nose was high-bridged, aquiline. Had his father from Mali had Hausa blood? Lydia wondered, closing her study door to shut out the endless sequence of French tapes and trying to immerse herself in her own work.

Why was she so hesitant? Why couldn't she just do what she wanted like other people seemed to? Izzy, for instance? 'Just ask for what you want and there's a good chance you'll get it . . .' Ironic that it was Richard who had said that, but she wasn't going to think about Richard any more.

'About us . . . making love?' Lydia said one evening, a week later, and wondered what her children would think, Marina for instance.

'What about it?' Jordan stared at her for a full half-minute. 'Changed your mind, did you?'

'Yes,' Lydia said softly. 'I think I did.'

'All right then. Let's go.'

'Has to be safe sex,' she said quickly. It was a long time since anybody . . . a very long time. Perhaps you could call it an interlude between the acts. 'You got a whatsit?'

'Condom,' Jordon said, following her up the stairs but making no attempt to touch her. 'Course. You take me for a yob or somethink?'

'I just take you for you,' she said, finding the retort neat. She switched on the bedside lamp, undressed quickly and slid into bed. Jordan was slower, already erect as he got in beside her.

'OK then?' he said, stroking her gently, his lips pink-brown like the underside of mushrooms mumbled her ears and neck but never kissed. 'Kissing is Hollywood. Africans don't kiss, it's not the custom,' someone had told Jordan once, making kissing disgusting to him for ever.

Everything he knew came from people telling him. 'Women like to be touched there, same as you boys,' his house-father whispered in his ears, 'touched ever so softly, softly.' Jordan listened; it was how you learned, listening carefully, touching softly. Plenty of practice night after night, boys in other boys' beds all round the dorm. Plenty of practice with Lois too. Same thing, same thing, almost.

His skin was child-soft, petal-soft, she was old enough to be his mother, Lydia thought, but wasn't his mother after all. His body heavy upon her, smelling of soap and coconut oil, exotic, exciting after so long, so long . . . She came almost at once, too soon . . . his body pumping on and on. Had she forgotten how it could be and quite often was?

Didn't he feel safe in her bed, fearful of the father in Mali, or Laius, father of Oedipus, lurking in the shadows of the hut? Husband of Jocasta – but Lydia was no Jocasta.

What was between them, what could be? she wondered. She liked him, was fond of him, felt responsible for him, felt guilt. His ignorance, his profound unknowing of everything she knew and cared about, how much did that matter? Copulation was always skin rubbing against skin but not necessarily an act of love. Put like that it sounded shocking but then the truth was often shocking.

'OK?' he mumbled afterwards, rolling off her, breathless, exhausted. Lying with his arms crossed on his chest.

'Very OK,' she said, and so it was. A relief, a new beginning, a sort of affection but not love. In the nineties everybody had sex all the time or so the media suggested. Was it all just pretending, a brave shouting to frighten the demons waiting in the blacknight dark?

Ten years since Ed, ten years since Richard. It had been a long time.

'You're not so bad yourself,' Jordan said. 'Tell you what, I could murder a cuppa tea.'

'If I must . . .' Lydia said, hostage to hospitality, pulling on her wrap and plodding downstairs. 'Your turn next time.'

'I done the 'ard work,' Jordan called after her. 'Three spoons o' sugar.'

It was the coldest November for years, also the strangest, Lydia thought. Nobody came to view the house and no wonder. The mauve-blossomed hebe, Midsummer Beauty, which offered autumn flowering too, turned brown in the wind, withered and died. Soggy amber leaves dropped from the apple trees. Mother had stopped phoning, a relief and a pain. Nothing between them had ever been right. Jordan arrived each morning.

'All right then?' he offered as she opened the front door, making his tea and disappearing to Ed's study. Suppose Ed arrived to collect his desk? What would he say? What would he think? What did it matter?

Each morning she considered the frosted garden from her study window and settled at her desk working on the poems, trying not to hear Jordan and his tapes, speaking his childlike laboured French. But his vocabulary and fluency increased from day to day. 'Getting on a treat, isn't he?' the ladies in the French conversation class fluttered and flattered round him, clapping at his first small sorties into speech.

Every day at twelve o'clock Lydia went through Jordan's written work, set him further exercises, worked through sections of questions and answers in his *Oral French*, heard him speak on tape and made suggestions for his afternoon's work. After that they had a snack lunch, speaking French together all the time.

They went to bed in the afternoon, timing which gave it a rakish flavour it actually lacked. Nostalgic too; hadn't she and Richard made love in the afternoon in the sad mad days of their affair? But comparisons do nobody any good. She and Jordan would both have preferred dusk but William occasionally arrived in the early evening after work and the possibility made Lydia jumpy, and besides, her classes at Park Lodge started at seven o'clock.

Making love with someone as young and vigorous as Jordan was often but not invariably pleasurable for her body but despite his physical beauty, the shining black of his eyes, it was not enough. Perhaps he felt something was missing too.

'*Je t'aime,*' he murmured once as if to improve things. '*Je t'adore.*'

'*C'est absurde, c'est ridicule,*' Lydia said crisply. 'We keep each other warm. *Nous nous tenons chaud, c'est tout.*'

What was between them could never grow. She needed a man in her head as well, a man who knew about sex and subtlety and words and nuance . . . fortunately her fantasy life had always been rich.

A shadowy figure lodged there waiting, a face she could never quite see. Who? A face she had glimpsed in a passing train, a professor she admired from a distance in her college days . . . or James released from an unquiet grave?

At the end of November, Lydia drove Jordan to South Bristol College to take his oral French and stayed, sitting in the car park, working and waiting.

'Done it,' Jordan shouted loudly, coming out at four o'clock, bursting with hectic joy. 'I bloody done it. Me, Jordan Errol Mackay.'

'*Excellent,*' Lydia said, sliding books into her briefcase, leaning to open the door. 'Good on you, Jordan.'

'*Il a dit "Ou est ta bicyclette?" "Ma bicyclette est dans le appentis."* Thass what I said. Over the moon!' he shouted, bouncing in and framing her face between his two hands. '*Dans la lune.*'

'*Non, tu ne peux pas dire ça en francais.*'

'Your place or mine?'

'Better be mine,' Lydia said, laconic, driving back through Bedminster.

A Mini stood on the drive in Cedar Avenue.

'William's here,' she said.

'William?'

'My son, William. There's a key in the garage, he can let himself in.'

'Never told me about no key,' Jordan said sulkily.

'William?' Lydia called, opening the front door.

'In the kitchen,' William said. 'Making tea.'

'This is Jordan, a student friend of mine,' Lydia said. 'Just done his oral French for GCSE.'

'Get on all right?' William asked politely.

'OK,' Jordan said, rocking from one foot to the other. 'Me 'eads goin' round and round. Clubbin', that's what I need, bit o' clubbin'. Look the chicks over, never know your luck.'

'Sounds like a good idea.' William regarded him soberly.

'Want to come, mate? Plenty of clubs Whiteladies Road.'

'Me?' William said. 'Well, why not? Do you mind, Ma?'

'Course not,' Lydia said, tucking herself perforce back in the mother role. 'Do you want something to eat first? Scrambled egg?'

'She could come,' Jordan said. 'You could come, Lydia.'

'Don't be ridiculous,' she said. 'What do you want to eat?'

Half an hour later she watched the Mini back up and shoot off along Cedar Avenue, Jordan's arm flailing from the window like a flag from a departing train. It was almost the end.

Jordan would come for a few days until his exams. After that he would bring his papers round for her to peruse, tell her in extended detail what he had put. She would listen and smile. She would get his results on a postcard in January maybe. At the end of next year a Christmas card would come from another town.

By then she would be painting again.

After that nothing but perhaps a sudden visit in five years' time, Jordan and wife and baby dropping in. That's how it would be.

As Lydia tidied the kitchen the phone rang.

'Hello, it's me,' Marina said.

'On Thursday?' Lydia said.

'Well, you teach on Friday evenings nowadays,' Marina said. 'Anyway, news at last, Ma. I'm pregnant.'

CHAPTER NINETEEN

ON THE FIRST Monday in December the house was quiet. Jordan was sitting his written French exam that day and his English literature next Wednesday. He wouldn't come to the Park Lodge classes after that. As Lydia had suspected the French conversation class was thinning out with the winter but the GCSE classes were holding their numbers quite well.

One more week and then it would be Christmas holidays and she would be able to paint again and Annie might come home. Everybody who had been round the house back in the summer had commented on Annie's water lily mural. Perhaps the two of them could paint together . . . or was that too much to expect?

Margaret and Bertie were cruising in the Mediterranean.

After announcing her pregnancy, Marina had listened in her monosyllabic way to Lydia's congratulations and then invited her to Christmas lunch at Frenchay, Annie too if she turned up. 'That'd be lovely, darling,' Lydia had said, 'but what about Grandma?' 'Oh, she's going to this four-star hotel with Vera for three days,' Marina had said. Evidently Mother and Marina kept in touch, dutiful granddaughter replacing less dutiful daughter. Why should she mind? Lydia wondered. But Mother herself phoned later, excited about the baby and convinced that her message to Marina had set the pregnancy in motion. Should she disclose she hadn't delivered the message? Lydia wondered.

She tidied her way through the penultimate draft of the poems by Eugene Gallant and Jules Vauclus, typed up a final version and composed the accompanying letter, trying to indicate how pleased she would be to do further work for them without sounding too creepy. Finally she took the package to the post.

Izzy was coming to supper and there was shopping to do. Izzy had given her vegetarian quiche, so what about cauliflower cheese, boring but all right with chopped boiled eggs, chrome yellow in an off-white sauce in the viridian green-blue casserole dish? Was Chris coming? She had asked him but Izzy had said, 'We're not joined by an umbilical cord,' which was neither 'Yes' nor 'No', and then started rabbiting on about the school dance club.

Izzy was tiresome like that.

When Lydia got back a postcard lay on the mat, the now familiar Morrab Gardens. 'Shan't be coming home for Christmas this year. Sorry. Love Annie.'

Lydia stared at the scrawled words. Children had to grow up, break away, she knew all that. She had made too much of Annie, spoiled her perhaps, she knew that too – Ed had told her enough times. But this was the last Christmas at Cedar Avenue and Annie loved Christmas. For years she had driven everybody mad, festooning the house with sticky and constantly collapsing paper-chains, insisting on doing the Christmas tree all by herself.

Something was wrong. But what?

Annie sat in the Morrab Gardens. She often sat there, sufficiently often for the people who used the path to and from work to nod as they passed. Sometimes the park keeper or the old lady stopped for a chat.

'Don't talk to anybody,' Jarvis said, but she had to talk to somebody or she just got miserable. The old lady was strange, whispered she was a 'pellar' and could cure sick people and Annie should keep away from yew trees for the baby's sake.

Jarvis didn't like Annie round the café and no wonder. Small café like The Lotus, great barrel like herself, couldn't bear to look. Annie hung a shawl on the dressing-table mirror.

She left Jarvis to run the café now. Not that there was much to run wintertime, no tourists was no dosh. Sophie had gone but Jarvis didn't want to be with Annie, who got bigger every day. He kept away like the babything was her fault, sitting inside and eating her up like a hungry monkey.

Lucky she had Clover in the market.

Lucky when she went to London.

Very lucky when she went to London for the last time. She didn't think about it much, the pain and that.

Such a beautiful cauliflower, Lydia thought, sniffing the creamy white head. You had to make the most of the passing moment, illuminate it if you could, what else was there? Freshness, super-markets were good for freshness. Freshness was everything in painting too, thinking about things made the idea stale, second-hand.

Soon she would get back to painting. One more week of classes, last class Friday and then the Christmas holidays and she would be free. Up in the study she stood the picture of the wild wood on the easel. It wasn't finished, but the wild wood wasn't like that any more. Except for the laurels it was not green at all, almost leafless.

It didn't matter because you didn't paint with your eyes or even your hand, you painted with your head and what was inside it. At least she had discovered that. Lots of people never did – Mother, for instance. Better not to think about it. You couldn't *make* painting happen; what happened or didn't happened in spite of you.

Like Annie and Christmas. Like love.

Later she rang William. 'Have you had a postcard from Annie? She's not coming home for Christmas.'

'That makes two of us,' William said cheerfully. 'I'm flying out to Hong Kong.'

'Ruby's in Hong Kong?' Lydia said. Suppose they came back married? she thought.

'Not yet but she will be.' William's voice was vibrant with joy.

'Can you afford it?'

'Got to, Ma. You can go to Marina's on Christmas Day, can't you?'

'Yes, thanks.'

'For goodness' sake, what's the matter now?' William said.

'Nothing,' Lydia said. She would like to tell him about how difficult it was not thinking about Richard but she didn't. It would only embarrass him; middle-aged love seemed foolish to the young, even indecent.

'Nothing at all.'

She assembled the ingredients for Izzy's supper on the kitchen table, grating cheese. How could Will possibly afford to fly to Hong Kong on his salary? Especially when what he needed was a new car with the journey from Pill and back every day.

Where was Richard, she wondered, Bath or Southsea? She

wasn't angry, it was nothing to do with her any more. Who was Richard? How much did you ever know about anybody?

In the middle of the cheese sauce the phone rang.

'Lydia?' Jordan said.

'How did you get on?'

'OK.' He sounded subdued. 'Listen, can I come over?'

'Sorry,' she said. How many *endings*, how much sadness had this word prefaced. Thousands, millions. 'My friend's coming, I'm just starting to cook.'

'What you mean, *friend*? Ain't I your friend?'

'Course you are . . .' she said briskly. She wanted to finish now and no messing. Jordan in her house all day every day for weeks, Jordan needing help with the past definite and Shakespeare's language and everything else. Pushing him out, she was setting them both free.

'Anyway I've got to go or I'll burn the sauce . . .'

'Don't you want to see my exam papers, Lydia?' he said, clinging like a limpet . . . a child and the last drink of water. 'Come tomorrow, shall I?'

'Jordan, I'm busy,' she said. 'You can work in the central library now. Lots of students work there.'

'Tellin' me to piss off, whacha think I am . . . nothink?'

'Goodbye, Jordan.'

Her heart was pounding as she hung up. Fortunately she had had the good sense to switch off the hob. She switched it on again and stirred the thick creamy mixture, sad but relieved. She was entitled to do what she wanted with her own life, wasn't she? Would it have been better for Jordan if what had happened between them hadn't happened? she wondered, chopping hard-boiled eggs. How could you know something like that?

An hour later Izzy's scarlet MG trickled on to the drive.

'Just the one of you?' Lydia said.

'How many were you expecting?' Izzy said, getting out. 'Know something, I love this house, even in midwinter. Can't think why it hasn't been snapped up.'

'We had offers earlier,' Lydia said, moving to the kitchen, 'Ed always says they're too low. Fancy a drink, white wine?'

'Why not?' Izzy said. 'Perhaps Ed wants to come back, you and him start all over, but he can't quite admit it.'

'You got to be joking,' Lydia said. 'Besides, he's been married to Leonie nearly ten years. Anyway, how's Chris?'

'Gone,' Izzy said cheerfully.

'Off in his new camper van?'

'Couldn't get one in his price range. Offered a job teaching English at a language school in Málaga just as that cold spell started. Went like a shot.'

'Violin time?' Lydia said. It was Izzy's favourite expression.

'Certainly not,' Izzy said. 'Place to myself, find out who I am all over again. Anyway, I'm flying to Málaga for Christmas.'

'Seems like the whole world is going nomadic these days,' Lydia said wistfully. 'A new age of hunters and gatherers. Is it the EU or what?'

'What we need are genetically engineered wings, preferably detachable. Think of the saving on air fares,' said Izzy, who had just bought her ticket. 'Did I tell you I've given notice at Stoke Bishop High?'

'You know you didn't,' Lydia said, lifting the green-blue casserole dish out of the oven. 'Whatever for?'

'Plans.' Izzy shrugged. 'Plan A is I'm signed up for this TEFL course in Bristol after Christmas, the RSA course for the prelimary certificate.'

'Teaching English as a Foreign Language? You're joking!'

'Thanks for the vote of confidence,' Izzy said, accepting her plate of cauliflower cheese. 'I'm *really* into language at the moment. This look good, tastes good too. What's the cheese?'

'Supermarket Cheddar, mature. You were *really* into classical Arabian dancing and camper vans last week.'

'Still crazy about them both,' Izzy said. 'But I'm selling the MG.'

'Oh Izz, you can't, you love it so,' Lydia said, following the scarlet vehicle in her head as she had done so many times in life. Did Izzy drive fast so nobody could catch her?

'Yesterday's love.' Izzy shrugged. 'You have to let it go. Nobody in their right mind stays here for an English winter.'

'Since when?' Lydia said.

'Since Chris, I have to admit,' Izzy said. 'He'll be home again by Easter. We're signing up for Voluntary Service Overseas, Malawi or Uganda, driving down through Africa . . .'

'A ferry across the Mediterranean?'

'Toe of Italy or the foot of Greece. Chris knows all that.'

'But VSO don't pay you, do they?'

'Board and lodging and a bit of pocket money. It's all we need. I'm letting the flat on a shorthold tenancy so we can get it back if we get fed up.'

'You getting married or something?' Lydia said.

'Might have to,' Izzie said. 'Lots of schools in Africa are mission founded. Málaga is crawling with black-robed priests.'

'I can't keep up,' Lydia said, collecting plates. 'Every thing changing so. Marina's expecting . . .'

'Congratulations, Granny. And how's the painting? Galleries fighting for your work yet? More to the point, how's Richard?'

'Gone,' Lydia said, and the word, tolling like a knell, summoned Izzy's eyes in her direction.

'The way of the world. Off with a blonde bimbo?'

'Something like that.'

'Tough toenails,' Izzy said. 'What's next?'

CHAPTER TWENTY

TOMORROW WAS CHRISTMAS Eve. No turkey to cook – it was all going to be so simple this year, Lydia thought. She had pondered over fresh or frozen, stuffed and basted for twenty-five years and that was enough. This year she would be at Marina and Jeremy's, their first Christmas in the new house, Marina happy to be four months pregnant.

Lydia was pleased too, her first grandchild due in May, a month of blossom and a good month to enter the hazardous world. Did Marina still feel her fragile fertility was Lydia's fault, telling Grandma first a sort of punishment?

Mothers made children and children made mothers.

This would be the last Christmas at Cedar Avenue and her painting life just beginning – the first glimmerings of the way she had to go. She had hardly spoken to a soul since term ended, just looked out at the Payne's grey sky each morning and painted all day, discovering red cadmium, an acrylic which glowed with such an intensity of red light, hot and dangerous. She was painting on paper as well as hardboard now. She had bought a complete set of brushes: *filberts* with their soft rounded tips; *brights*, as springy as a gym instructor; *rounds*, long, tapered at both ends, elegant and almost decadent.

The brushes were a present to herself. She wasn't giving individual presents this year, no wondering what for whom. Instead she had chosen and bought eighteen scarves one afternoon three weeks ago, a scarf for everybody – Izzy's idea – telling them beforehand, choosing silk, wool or man-made fabric and whatever colour seemed most appropriate.

Early though it was, she had seen Father Christmas in several department stores that afternoon. She had liked him well enough in the days when the children insisted on visiting his grotto and had always gone along, pleased that elderly unemployed men should have a few weeks' wages but alarmed by the talk of paedophiles. So why the sudden dislike of him now?

Something to do with comfort promised but not actually redeemable? Something to do with Richard?

Still, Christmas was a time for children, and loaded with her eighteen scarves and alarmed at her own disaffection, Lydia had wandered into a shop and up a wide staircase to a place where toys were piled in a huge hill, plastic replicas of Snow White and Pocahontas, polyester replicas of the Lion King, a hundred and one Dalmatian pups, the hill encircled by children stretching out their arms or scrambling to get a foothold.

To Lydia it had seemed horrendous, Yeats' rough beast slouching towards Bethlehem. It was a relief to get home, close the front door behind her. Since then she had managed to forget Christmas. There was no room in her life for anything but painting.

She had painted the wild wood as it had been and followed the reality with different abstractions, extending the idea and making it her own. Sometimes straight tree trunks enclosed her like a cage, sometimes she was outside the cage trying to get in. Hadn't the sun shining through the bars of the cot a few weeks back created a prison cell?

What made her emotional life so full of the symbols of constraint, apart from Ed, apart from Mother?

Lydia had been out that morning early to stock up for Christmas with more acrylic paint and hardboard as well as food. Coming in, she made herself tea, scooped mail from the doormat and wandered to the sitting room where Christmas cards marched across the mantelpiece in red, green, gold, blue.

She sipped her tea and opened envelopes: cards from Margaret and Bertie, who were going to Rye, and the Newtons, the other side, and an Oxfam card: 'Just off to Southsea. Wish me luck. Love Richard.'

Wish him luck, what a nerve!

It was typical, she thought irritably. He just didn't believe people got fed up with him. And why go to Southsea anyway? Much better let Yolande and her poor young husband sort things out. No doubt he would say she needed his support because Richard needed to be needed. Some people were like that, didn't feel alive unless they were needed. Only a child would ask her to wish him luck. Lydia tucked the card at the back of the mantelpiece.

Would Annie phone on Christmas Day? Lydia understood now how totally absorbing painting could be, how it haunted you night and day. Was it like that for Annie? Maybe she had exaggerated Annie's talent, pushed her too hard but the truth was Annie would never have got anywhere if she hadn't been pushed, certainly not into art school.

The phone rang.

'Merry Christmas, Lyddy,' Mother said. 'Lovely news about Marina. Looks like my advice did the trick.'

'Things do sometimes happen without your help,' Lydia said tartly.

'Feeling like that, are we?' Mother said after a pause. 'Got the hump? You should go away. I'm off with Vera for three days tomorrow. She's picking me up Christmas Eve.'

'Yes, you told me.'

'Three days at this four-star hotel, waited on hand and foot. Course, I'm sad to leave The Cottage, first Christmas without James. Did you get my card and the little present?'

'Yes. Both on the mantelpiece.'

'What have you been doing then?'

'Painting.'

'Painting you call it, *moping* if you ask me. You want to get out and about like I do.'

'I'm not moping, Mother, I'm painting. I *want* to paint.'

'But you need to meet people. With all this divorce about there must be lots of middle-aged men . . . you should think about it, dear. I mean you're not bad-looking for your age. Anyway, Happy Christmas. I'll phone Christmas Day from the hotel. It's only two miles, I could phone when I get there.' Mother's voice was rising.

'Shouldn't bother, unless something's wrong.'

'What do you mean *wrong*? Vera's a very careful driver.'

'Course she is,' Lydia said. 'Good night then.'

She wanted to get back to painting – back to the *studio*, as her study had become. But she phoned Margaret first.

'Thanks for your card. You're off to Rye then?'

'Yes. Leaving early in the morning. Bertie loves driving but we try to get away before the traffic builds up. After Christmas we're pottering back, stopping off for a night in Savernake Forest. There's a hotel miles from anywhere, Bertie says. I shall miss my swimming pool, of course.'

'You're not still swimming this cold weather?' Lydia said.

'Have to, don't I, after all the hard work Bertie put into the cover? It's important to be grateful and I'm so grateful to Bertie for all the marvellous things we do together. He looks so disappointed if I don't have a dip every day. Such sad doggy eyes . . .'

'Well, you mustn't let him bully you if you don't *want* to swim,' Lydia said. Had Margaret's attachment to Bertie impaired her sense of reality? Bertie's blue eyes suggested Siamese cats, or sapphires perhaps, but could not be described as *doggy*. Could swimming in a heated pool on a cold day precipitate a heart attack in an elderly person? Besides, she didn't much like the sound of a hotel miles from anywhere in Savernake Forest, especially since Margaret had recently changed her will leaving nearly everything to Bertie.

'Bully me! Oh, Bertie could never do that,' Margaret said with an edge to her voice. 'Gives me everything I want and more but I must get on with the packing. You've got the children Christmas Day?'

'I'm going to Marina's,' Lydia said.

'Lovely,' Margaret said. 'See you when we get back.'

William lay pinioned, one right arm under Ruby's neck. He had arrived at the Peninsular Hotel that morning. The watch on his left wrist indicated it was two o'clock in the middle of the night now. Did the flashing lights of Hong Kong, the noise of traffic, gongs, the click of mah jong go on until dawn?

'It's been such a long time, Ruby,' he whispered.

'Five months,' she said, sitting up, smiling at the lift of her breasts in the dressing-table mirror, flicking back her long red hair. 'Think I've changed, do you?'

'Bit thinner.'

'It's the heat. And the Sanderson kids. That Tarquin, talk about hyperactive. Shouldn't have fizzy drinks, I keep telling them, but nobody takes a bit of notice . . .'

'I do, Ruby,' William said, curling a strand of red hair round his fingers. 'I notice everything about you and I bet you handle Tarquin OK . . . and the Sandersons.'

'You don't *really* know anything about me.'

'Marry me, Ruby?' William said softly, but the words seemed to bounce in his stomach like small pebbles.

'What?'

'Let's get married, you and me, soon as possible.'

He had to say it, he couldn't live without her. He had tried, hadn't he? Was anybody ever absolutely free?

'Changed your tune a bit.' Ruby looked round at him.

'Yeah, well . . . I always knew I loved you but now I know I can't do without you,' William said, thinking as he said it that it would be better not said.

'Well, you might have to,' Ruby said, pulling a blue silk wrap round her, watching their reflections in the mirror. 'Nobody gets everything they want this life.'

'OK, Nanny,' he said with his eyes on the silk. 'Where d'you get that blue thing?'

'What's it to you?' Ruby said. 'Bought it Kowloon market.'

'Yeah?'

'Yeah,' Ruby said. 'Like silk, don't I?' Her green eyes watched him. 'I got faults, you know. Well, everyone's got faults. I like things my way.'

'Tell me about it,' William said.

'Cheeky!' Ruby said, flinging round to tickle him. 'You're supposed to think I'm absolutely fabulous.'

'I do, I do,' he said, rolling out of the range of her small strong hands. 'Ab fab, ab fab. Let's get married, Ruby.'

'You mean it? Cross your heart and hope to die?'

'Cross my heart and hope to die.'

'Won't always be like this,' Ruby said, looking at him seriously. 'I mean we always squabbled, didn't we?'

'Long as we're together,' William said. Simultaneously they glanced towards the window, trying to see the way ahead beyond the flashing lights.

'Know something? We wouldn't squabble if you did what I said,' Ruby suggested.

'No chance,' William said. 'Unless you promise to do what I say too.'

163

'Another thing ...' Ruby said, dreamily. 'I'd like to be rich. Really rich like the Sandersons ...'

Lydia went upstairs, lifted the last version of the wild wood from her easel and selected a new piece of hardboard. She wanted to paint the hill of presents, the scrambling children ... but not thinking about it, just painting.

She painted until two o'clock that night, already Christmas Eve, and dropped into bed exhausted. She didn't wake until ten o'clock next day and after breakfast selected another hardboard and painted on through the day. Her wet palette kept the acrylic soft, workable for a day at least. She had discovered that though you couldn't put acrylic on oil paint, you could put oil on acrylic. No problem.

The night painting was dark, sombre. At first she hadn't known what it was that was disturbing her mind but then she had. Jordan lying flat on his back on a bed she had never seen; Jordan in the late night café where she had never been, sleeping in his crummy bedroom.

Was Jordan all right?

Would he have gone home for Christmas?

Lydia was washing her hair when Jeremy phoned.

'Everything OK?' she said, a towel turbanning her head. She recognised a knife-edge of fear in her voice.

'Not really ... Marina's not well, been in bed all afternoon. I had to get the doctor out.'

'What did he say?'

'Stay in bed. So I'm afraid we have to cancel. I put the turkey back in the freezer. Sorry, Lydia. Just don't feel like cooking it now. Maybe we can have it in a day or two?'

'Is she bleeding or anything?' Lydia said.

'Not so far, but she's very pale. What'll you do?'

'Make myself a sandwich. Long as Marina—'

'I'll phone tomorrow, let you know.'

Lydia abandoned painting, wandering through the house from room to room. Her house, wasn't it? It was weeks now since anybody had been round, and it needed dusting. Outside the garden looked desolate. Why did evergreens have to be such a dull dark green? From upstairs she could see over the hedge to Margaret's garden.

The silver cover right across the pool was a symbol of love. Had they switched the electricity off? Lydia wondered, imagining flying over the hedge and dipping a finger into the still warm water.

Was Marina going to miscarry?

It was good to express your feelings when you lived alone, Izzy said. Lydia turned from the window and moaned aloud. Was another baby going to be lost? And would that be her fault too, ringing for ever down the generations?

Had Marina told Ed about the baby?

Why had Ed never collected his desk? Once or twice a year he promised to do so but he never did. Did he secretly want to come back, had kept a foot in the door, as Izzy suggested?

Lydia wandered on to Annie's room and stared at the mural. The central water lily was robust, a heroine in its rampant foliage twisting through the water, but not like Annie.

Was it the way she wanted to be?

The Lotus didn't open Christmas Day. It was good, just the two of them, all right lying in bed, the street quiet outside, nobody to smirk and wink: 'What you two been up to then?'

She loved Jarvis but she mustn't let him lie on her now, Dr Rinde-Smith said. Jarvis could do it from behind if he wanted, Dr Rinde-Smith said, and Jarvis did want. Ever since the scan Dr Rinde-Smith said things like that. They stayed in bed till dinnertime. Really cool.

'Poor little babything,' Annie said. 'All shook up on his Christmas Day.'

'He's all right,' Jarvis said.

'Ought to get up now,' Annie said. 'Got to phone Ma.'

'What for?' Jarvis said. 'You'll only say something.'

'Like what?'

'You tell me, girl? You wind her up, you do. Got enough on me plate when I can't find the rent without 'er berserking down 'ere.'

'Guess you're right,' Annie said slowly. 'Yeah?'

All Christmas Day Lydia was painting and waiting. Painting the pool next door, secret under its silver cover. Didn't Hockney paint a blue pool over and over, his own pool in California?

Lydia painted Annie in a pool, Annie and her yellow-as-gorse hair, streaming out like water weed. Ophelia's hair.

On Boxing Day Marina was better, got up a couple of hours in the afternoon. She phoned and so did Mother. The day after that the post came with a package postmarked Penzance.

How could she open a package addressed to Annie Kemp? Lydia wondered. How could she not?

She inserted her thumb under the lip of the thick brown envelope. Inside, her own letter sent to Annie last September and several Christmas cards addressed to Annie Kemp at the art school fell out. One had a pencilled message on the back. 'Haven't got your address. Hope they send this on. We miss you, Spike and Joss and me, especially coffee time. Hope you and Jarvis works out. Me and Ben split, cried buckets but I'm over it now. Love Helen.'

CHAPTER TWENTY ONE

T HE ALARM CLOCK waking her surprised Lydia. It suggested she had slept when she seemed to have tossed and turned all night, gnawing like a dog with a bone at the enigma of Annie and the Christmas cards sent back from Penzance.

Had Annie left art school, left Penzance even before Lydia's letter? Where had she gone and who was this Jarvis?

Endless speculation was useless. Lydia must go to Cornwall. She had to, she wanted to. It would have been different if she had someone to talk to but everyone was away – Izzy, Margaret, William . . . and Richard of course.

It was dark when she left home, crossing Clifton Suspension Bridge and travelling towards and then on to the M5 motorway. An occasional lorry thundered out of the darkness behind her as if her journey, her presence there, was untoward, overtaking her and disappearing into the darkness of the west ahead.

The sky lightened to dustsheet grey. At first small sloping fields and straggling hedges bordered on either side, but soon everywhere was flat, frosted grass intersected with straight black leats, a single ploughed field like dark chocolate. Lydia had never seen the countryside like this, the countryside in winter, an omission which now seemed feckless.

She passed a park of mobile homes, checked with squares of yellow light. Izzy's idea, wasn't it, the whole world going mobile, turning into bohos of no fixed abode, rejecting ownership and goods, wandering nomads, desecrating the countryside with litter and scrap iron, then moving on to fresh green pastures?

Was that the way it was going to be?

An older generation had neither the right nor the opportunity to control future patterns of life. But surely the pressure of population would soon exceed the dwindling supply of food from land and air mistreated and polluted? Sick cows, sick chickens, carrots, lettuce and what else contaminated with organo-phosphate, hundreds of plant and animal species lost each year. Elm trees gone, what next? Lydia wondered.

What would Richard say about this? But she wasn't going to think about Richard or Southsea. Not any more.

Ahead of her was a huge skeleton greenhouse with its plastic torn away, flapping in the wind like a monstrous scarecrow. The experiment, whatever it had been, had evidently failed, progress regressing into decay.

Further on more farms, real farms with black and white cows and hedges neatly trimmed, blackberry keeping its purple leaves through winter, plantations of pine. The sky lightening, bits of blue and yellow gleaming between straight lines of cloud, white-edged like white fur. Under the brighter sky the grass looked greener. Another breaker's yard, heaps of derelict cars and black tyres piled up like cans of supermarket beans.

Lydia stopping near Exeter for coffee and petrol, left the motorway soon after for the A30. Suppose she couldn't find Annie, should she go to the police? At sixteen you had the right to leave home, disappear for ever if you wished. And Annie was already twenty.

Lydia drove on. Jersey cows, fawn coats soiled in a deeply muddied pen, more piles of tyres but more green too, cypress and spruce, a flock of grey sheep, heavy with lamb. Dartmoor and its bleak hills capped with granite, a herd of ponies, furry as squirrels, stretching long-maned heads to search for food. A gorse bush blooming, yellow as baby Annie's hair.

William tried the number again, listened to sounds of wind and sea, high-pitched female voices speaking Cantonese. He ought to tell Ma at once. Ruby had phoned home straight away. Ma didn't like Ruby, none of his family did.

The beginning of a great charade. William sighed, would it always like this? People had to get married; Ruby wanted to get married. Ruby was so much herself, liked being herself. Was that why he loved her, why she was the only girl he had ever wanted for more than a week?

'Operator say no reply that number,' a voice with a Cantonese accent said. 'Please try later.'

William hung up. Where the hell had Ma got to?

* * *

As Lydia crossed the Tamar she felt a lift of the heart. Cornwall, she had loved it since the holidays of childhood but her hands were shaking and her knees felt weak. Was it sleeping badly or driving so far or was it Annie?

Why shouldn't she drive to Cornwall? As Izzy said, the whole world was there, waiting to be explored. You could go anywhere, everywhere; she could go anywhere, everywhere if she wanted, stop where she liked, live in Cornwall if she liked. It was a different way of thinking. 'Where have you been, may I ask?' Mother would say. 'Whatever did you have to go there for?'

Lydia stopped at Launceston for lunch, a ploughman's at Keppels Head, and drove on.

The sky was clear blue now. Sun on the grey slate roofs of cottages shone like pewter; sometimes grey slates were veiled with white cement against the Cornish gales. Even in December everywhere was green with ivy, laurel, rhododendron, holly, conifer, camellia almost in bud.

Across Bodmin Moor dusk was already descending and by the time Lydia reached Penzance it was dark. She parked behind The Longboat Hotel, pottered to stretch her legs and buy a street map of Penzance before she booked in.

The following morning she breakfasted and went out as soon as it was light. She would have to start at the art school but not just yet. She needed to walk about a bit, breathe fresh sea air, experience the place. Besides, she was afflicted with a sudden unease.

Suppose Annie didn't want to see her?

She followed the road to Market Jew Street, walked along North Parade and then South Parade. Penzance, sited on an isthmus, had sea and beach on either side. There were a couple of supermarkets but most of the shops were small, dedicated to the tourist trade: gift shops, bric-a-brac, craft jewellery, hand-knitted jerseys and antiques. There were numerous cafés too. 'Closed' signs on several dusty glass doors looked semi-permanent.

People were very friendly. It was like a village, Lydia thought, everybody offering good morning to everybody, including strangers like herself, children smiling.

'Excuse me,' she asked a boy with a gold earring and startlingly black hair – Spanish ships had been coming here since Armada time. 'Do you know the art school?'

'Up the Causewayhead there,' he said, pointing.

The Causewayhead went uphill, a wide pedestrianised lane with small shops either side, a covered market full of craft stalls. How did people make a living with so many sellers and so few buyers?

At the top of the Causewayhead a circular car park. Beyond, the art school, a red-brick building, Victorian Gothic.

The front door opened but the building struck cold after the sun, the foyer panelled in dark wood, to the left a cubicle with pigeonholes fronted by a counter. A porter was sorting letters.

'Did you want something, madam?'

'Yes,' Lydia said, trying to appear calm. 'I'm looking for Annie Kemp. She's a student here.'

'Annie Kemp?' the porter said. 'Thass right. Cleared out they pigeonholes, load o' stuff for Annie Kemp. Took 'im to the office . . .'

'They were sent to my address,' Lydia said. 'I'm Annie Kemp's mother but Annie's not with me.' Her voice quavered but she cleared her throat firmly. 'I thought somebody here might know where she is . . .'

'If you was to come back beginning of term . . .'

'But I'm only down here for a day or so. Surely somebody must know where she lives? I mean she must have a tutor?'

'Could try Mr Lukes,' the porter said, turning reluctantly to study a list on the wall.

'If you let me have the number . . .?'

'Can't do that, Mrs Kemp, it's not public information.' The porter lifted the phone. 'I'll give 'im a bell.'

Lydia nodded.

'Mr Lukes? Yeah, Tom from the art school. There's a lady 'ere asking for Annie Kemp . . .' he murmured, turning his back.

'Tell him I'm her mother,' Lydia whispered into the ensuing pause.

'Annie Kemp's mother,' he offered into the phone. A pause. 'OK then.' He held the receiver towards her.

'Er . . . Mr Lukes?' Lydia said.

'That's right. I understand you're Annie Kemp's mother?'

'Yes. And I want to know where she is.' Despite her resolution her voice was rising. 'Where's Annie gone?'

'Can't help you much. She dropped out of art school ages ago. Last Christmas – well, before that really . . .'

'Why?' Lydia said, her heart thudding. 'I mean why did she drop out?'

'Lot of 'em do. Not much motivation, go down at the first fence. We try to pick the sticking-at-it types but we don't always get it right.'

'But . . . but I think Annie's still down here,' Lydia said. 'I mean she sends me postcards marked Penzance.'

'Yeah, think she is. I see her about sometimes.' His tone was irritatingly laconic. 'Hangs round the market afternoons.'

'Why didn't they tell me about it?' Lydia said. 'Surely somebody from the art school should have got in touch?'

'Eighteen, nineteen? Girl's got to do what a girl's got to do these days, Mrs Kemp.'

'Do you know somebody called Jarvis?' Was it a first name or a surname?

'Student, was he? Can't say I do. Hope you find Annie then.'

As Lydia walked down the Causewayhead she glanced left and right at girlish faces. If Annie was still in Penzance it shouldn't be too difficult to find her. Especially if she hung round the market.

She turned into Chapel Street and stopped suddenly outside a café called The Lotus. 'Closed' hung on the door and the café windows were dirty but on the back wall behind the coffee urn was a wall painting. A water lily rampant, curling up through blue waves, almost a replica of the one in Annie's room at Cedar Avenue.

Lydia pressed the bell. It rang loud and shrill but nobody came. She rang again, banged on the door with the flat of her hand, stepped back on to the street to look at the upstairs windows, saw the curtains twitch.

'Annie?' she shouted, slapping at the door again. 'Annie?'

A young man in jersey and jeans came into the back of the café and wearily unbolted the door top and bottom.

'Did you want somethink?' He was dark-haired, dark-eyed, olive-skinned, late twenties perhaps.

'Jarvis? Where's Annie?'

'Who's asking?' His brown eyes studied her carefully.

'I'm Lydia Kemp. Her mother.'

' 'Fraid she's not here at the moment. Want to come in?'

'You're Jarvis?'

He nodded and stood back.

'Where is she then?' Lydia hesitated and then followed him into the café and through a doorway hung with plastic ribbons and then up narrow, uncarpeted stairs.

'Away.'

'Away where?' She faced him across a kitchen table littered with remains of breakfast. Behind him the sink was full of unwashed crockery.

'London. Fancy a cup of tea?'

'No, thanks,' Lydia said, but her throat felt dry. She glanced into the room next door, a large unmade bed, what looked like a shawl hung over the dressing-table mirror, a dressing gown she knew.

'You're her boyfriend?'

'You could say.'

'Tell me where Annie is or I'm going to the police.'

'Shouldn't do that, missus,' he said with a grin. 'Annie wouldn't like that. Got this contract, business deal, dicey, know what I mean?'

'What *do* you mean?' She stared into his tawny eyes.

'Leave off about the old bill or Annie could be in big trouble,' Jarvis said. 'Tell you what, if you was to meet her off of the train from London first thing tomorrow morning, be a real help, that would.'

CHAPTER TWENTY TWO

Dr RINDE-SMITH WOKE in the night. He had been restless since the scan, suggestive certainly but not proof positive. Foetal development showed minor variations and at least Annie Kemp was only carrying one child. Beside him Hermione breathed steadily. Dr Rinde-Smith sighed, turned over and fell asleep.

Lydia leaned her elbows on the brick wall. The station below was quiet and seemed empty. She stared down at the straight rails, bright as silver under the lights. It was still dark but beyond the station she could hear the invisible black sea, and faraway St Michael's Mount showed a lighted window.

If you didn't really live anywhere, she thought, you were free to imagine you lived everywhere.

She tried to stay calm, experience this moment which, like the millions of other moments of her life, would never come again; feel the ambience of the place round her, imagine the colours appearing with the light and how she would paint them.

She tried not to think about Annie but questions zizzed in her head like wasps. Who was this Jarvis? Why did Annie have to live in that awful café? What was she doing in London anyway? Trying to get herself into another art school, St Martin's or Camberwell, for instance? Both had excellent reputations. Was she visiting galleries? London was the centre of the art world in the UK, that would be positive. But how could she afford to go up from Penzance every week?

Away to the left signals clicked in the darkness and now she could hear the distant rumble of an approaching train. She walked quickly downhill along the pavement and turned into the station. A guard appeared and strolled nonchalantly towards the barrier. The lights in the station buffet had come on. Outside the sky was lightening to grey.

The train slid slowly alongside the platform, stopped against the buffers. Carriage doors swung open, a dozen passengers stepped down with their luggage and started towards the barrier, some towing suitcases on wheels. Lydia's eyes combed the platform. Had Annie been on the train? Could she have missed it?

But suddenly a carriage window slid down, a fair frizzy head leaned out, a hand released the brass handle. The door flung open and Annie stepped on to the platform.

Lydia stared silent. In the last few months she had contemplated a variety of alarming possibilities for Annie. Pregnancy had not been one of them. But here was Annie, hugely pregnant, walking towards the barrier, clad in a long black coat which swung open as she walked, black skirt, black beret, a pigskin weekend bag hung from her shoulder.

Since they had last met Annie had evidently grown up, however precariously, broken free, changed her entire life. Suddenly Lydia felt her presence there unwelcome, intrusive.

If she kept quiet would Annie walk straight past?

Annie came on slowly, deep in thought. She hated London. It was up and down every week now. Why should she when she couldn't sleep on the narrow bunk? Couldn't blame the babything, wasn't his fault, he was quiet all night. Quiet as a mouse all week come to that, but she hadn't told Dr Rinde-Smith – why should she? As it was he was going on about the date of her last period and was she quite certain all over again, like she was some sort of moron. Like it was all starting from the beginning again, which it never would. No way. Never again.

Jarvis always waited at the entrance nearest the sea but he wasn't there today. Annie clutched her coat together, cold inside. Where was he? Suppose he had run away? As she reached the barrier, she stopped and looked all round.

'Ma? What you doing here?'

'Came to see you, darling. It's been such a long time. I was worried,' Lydia said quickly, breathlessly. Girls got pregnant every day, she knew, but somehow Annie's condition was different, entitled her to special consideration, mother-to-be of the first grandchild. Lydia had expected to throw her arms round Annie but that was not now possible or quite suitable.

'What about it?' Annie said, shifting the pigskin bag to her other shoulder and still looking round. 'I am grown up, you know. Free, white and twenty-one next month.' Her face was pink but her eyes, dark grey as the sea, were defensive. 'Jarvis is my life now.'

'Yes of course,' Lydia said, looked away apologetic. 'You've got your own life . . .'

'Too right!' Annie said, flinging her coat open like a flasher. 'Got your eyeful, have you?'

'It's all right, Annie,' Lydia said. 'I'm not getting at you, not criticising or anything. I've met Jarvis, been to The Lotus . . .' Was Jarvis her common law son-in-law?

'Where is he then?' Annie said. Was he going off her? He couldn't, he mustn't . . . 'What's he been saying?'

'Nothing. He just asked me to come instead,' Lydia said. At least it had given her the chance to meet Annie on her own. But her arrival in Penzance seemed more than ever intrusive. She had seen Annie sad, disappointed, cross, but never quite like this. What about the baby if Annie was already so distressed? 'Shall we have a coffee or something, sit down a bit?'

'If you like,' Annie shrugged. They walked to the buffet. A middle-aged women with bright blonde hair was wiping the counter.

'Would you like some breakfast?' Lydia said. 'An egg or something? Orange juice?'

'Wouldn't mind a Danish pastry,' Annie said. Jarvis never let her eat things like that now.

'Apricot or pineapple?' the woman enquired. Her grip on the cake tongs seemed inexperienced.

'Apricot, thanks.'

Lydia paid and carried the tray to the distant table where Annie had settled. 'Feeling all right, are you?'

'Course,' Annie said cool.

'Won't be long?' Lydia said, pulling at the top of the small carton of milk with too short nails. 'I wish you'd let me know – your first baby, my first grandchild . . .'

'No, it's not,' Annie said, swallowing a mouthful of Danish pastry. 'Got nothink to do with you, nothink to do with me or Jarvis.' The blonde woman at the counter was staring in their direction. Annie lowered her voice.

'Kid Spenser, that's what Jarvis calls it. Kid Spenser out of Annie Kemp by IVF courtesy of Dr Rinde-Smith, that's what Jarvis says. It gets born and I get ten thousand pound.'

'What? Surely if you have a baby it's *your* baby?' Lydia whispered.

'Hush up, will you?' Annie said, jerking her head towards the counter. 'People here got big ears. Dr Rinde-Smith at this clinic says a surrogate mother's got to be discreet. That's what he calls me, "surrogate mother".'

'What clinic?'

Annie shrugged. 'In London. I'm not allowed to talk about it nor nothing. I have to go there every week now.'

'But it's illegal surely, when you get paid?' Lydia whispered.

'You going to turn me in?' Annie said, but her defiance was flagging. 'Jarvis was the start of it.' Her eyes gazed across the station towards the sea as her thoughts moved back to the dream-time. Jarvis had loved her then, said it every day, proved it every night, but now . . .

'Couldn't pay my rent to Mrs Trewartha, that was the start of it, so I got this job waitressing evenings and weekends at the café. Next thing I'm in bits about Jarvis and he's in bits about me, so I move in but trade was down wintertime and Jarvis couldn't pay the rent nor nothing . . .'

'So?'

'So I went to London, didn't I? Had to. I got this job at a hotel, cleaning the bedrooms, putting on clean sheets, £3.35 an hour, plus bed and board, talk about slave labour. Sent the money to Jarvis, most of it, but I didn't see him hardly at all, which was really miserable. One night there's this lady over from Jersey, Drina Spenser, crying her eyes out and I fetch her a cup of tea and she tells me about how she can't have a baby and it was all fixed at this private clinic with her husband's seed and hers ready mixed and everything. A surrogate mother had agreed to have the baby for them for ten thousand pound but she'd dropped out and that's why this Drina Spenser's so upset, crying all the time.'

'She told you all this?' Lydia said.

'Not right off,' Annie said. 'Just crying like she was a poor animal shut in a cage, made me feel mega-miserable, so I said I would have the baby. For ten thousand pound.'

'Oh Annie . . . Annie.'

'So I went to this clinic. Dr Rinde-Smith didn't like me at first. Said I was too young and they didn't know anything about me but Drina Spenser kept crying and crying and after a bit Dr Rinde-Smith started asking questions like, 'Do you have a boyfriend?' and I said, 'Not at the moment,' because I knew that was what he wanted. 'Best keep it that way,' he said, and then he was asking stuff like when was my last period. Said it was good I wasn't on the pill and he looked inside me, know what I mean? Then he said to come to the clinic in exactly three days so I did and he had this long silver thing and he put the speckything inside me, no anaesthetic nor nothing. IVF they call it.'

'And you went back to Penzance?' Lydia said. Her cherished child, her baby – they had been so close once, but what was between them now? How could Annie experiment with herself and her life so perilously without Lydia even knowing?

'You went back to Jarvis?'

'Yeah, well, the ten thousand pound was for him. Course, trade picked up with the season and The Lotus was OK and me and Jarvis were OK too.' Annie blinked. 'But then I started getting big and people whispered and Jarvis hated that.'

'Hated what?'

'People smirking, making jokes. I mean Jarvis was in bits about me one time.' Annie's eyes filled with tears. 'Couldn't tell them it wasn't our baby. Couldn't tell them anything, still can't.' She blew her nose. 'Anyway, what's happened about the house?'

'Nothing,' Lydia said. 'You could come home if you like. After the baby's born, you're bound to feel limp. I've still got the old cot.'

'Don't you understand anything?' Annie said. 'It's not *my* baby to take home. Once it's born it's nothing to do with me.'

'But having a baby is a great upheaval. You can't just—'

'Tell me about it,' Annie said, staring out of the window. In the distance rough grey sea, edged with white, was angry like everybody was angry at her, angry and disappointed, expecting what she wasn't and could never be.

'So what'll you do then, after the baby?'

'Go back to the café. Get the rent paid and council tax, redecorate . . . Jarvis and me. You won't tell Dad, will you?'

'Don't you think he has a right to know?' Lydia said.

'Why? Why should he have rights over me? It's got nothing to do with him or Marina or William or Grandma or anybody. Promise me you won't tell *anybody*?'

'Well, all right. You don't want to go back to art school?'

'Don't see it, do you? What you think I am?'

'But you seemed so keen, Annie.'

'It was you that was keen, Ma, keen enough for both of us. I didn't want to go in the first place. But you were so set on it, going on about my talent, twisting my arm like I had to go. I went for you.' Her eyes were bright and angry now. 'But inside my head isn't yours, Mrs Kemp. I'm not like you, I'm like *me* and I haven't got any talent. All the tutors think I'm crap. I can't paint and I don't want to and I'm not going to any shitty art school ever again and that's that.'

'But you do have talent, Annie. The water lily on the café wall –' Lydia's voice faltered – 'soon as I saw it I knew you had painted it.'

'Only because it's just like my bedroom wall.'

'Yes. But everybody going round the house notices it, says "Very original" or "Very unusual", something like that.'

'Load of crap from a load of thickies and you just swallow it,' Annie said. 'Copied it from an ad in a Sunday supplement, didn't I, an ad for selling aquariums. Do us both a favour, Ma, get real. Sell the house and get yourself a life and just go away and leave us alone, Jarvis and me. Please.'

CHAPTER TWENTY THREE

IT WAS STILL early when Lydia left Penzance and turned on to the A30. She would have liked to go back a different way, just as she would have liked to start a different life but for the moment she lacked the energy to contemplate, let alone accomplish either change.

Outside wind buffeted the Fiesta and chased bruise-coloured clouds across the sky. Inside something which felt like a slab of concrete wedged in her chest so that breathing was an effort. What Annie had said ran round and round in her head. ' "It was you that was keen, keen enough for both of us." ' But it wouldn't go on for ever. Lydia murmured aloud, ' "All passes, so will this" ': the only bit of an Anglo-Saxon ballad she remembered from school days. It had been a comfort ever since.

The quest, coming down the journey to Cornwall in midwinter to find a lost daughter, had seemed like a fairy tale, driving to the edge of the known world. But Annie had been found and lost again because she *wanted* to be lost. 'Do us both a favour, Ma . . . just go away and leave us alone. Please.'

How could she live with this grief? Lydia wondered. How could she paint? Yet she had to paint just as birds had to sing. It was her territory even if she was inexperienced, naïve as to its nature and her own direction.

Suppose she never saw Annie again? She had promised not to tell the family but the way she felt she had to tell somebody. Talking was for friends. Not Margaret – her head was swamped with Bertie; not Izzy, who loved gossip and would sell her soul and yours for a juicy disaster. Richard was kind, cool, a good listener. If he had abandoned his role as prospective lover, hadn't he also described them as good friends?

She had gone down to Cornwall with anxiety but some excitement. Going back the excitement had gone, the house in Cedar Avenue seemed suddenly fragile, not bricks and mortar but a mirage floating in the air.

It would sell sooner or later – houses sold best in spring – but with her job abandoned and the children grown, the house no longer defined her, told her who she was or where she belonged. There were plenty of flats and houses for sale round Bristol but she had lived in Cedar Avenue for twenty years.

Where could she go? Where could she live? Where did she want to live? How could she paint in a situation so fluid, a landscape so unfenced, time without fixtures?

The wind whistled across Bodmin Moor, gnarling and sculpting the hawthorn trees to grow horizontal, reminding her of James lying in hospital gnarled and sculpted by his years. James who had driven them all across Bodmin Moor late one summer evening to a holiday flat in Newquay; James who had done his best for his stepchildren most of the time.

Last day of December but the gorse was already in bloom.

'Get yourself a life,' Annie had said. Had it been the worst moment she had ever experienced? Lydia wondered, but then remembered Ed shouting that night, smashing the last of the wedding-present glasses, the Citroën backing up the drive. But replaying old dramas was childish, words eventually lost their sting. 'All passes, so will this.'

'Just go away,' Annie had shouted. And so she had and somehow she knew it was what she wanted too. She had worried about Annie for so long, tried to protect her, enhance her prospects but only succeeded in damaging her confidence, her sense of her own worth, confusing their identities just as Mother had confused her own and Lydia's.

What was Annie doing now? But she had to stop wondering, release them both. How could she paint with Annie always in her head? Annie absent would leave a wilderness of empty space but wasn't that space called *freedom*?

Launceston, Okehampton, stopping for a late lunch in Exeter – it was dark when Lydia reached Bristol and crossed the Clifton Suspension Bridge which hung across the gorge outlined with a thousand lights. She drove towards Stoke Bishop.

People spreading across the pavement from pubs, people in the streets . . . suddenly she realised it was New Year's Eve.

'Home at last,' she murmured, turning into Cedar Avenue,

smiling at the familiar house, white-walled and brown-roofed in the streetlight, letting the car run down into the garage.

The 'For Sale' sign floated confidently above the gate but the absence of lights next door suggested Margaret and Bertie were still away. Lydia carried her case to the front door, switched off the alarm, switched on the heating, and, tired though she was, felt the warmth and comfort of the house enfold her as she drank tea, picked letters from the doormat and carried them to the sitting room.

Belated Christmas cards and a bill from BT for £79.52.

Now she was back she had to talk to somebody about time. Izzy was in Málaga but she could phone Richard. She had already given herself permission to phone him as she travelled back. But his voice on the answerphone informed her coolly that he wasn't available at the moment and invited her to leave a message. Was he still away in Southsea?

She phoned Marina. She was tired, so tired she could weep, but at least she could play the part of Marina's mother again now.

'Happy New Year, darling. Are you all right?'

'Fine, Ma,' Marina said in her small cool voice.

'The pregnancy and everything?' Lydia said. She would have liked to know what Marina was wearing, so she could picture her but decided not to ask.

'Fine,' Marina said.

'I won't keep you if you're just getting the meal.'

'It's OK, Jeremy's getting it. Did you find Annie?'

'Yes but . . . well, she's dropped out of art school.'

'I think I guessed that,' Marina said.

'And she's living with this young man, Jarvis. Working in his café.'

'I guessed that too, didn't you?' Marina said.

'Seems I'm a bit slow,' Lydia said.

'Not slow . . . just prejudiced,' Marina said.

'What's that supposed to mean?'

Marina ignored the question. 'Have you heard from William? You're not going to like this, Ma. He and Ruby are engaged.'

'Up to him, isn't it?' Lydia's voice was brisk. 'He's a big boy now.' 'All my pretty chickens,' said a voice in her head but no one must hear her lament. Ruby must catch no hint of reservation. Was all continuing family life such a sham?

'Quite,' Marina said. 'Would you like to come to lunch on Sunday?'

'Yes, thanks,' Lydia said. Was it meant to cheer her up, compensate for Christmas lost and Ruby gained? 'You know the old cot, the one you all slept in, would you like to have it?' she offered. Her stepping stone to painting, it would be a wrench but it was the season for wrenches.

'No, actually,' Marina said. 'I've seen this antique cot, shop in Alma Road. Bit pricey but I'm talking Jeremy round.'

'Oh,' Lydia said, saddened but relieved.

'Must go, he's dishing up. Happy New Year, Ma.'

Lydia was making herself a sandwich when the phone rang. Richard or William or Mother or Ed?

'Hi, Lydia, it's me,' Jordan said. ' 'Appy New Year, innit?'

'Thanks,' Lydia said. 'Had your results yet?'

'Nah. Think I passed OK, done the biz, know what I mean? Can I come round?'

'No. Sorry. Happy New Year,' Lydia said.

'Fancy a pork?'

'Get lost,' Lydia said, putting the phone down. It was nobody's fault, it was just what happened if you hurt people. 'All passes, so will this.'

Five minutes later it rang again.

'Yes?' she said tartly.

'So you're back,' Mother said in her telephone voice. 'Just phoned to wish you a Happy New Year, dear. Marina said you'd gone to Penzance.'

'Just back. Annie's dropped out of art school,' Lydia said, and took a deep breath. 'She's living with Jarvis, a young man who runs a café down there.'

'Only hope she knows what she's doing,' Mother said after a pause. 'She is my granddaughter after all!'

'She certainly is,' Lydia said, too tired to be forbearing. Was New Year's Eve the time for home truths? 'Ironic really.'

'What is?' Mother said. 'What you talking about now?'

'Annie saying she only went to art school because I *wanted* her

to, and me complaining I didn't go to art school because you *didn't*
want me to,' Lydia offered.

'Oh you. You were always difficult.' Mother was launched. 'Quite
different from Unity, chalk and cheese. Difficult right from the start.
All I wanted was for you two girls to have a good education.' Her
voice glided along its familiar track. 'Wanted you to have the chances
I didn't have but you're never satisfied, that's you. How was I to
know you wanted to go to art school?'

'I told you,' Lydia said wearily. 'I told you but you wouldn't hear
it.' Had it been like that for Annie too?

'Digging up the past, where's the sense in it? No wonder Annie's
throwing herself away. How's she's going to get a decent husband,
may I ask? That's what Annie needs – a decent husband. Worked my
fingers to the bone for you two but nobody cares tuppence what I
think, because I'm old.' Her voice was tremulous now. 'Where's the
sense . . . upsetting people New Year's Eve?'

'Sorry, Mother,' Lydia said, relenting. 'I'm tired, driving up from
Cornwall. Like they say, "A mother's place is in the wrong." '

'Who said that?' Mother said after a pause. 'Polly Toynbee, was
it?'

'Katherine Whitehorn,' Lydia said.

'No, Shirley Williams, I saw it in the *Radio Times*,' Mother
asserted. 'Mind you, Fergie's always *saying* things but she hasn't had
the education . . . not like my girls.'

'Happy New Year, Mother,' Lydia said, putting down the phone.
She was tired, exhausted, but that didn't give her the right to upset
people. Why did she always have to upset people?

She considered the television, the custom of the country. A
minority went to the pub, the majority stayed home and saw the
New Year in by proxy.

Were Annie and Jarvis watching right now? Had there been a
television in the flat above The Lotus? Lydia found she could already
contemplate Annie's home with some equanimity.

The phone rang again. 'Wanted to wish you a Happy New Year,'
Margaret said. 'We've just got back.'

'How was Savernake?'

'Wonderful,' Margaret said. 'This little hotel Bertie knew, so
quiet. We went for walks and Bertie was so good with the wild

ponies, he worked in a circus once, you know. He's had the most amazing life. But I did miss my swimming.'

'Happy New Year to you both.'

'Oh, I'm sure it will be. Good night, Lydia, dear.'

At nine o'clock the front doorbell rang. Jordan or William or Ed or what? Lydia wondered, as she switched on the porch light.

'I don't usually open the door late as this,' she said quite calmly, though her heart was pounding.

'You should get yourself a peephole,' Richard said, holding out a bottle of wine as a peace offering. 'You didn't sound quite yourself on the answerphone. I thought we might see the New Year in together.'

'That's a very good idea,' Lydia said, heavy with fatigue but pleased to see him.

'We can lick each other's wounds,' Richard concluded.

'That sounds disquieting,' Lydia said, fetching a corkscrew.

'I shall take it in my stride,' Richard said.

'Have you eaten?'

'Not specially,' he said. 'We could go out.'

'Too late,' Lydia said. 'Everywhere will be crowded out.'

She drank a second glass of wine and made scrambled egg enlivened with Parmesan and accompanied by salad. While they ate she told him about Cornwall and Annie dropping out of art school, Annie pregnant with a surrogate baby. Lydia had promised not to tell anybody but she had to tell Richard. She even told him the awful bits, the 'Leave us alone', 'Get yourself a life', 'I'm not like you, I'm like me' bits. She even told him about Carmel and the BT bill in September for £255.24. She wanted to tell him everything and she wanted to be in his arms but that was impossible because of Yolande. She was weeping now, she couldn't help it.

Richard listened and they finished the wine and were quiet.

'You have taken a buffeting,' he said, taking her hand. 'But it'll work out, you know. Easy things first. You get copies of the BT bill and send them to the language school and Carmel's father. That'll probably produce something and if not you'll have to try the small claims court.'

'You're right, of course,' Lydia sniffed, oblivious to her red eyes and nose. 'But poor little Annie, what a dragon I am.'

'You're not a dragon, Lydia, far from it,' he said, stroking her fingers. 'Try not to worry. Young women have babies every day and the clinic doctor will take good care of Annie because it's in his interests, isn't it?'

'It's not the baby so much,' Lydia said. 'It's what she said. That I made her go to art school . . . all that.'

'Girls will be girls,' Richard said. 'But you couldn't really do that, nobody could. Girls have to break away from their mothers, do their own thing, but we are all ourselves. Even a three-year-old has free will.'

What good manners, what good nature, Lydia thought sadly. Didn't the two together make grace?

'How selfish!' she said. 'I've been on about my problems all evening. Your turn, Richard. What about your wounds?'

'Nothing to report but superficial abrasions to the ego,' he said, putting down his glass. 'Yolande made it up with her husband at Christmas. She's off to the South China seas.'

'Leaving poor old you with a broken heart?'

'Wouldn't say that. Fun while it lasted. What's that?' He jumped up suddenly.

A church clock struck the first stroke of midnight and far away in the harbour ships hooted, a rocket exploded above them, green and red stars falling against a black sky towards the garden.

'Happy New Year, Lydia,' Richard said. He kissed her lightly and stepped back.

'Happy New Year,' she said as the phone began to ring.

'Happy New Year,' Ed said. 'I've sold the house. Phoned this morning but you were out.' Richard stepped in to the hall.

'This morning?' Lydia murmured. Was that why the house had suddenly felt so fragile? 'How much?'

'The Holroyds – you remember, in the summer – well, they upped their offer, two hundred and eighty-five thousand.' Ed's tone was jubilant. 'OK?'

'Suppose so,' Lydia said. Richard picked up his raincoat.

'You don't sound very pleased.'

'Well, it's where I live,' Lydia said. Richard opened the front door and whispered, 'Thanks.'

'Wait,' she said, but the front door closed.

'Where we both *used* to live,' Ed was saying. 'I'll be round to discuss details tomorrow if that's convenient?'

'Quite,' she said. The Astra was backing up the drive. Lydia dropped the phone and sprang to the front door.

'Wait.' she shouted into the cold darkness, but the Astra was already moving along Cedar Avenue and it didn't stop.

PART FIVE

Beginnings and Endings

CHAPTER TWENTY FOUR

Richard's sensible advice about copies of the BT bill for SHSE was calming. Lydia hadn't realised he was so practical. She proceeded to get photocopies of the bill enclosing them with letters as he had suggested. Now she awaited events. She felt cleansed somehow by the evening they had spent together. Was it all that weeping?

Talking about Annie might be good for her but what about Richard, leaving on the stroke of midnight New Year's Eve and not phoning since?

But she had to get on with house-hunting now. Cornwall was out of the question. Lydia abandoned the idea of leaving the area and approached agencies about flats for sale, eschewing houses as a greater commitment and more difficult to sell should she want to move on. She tramped the hills of Montpelier where loud music proclaimed territorial rights and vistas of eccentric roofs reminded her of Paris.

Maybe she would contrive to live in Paris one day?

Meanwhile there was Clifton Wood and then Hotwells, grey terraces mirrored in the grey water below like great iron ships. How she longed for somewhere green, a cottage perhaps. But at least she had already cleared the cupboards in Cedar Avenue though she wasn't sure what furniture to keep until she found a flat.

January was mild, the garden sap already rising, snowdrops pushing through the earth, the pieris presenting bunches of buds like tiny green grapes which would blossom white as lily of the valley in March, smelling like incense. The Holroyds visited several times, ostensibly to measure up for curtains and make offers for fitted carpets and the dishwasher, but actually, Lydia suspected, to assert and savour the pleasures of ownership. They seemed in no great hurry to move in.

William came to supper.

'Pity about the garden,' he said, standing at the French window looking out. Ruby was still in Hong Kong working out her notice. The Sandersons had not been pleased at her defection. 'Pity you can't take it with you.'

'Thanks for all that grass- and hedge-cutting over the years, Will,' Lydia said.

'Think nothing of it, Ma.' There was a nervousness about him now, unfortunate in a solicitor; he had always been so confident.

'I was thinking of taking the pieris with me.'

William raised his eyebrows. 'Bit big for a window box.'

'All right for a balcony, though. Loads of flats have balconies,' she said, deciding to add it her list of essential requirements. 'Have you heard from Ruby?'

He frowned. 'Phoned yesterday but she'd gone out.'

Making hay while the sun shines, Lydia thought, but could she afford such critical embroidery? Ranks had to close now.

'Do you want to try again while you're here?'

William glanced at his watch. 'Wrong time of day,' he said. 'Anyway, when are you actually moving?'

'End of March.'

'Thing is, we were wondering, Ruby and me, if we could have our wedding lunch here, sort of reception-cum-party.'

'Isn't it the bride's family who does all that?'

'That bride's family stuff is feudal now, Ma. Not talking about anything grand, just family and friends, us and the Fields and Dad and Leonie and Grandma and old Mr Beavis – well, it was Ruby's idea actually. We'd get caterers in. You wouldn't have to do anything except be there.'

'Sounds like the Last Supper,' Lydia murmured gloomily.

'What last supper? Oh, the Jesus one. This is a festive occasion, Ma, more a *grand finale*.'

'I hear you,' Lydia said. 'Who's going to pay?'

'I should think Dad will . . .'

'Well, you'd better make sure first. I suppose it's OK if you get the caterers organised. Dare say I'll have got my flat by then . . .'

'With balcony?' William said.

'With balcony. Or I might get a cottage.'

'Bit pricey. Don't go and saddle yourself with a big mortgage.'

'Half the money from this house should do me,' Lydia said

boldly. 'After the wedding lunch you children and Ed can take any furniture you want and I don't. The rest goes to the auction rooms. I move out and the Holroyds move in. End of story.'

'Great,' William said. 'If you had a big pot I could dig up that pieris for you now, diminish the shock to both your systems.'

'But I *have* got a big pot,' Lydia said. 'Bought it a week ago. It's in the garage. No time like the present.'

'Right,' William said with rather less enthusiasm.

The pieris duly potted and William gone, Lydia began painting again, found that she could. Was it because the sale of the house was definite that its loss had turned from alarming fantasy to an actual reality offering choices she had never had before?

The study was more like a studio every day, her desk concealed under layers of newspaper spattered with paint, an equally spattered groundsheet covering some of the fitted carpet, the only one the Holroyds had declined to offer for. Jars of water stood all along the windowsill and piles of hardboard ready for painting were stacked against the walls.

For the moment Lydia abandoned her intuitive journey towards abstraction and gave herself up to nostalgia, sketching what she could see from the windows: the wintry garden, the slope of the grey-green lawn, the silver cover of the blue pool next door, the stark black trunks of the wild wood. The house itself she painted from memory, occasionally running out to look, finding angles and attitudes she had missed for twenty years. Painting had sharpened her powers of observation, her way of seeing, for ever.

A fortnight into January evening classes started again. Jordan didn't return – she had not expected him – and only four students arrived for the French conversation class on Friday night. Mr Sharpe had evidently noticed and emerged from his office to say, 'May I see your register?'

'Of course.' She tried to sound casual.

'Only four students . . . you'll have to do better than this, Lydia,' he said.

Lydia juggled, 'If you think you could do better . . .' and 'It is midwinter' in her head but decided not to risk either and offered an apologetic smile instead.

'People go away for Christmas. I expect next week numbers will be better.'

Fortunately the GCSE classes held their numbers.

'Where's our Jordan?' one of the girls asked, smiling round. 'Had his results?'

'No idea, I'm afraid,' Lydia murmured casually. Had the smile been knowing? Once she had relied on Jordan's discretion but she couldn't now.

Three days later a postcard arrived with the message, 'French=Pass. English lit=Failed. Keep your knickers on. Jordan Errol Mackay.' She sighed and tore the postcard in half. She had hurt him but at least she had got him through his GCSE French, despite the odds, and fortunately she hadn't expected thanks.

Annie lay on the bed and stared at the top of the cypress tree, framed by the window, a pyramid of green. It grew in the back garden. She had never seen it before, never thought of the clinic as a terraced house with a back garden.

'Now you're here I think you'd better stay, Annie,' Dr Rinde-Smith had said after he had examined her. She stared at him. She hadn't said anything about the pains in her back – well, they were nothing much really, coming and going, but somehow he seemed to know. Could he read her thoughts like a sort of magician?

'But I can't,' she had said, suddenly scared. 'My boyfriend is expecting me back. Waiting at the station.'

'You can phone him, can't you? Tell him the doctor says the baby may arrive any time now,' he said, smiling as if it was nothing.

'The baby . . . You said mid-February, isn't February yet,' Annie stammered. 'It's January.' Early. Annie had been born a month early herself, Ma said.

'Nothing to worry about, babies make their own rules,' Dr Rinde-Smith said soberly. 'And young women are often mistaken about the date of their last period, leads to confusion. Shan't mention it again. Best you don't mention it, not to Jarvis, Drina or anybody. Understood? Silence is golden.'

Dad used to say that when she was a little kid, Annie thought. Funny that. *Silence* was Dr Rinde-Smith's favourite word. Silence and discretion.

She nodded and he passed the phone across the desk and went on sitting there, his eyes watching.

'Shall I phone Jarvis now?'

'Of course,' he said. 'Tell him you'll phone him every day but *do not* give him this number.'

Jarvis seemed relieved she was staying up. He'd miss her, course he would, but he'd been worried. Suppose the baby started sudden in the night . . . Setting off for London in the old van they might never get there.

'Kiss kiss,' Jarvis whispered and his lips plashed on the plastic receiver. 'Good luck, love.'

She loved him, course she did, but how could she send kisses with Dr Rinde-Smith sitting there?

' 'Bye then,' she said.

'Tell me,' said Dr Rinde-Smith, 'your young man – what colour are his eyes?'

'What's that got to do with anythink?' Annie said. 'Chocolate brown. I got pains in my back.'

'Nurse'll take you up to your room.'

So Annie's eyes fixed on the top of the cypress swaying in the wind like a green flame; downstairs Dr Rinde-Smith stared at the bole of the same tree. He dealt with Annie Kemp by the book, had to when the girl herself wasn't reliable. Quite likely she had been having Braxton-Hicks contractions which were often mistaken for the onset of labour but he could hardly let her leave the clinic under the circumstances.

Why couldn't her boyfriend have blue-grey eyes like the bulk of the population, eighty per cent was it? Chocolate brown indeed.

'How you feeling then?' the nurse asked, collecting the untouched tray.

'Pains have stopped,' Annie said.

'They'll be back, don't you worry,' the nurse said brightly and as if she'd ordered it, suddenly they were. Stabbing pains in her back and a griping pain in her belly. Annie moaned.

The nurse came again. 'How're you getting on? Let's have a look, shall we?' She burrowed under the white gown.

'How long?' Annie whispered. Nobody told her it hurt like this.

Not Ma, not Mrs Ward who did the sex class at school.

'Long time, dear. Dilation's only just started. Just have to wait,' she said with an encouraging smile. 'Let's see what the doctor says, shall we? Fancy a cup of tea?'

'No, thanks,' Annie said.

'Got to keep our fluids up. I'll bring you a cup.'

'OK,' Annie murmured. 'Sorry.' Always got everything wrong, didn't she? 'Sorry.'

The pain subsided and she sat up and looked out of the window. Little white dots in the grass below, snowdrops like in Cedar Avenue, remembered Ma saying, 'Such dear little things,' Annie running out and picking them. 'Thank you, darling, but leave them another time. I like to see them growing, little buds coming out.' 'Sorry,' Annie had said.

Waiting. Long waves of pain. Waters breaking. 'Hello, Annie.' Drina's eyes hot with excitement, sliding on to the bulge below. The Spensers' baby, little bud coming out.

Whose baby? Solomon's baby? Annie's baby but it wasn't really and how could she pay the money back?

Downstairs Mr Spenser waiting with his bag of gold, cheques not accepted here. Upstairs Annie waiting for the next pain. Drina saying, 'Shall I stay?' Annie saying, 'Go away.'

Hot red pain, tight metal bands round her belly. Hotter and hotter, tighter and whiter, hard as diamonds. Annie moaning.

'All right?' The nurse put another cup of tea beside her. 'Be quiet now, you're upsetting people.'

Annie drinking tea, Annie throwing up. Rising pain, a boiling pain. Midwife saying, 'Breathe slowly. Try and breathe slowly now. Where's the gas and air?'

'Slowly,' Annie said, and heard a noise she didn't know. A howling noise like the wolves at Whipsnade Zoo but this howl was coming from her throat.

Like I'm mad, Annie thought, up shit creek with no sandwiches. Helpless, hopeless Annie. A prick in her arm.

'Diamorphine,' the midwife said. 'Helps you to relax. Monitor the baby's heart, Bridget.' A strap on Annie's belly.

'Ah . . . ah,' Annie howling, nurses bustling trolley into lift. Gliding sliding down. Drina's frightened face. Door opening, trolley bumping, feet running. White masks and a bright white light shining down.

'Had diamorphine.'

'Wait, Annie, wait. Don't push yet. Don't push.'

Changing. Everything changing, a hurricane raging through her body, shaking her like a dog with a rat.

'Push now.'

Gasping, 'I am.'

'That's right.' Dr Rinde-Smith's eyes bright above the mask. 'Push again, Annie, push.'

'Can't. Can't.'

'Like you're doing a great big pooh. Push, Annie.'

'Ah . . . ah.' A long low moan.

'I can see the head.'

'Push, Annie, push.'

'Ah . . . ah.'

'A lovely little boy,' the midwife said. The doctor holding the red-streaked child by his ankles, rubbing the soles of his feet, baby wailing. Annie closed her eyes as the door opened.

'A perfect baby boy. See to the afterbirth, nurse,' Dr Rinde-Smith said. 'And watch that uterus, too much blood.'

I'm going to die, Annie thought, feeling the hot wet rush on her legs, a hand massaging her belly. A prick in her arm.

'Helps the uterus contract,' the midwife said. Dr Rinde-Smith had gone. Stitches and white pills and back to her room.

'How's the baby?' Annie whispered.

'Fine, dear,' the nurse said. 'Like a cup of tea?'

'Can I see him?' Annie said, but her head was full of mist.

'Get some sleep now, Annie.'

'Sleep?' Annie said. She looked at the window but sky and cypress tree were black now and the cup of tea grew cold.

Dreaming, waking, hurting. Speckything, babything gone.

Downstairs Drina's voice trilling like a nightingale.

'My baby?' Annie's feet slapping on cold lino. Downstairs a taxi pulled away. Annie heard but couldn't see. Couldn't.

'Whatever are you doing, dear? Back to bed at once. Don't want you haemorrhaging, do we?'

CHAPTER TWENTY FIVE

T HE THIRD WEEK in January a letter of apology with a cheque for £93 arrived from SHSE, which claimed to be still negotiating with Carmel's family. It covered the cost of the phone calls to Naples in August. A day of celebration, and with one thing fewer to worry about, Lydia phoned Richard to thank him for his advice and invite him to dinner. 'Took their time about it,' Richard said.

She would do something special: *boeuf Strogonoff,* for instance. They had known each other for a long time. Why shouldn't they be friends? She needed a special friend to confide in. She could tell Richard anything because he was nonjudgemental. She had told him everything – a kind of loving and a kind of therapy.

Richard accepted the invitation and in the afternoon two days later Lydia stopped painting and applied herself to the recipe, assembling and chopping onions, green pepper, mushrooms, lemon and yogurt, better for both of them than the traditional sour cream. A really nice meal was no more than he deserved for listening to her Annie story. She was still anxious with the day of Annie's confinement approaching. She had got the number of The Lotus from directory enquiries and phoned twice but nobody answered.

She hadn't so much chosen a different life, a painting life, as been precipitated into it. It could surely include Richard as friend and lover, but not all the time, not marriage. She had never really liked being married, a life so limited by another person's expectations. Besides, she had never been good at it.

Dinner in the oven, she went upstairs to change, selecting a white polo-neck jumper and black velvet trousers, practical for handling an iron casserole, elegant and an antidote to tears and problems, but not too blatant a come-on.

'What about the maniac with the blue paint?' Richard said on the doorstep, glancing back at his Astra.

'Haven't seen her for ages. She's turned over a new leaf.'

'Something smells delicious!' he said, coming in but making no attempt to kiss her.

'*Boeuf Strongonoff*,' Lydia said. 'And don't worry, the *boeuf* is Scottish, cross my heart. Cross my butcher's heart too.'

'I'm not worried,' Richard said, dropping his coat on the hall chair. His grey-blue corduroy jacket looked new. 'What news of Annie?'

'Not a peep!' Lydia said.

'You haven't phoned?'

Lydia shook her head. 'The way I see it a young woman pregnant or otherwise has a perfect right *not* to see her mother. Besides, I couldn't get through.' She couldn't quite control the tremor in her voice either. 'Get lost, Ma', 'Get yourself a life' – how long would Annie's words go on echoing in her head?

'A girl facing childbirth, I'd get in touch if it was Fen,' Richard said. 'I mean mothers and teenage daughters, it's crisis time, isn't it? Fur flying?' His smile was tender.

'But Annie is nearly twenty-one,' Lydia said, separating each word. 'And you're nicer than me, more tolerant. Red wine?'

'Great,' he said. 'Are we eating in the kitchen or what?'

'Dining end of the living room,' she said, crossing to the sideboard, where bottle and glasses stood. 'While I've still got a living room with a dining end.'

'Cheers,' Richard said, accepting his glass. 'Here's to solutions, or do I mean resolutions?'

'Solutions will do,' Lydia said and sighed. 'If only . . .'

'If only what? You can do what you like now, can't you? Any progress with a flat?'

'Don't let's talk about flats,' she said. 'I've been round dozens in the last two weeks.'

'Did I tell you I'd got this part-time job . . . two mornings a week at a mother and baby clinic?'

'In Bath?'

'Bradford-on-Avon. Not far. Nice little town.'

'Good for you. Remember your talks on *Woman's Hour* years ago, "The Wakeful Baby"?' Lydia said. Was she reproaching him for what had been between them then?

'Fancy you remembering!' Richard said. His furrowed brow suggested he did so only with difficulty.

'Course I remember,' Lydia said. He looked up then, his eyes hazy blue like bonfire smoke, his hair pewter grey.

'Ah, yes.' His smile modified to his 'men-are-deceivers-ever' smile, which wasn't how she wanted the evening to go.

'Happy days.' He raised his glass, sipped and moved across to the French windows, looping back the curtain and peering out. 'Garden's looking good even now, what I can see of it.'

'If you're ready, I'll get the dinner started.'

'Need any help? Or shall I just refill the glasses?'

'Please do,' Lydia said. Sometimes his imperturbable composure was maddening, she thought, lifting the casserole out of the oven, pouring new potatoes and peas into their respective dishes and carrying them through. The trouble with cooking was it gave you that bothered look.

'What a magnificent feast!' Richard said. 'Should I have worn my bow tie?'

'Some of us like you as you are,' Lydia said, removing lids. It was *his* treat, his thank-you-for-listening present. He liked talking about his son, more than anything.

'How's Sean?'

'Fine. Been asked to write the music for the television version of *Dombey and Son*. Filming in Gloucester at the moment, keeps him pretty busy. This *Strogonoff* looks good.'

'Help yourself to vegetables. Ages since I read *Dombey*.'

'Afraid I've never read it,' Richard said with mock humility. 'Complete Philistine, according to my children.'

Was he actually proud of it?

'Doctors don't get time, all that anatomy and physiology to get in their heads. Must be a nightmare keeping up to date.'

'Impossible!' Richard said.

'Papa Dombey is a shipping magnate. He loves his son but his son dies.'

'Not a work designed to raise the spirits?' Richard said.

'Dickens was into moral and social criticism,' Lydia said. 'Isn't it about the railway age . . . ?'

'Sean did say something about railways . . .'

Lydia tried to listen but what would it be like to have Sean for breakfast, lunch and tea? An unfair question when Richard had listened so patiently to hours of Annie. He had an advantage in that he didn't seem to remember beyond a day or two, but at least he was sensitive to other people's feelings.

'Excuse me.' She got up to collect the plates and dishes. 'No. You sit still.'

'Phew!' Richard said, as she returned with apple and lemon tart, nicely browned on top. 'You're spoiling me.'

'Good!' she said, surprising herself as she sliced the tart. 'The way to a man's heart . . . ' But that was tactless.

'Is through his stomach,' Richard said, refilling her glass.

'What about *your* glass?' she said.

'I have to drive home, don't forget,' he said.

'Ah . . .' Lydia smiled. *Please stay* and *you don't have to go* slid through her head. Were they sliding through his?

Spoons clicked on plates in silence.

'You're going to miss this house,' Richard said.

'I love it,' she said. 'Because I've lived here twenty years but it's not really that special, just a suburban house with bits of vernacular Tudor, sort of sub-Lutyens.'

Was the house listening to this disloyalty?

'Moving is always an upheaval,' Richard said. 'Leaving Chippenham was awful, so many things, items, decisions, better once it was over...'

'You can care too much about *things*,' Lydia said. Did she sound like Izzy, the old Izzy, whose live-ins lasted about as long as her tights? Where was Izzy at the moment?

'But this room, all this . . . ' Richard glanced across at the large sofa and two easy chairs loose-covered in a Jacobean pattern which Lydia had chosen as representing continuity and family stability for the children. Several smaller chairs, the kneehole desk, coffee table, it all had to go somewhere.

'I shall keep things for my flat,' she said. 'Then Ed and the children can choose what they want. What's left goes to auction. Did I tell you William's getting married?'

'I gather you're not too happy about it?'

Lydia shrugged. 'What can you do? Anyway, I'm hardly an expert on choosing a partner, am I? I'll get the cheese.'

'Not for me,' Richard said.

'Stilton?'

'Ah, well, if you're twisting my arm . . .'

Lydia carried plates out to the kitchen and returned with green grapes, Stilton, oatcakes carefully arranged in three hollows of the same dish. All this palaver, she thought, wasn't what she meant, wasn't really *her*.

Richard helped himself to three green grapes and a morsel of cheese. Why was he always so obliging, so well-mannered? Was it something to do with his mother?

'I'll just get the coffee,' she said, and moments later set the tray on the coffee table. 'I haven't made proper coffee for ages.'

'I'm honoured then,' Richard said. He settled himself in an easy chair with his arms spread either side in repletion.

'How's Fenella getting on?' Lydia said. His daughter was Richard's other favourite subject and he had listened so patiently to her account of Annie amok.

'Expecting again,' Richard said.

Lydia smiled. When she had arranged the evening, the possibility they would end up in bed had occurred, but not particularly enticed her. Now the likelihood was disappearing fast, it was suddenly what she wanted.

'More coffee?'

'No thanks.' He glanced at his watch. 'It's getting late, Lydia. Working day tomorrow, my first clinic.'

Suppose she just said it straight up? Women were allowed to, according to contemporary mores.

'Was Bradford-on-Avon your first choice?' she said.

'Fitting in with local needs, I was lucky to get it actually. Anyway, how's the painting going?'

Lydia shrugged. 'Mostly sketching the house at the moment, *aide mémoire*, not that I'm likely to forget. I think about houses a lot anyway. Sometimes I visit all the houses where I've lived in my head, wander through the rooms.'

'Amazing! But you can't have had many places if you've been here twenty years?'

'A semi and two flats when the children were small, before

that student digs. But I go back to Mother's house sometimes. Do you remember that hotel room at Weston?'

'What hotel room?'

'The only night we spent together,' Lydia said. Surely he couldn't have forgotten? 'Right on the road, cars going past all night. Wardrobe with a cracked mirror . . .'

'Doesn't sound up to much,' Richard said. He glanced at his watch. 'Time I took myself off.'

'Already?' Her heart was thumping; surely he would hear it. 'Why not stay the night?' she said, breathless.

'Well . . .'

'I mean make love . . .'

'Of course you do, but you've taken me by surprise.' Richard's eyes had brightened. 'That's not a bad idea, in fact it's a very good idea. I just didn't think you—'

'I was worried about your heart,' Lydia said. 'And Yolande.'

'No need,' Richard said, and got to his feet. 'Let's go, shall we?' He held out his hand.

'Only if you want to. I mean . . .'

'Know something, Lydia? You talk too much.'

'Sorry . . . ' He put his arm round her as they went upstairs. The studio door stood open, he paused and looked.

'See what you mean,' he said. One wall was covered with sketches on paper of house and garden. A montage stood on the easel, a wash of ochre acrylic, almost covered by stuck-on fragments of wallpaper, school reports, nursery rhymes, crisp brown leaves from the wild wood, the whole framed with new strips of the dust-pink carpet fitted downstairs twenty years ago and trampled now to donkey brown.

'I rather like that,' Richard said.

'It's an obsession,' Lydia said, not sure she cared for Richard in her studio. It was too intimate, more intimate than love. 'The whole house is an obsession.'

'Can't argue with that.' Richard moved into the bedroom, closing the curtains. 'Your neighbours are early to bed.'

'Margaret and Bertie are a wonderful advertisement for wedded bliss,' she said. It was enough for now.

Richard took off his jacket, Lydia kicked off her shoes. Like a married couple themselves, she thought, no rush, no need to pretend urgency.

'We'll have the light off if you don't mind,' Richard said. 'My chest is not a pretty sight except to my surgeon . . .'

'I don't think I'll mind,' Lydia said into the darkness, laying her clothes across a chair. Nothing was what you expected. Let the night keep its secrets.

In the faint glimmer of the landing light she could see his body white between the sheets and as she slipped in beside him his arm came out to receive her.

'It's been a long time,' he murmured.

'Too long,' Lydia said. But this was no homecoming, it was quite unlike that other time so long ago, the night of buttons scattering, gasping, the time of passionate love. It was the warmth of his arm round her as the tips of her fingers gently explored his bypass scars.

What did she expect? Not this exactly. She wasn't so young and she wasn't so old, neither was he.

'Long as it doesn't alarm you,' he whispered.

'Not at all,' she said, kissing his chest. 'Course not.' His hands stroking, his delicate but confident hands, excitement rising and warmth but with it something else. Fear.

Oh God, she thought, as he slid into her, suppose his heart, suppose he . . .? But she mustn't think like that, shouldn't, couldn't with him moving inside her, mustn't think at all . . . out of her body . . . lost.

Resting, dreaming, his kiss as he rolled off her. 'All right?'

'Mm,' she said.

A sudden scream split the darkness. 'Bertie!'

'Oh my God,' Lydia said.

Richard was already out of bed, light switched on, pulling on his trousers, seizing his jacket.

'Stay there.' Running downstairs, front door slamming, footsteps, knocking at Margaret's door. Lydia leaned on her elbow, saw him go in, the door slammed shut.

An ambulance siren, the ambulance arriving. The front door opening. A stretcher carried out. The ambulance leaving, driving slowly now. Silent in the darkness.

Lydia waited but Richard did not come back.

Presently she slept and woke to daylight and the doorbell ringing.

'Bertie's dead, heart attack,' Richard said as he came in. His face was drawn. 'Poor chap had a heart condition. Bluish extremities, cyanosed, fingers and nose quite blue. Wouldn't see a doctor apparently.'

'Poor Margaret.'

'She wanted to talk. Told me all about Bertie, how she loved him, showed me some family photo album ... ' Richard yawned. 'His grandmother's funeral? Four black horses ...'

'Try not to touch your breasts, Annie,' the nurse said. 'Don't want them filling up with milk. Very uncomfortable if we have to bind you up tight. Doctor's on his way ...'

'How are you feeling today?' said Dr Rinde-Smith.

Annie didn't answer. She had slept for a long time and woken not quite sure who she was or where.

'What day is it?'

'Thursday. Er ... the baby was born Monday night. The Spensers took him back to Jersey. Delighted with him, they both were. I've got your money in the safe,' he smiled. 'Ten thousand pounds in cash makes quite a parcel.'

'Did you get ten thousand pounds too?' Annie wondered out loud. She felt strange, newborn herself, as if she had to learn to sit and walk and speak all over again.

'That's what is known as "confidential information",' said Dr Rinde-Smith. 'I'd like to see you up today. Lying in bed never did anybody any good. Are you going to go back to Cornwall – when you're fit and ready, that is?'

'Can't,' Annie said, and her voice sounded odd, thin, as if she was a phantom in someone else's head. 'Not Cornwall.'

'Y OU'D BETTER HAVE the front door key. I've got a spare.' Lydia said on the doorstep. Did it sound like a thank-you-for-having-me present? she wondered, mildly irritated by the idea. Actually it was more of a bonding present as well as an invitation to come again. Their first night together after ten years should have been dramatic but had been diminished and overlaid by Bertie's death.

Life was short. You had to live as much as you could.

'Thanks for everything,' Richard said, accepting the key with a kiss, by no means the first such key his pocket had accommodated. 'Clinic today and I want to phone Sean. So see you when I see you? I told Margaret you'd go over this morning, hope that's all right?'

'Course it is. She probably wants me to drive her to the hospital. She's bound to be upset, may need help with undertakers and all that. Fortunately I'm free this week. Teaching Tuesday and Thursday evenings starts next week – not Fridays any more, class collapsed . . . failed.'

They had to sort things out, establish a pattern. She wanted to see him, wanted to make love, but how much *time* did she want to be with him? She was used to living on her own; friendship, a good listener and a once-upon-a-time love affair was a slender basis for permanent love.

'Class collapsed – doesn't sound like you,' Richard said. His eyebrows lifted slightly above eyes dark-ringed with fatigue. If he had found dealing with a heart attack particularly stressful, she thought, he wasn't likely to admit it. 'Bye for now.'

Richard backed up the drive, waved and disappeared along Cedar Avenue. Had he been disappointed by their first night together? she wondered. How could you tell? He certainly seemed keen to get away. People – well, *men* – were mysterious creatures, acting polite, hopeful and helpful, appreciative, loving until suddenly they stopped and were gone.

Poor cyanosed Bertie, poor Bluebeard. How she had misjudged him.

Lydia fetched her coat and walked up the drive. A blue Mini stood in front of Margaret's house, and Mrs Crabbe, subdued and red-eyed, opened the door.

'Ever so glad you've come, Mrs Kemp,' she whispered. 'Keeps asking for you, doesn't seem quite herself, know what I mean? The shock of poor Mr Stringer going so sudden . . .'

Margaret sat on the rose-patterned sofa, staring down at her feet on the Chinese rug as if she didn't quite recognise any of them.

'Margaret dear, I'm so sorry . . . ' Lydia murmured.

In the hall the vacuum cleaner started up.

'Shut the door,' Margaret whispered huskily. 'I have to tell you something, Lydia.' Her eyes gleamed tiny and dark as melon pips in the swollen pink of her face. 'Lydia, I killed Bertie.'

'That's ridiculous, of course you didn't . . .'

Margaret raised her hand. 'I must tell someone, it's driving me mad. I loved him to death. I did.'

'But—'

'Terrible to say and terrible to know. There was love between us, so much love, the love I'd longed for all my life. Bertie was trying to please me every minute of the day and loving me all night. I wore him to ribbons, shreds. He wasn't young, you see. I loved him to death.'

'Listen to me, Margaret,' Lydia said. 'It wasn't like that. His heart was in a bad way, that's why his skin was so blue. Richard, Dr Foy, was amazed he'd kept going so long,' she improvised.

'He was so kind, your Richard,' Margaret said.

'You've been happy together, remember. That's something, isn't it? You loved each other and made each other happy, nobody can take that away. You gave Bertie the best year of his life.'

'I wonder if I did.' Margaret smiled a pale, tentative little smile. 'He used to say that . . . but I wonder.' Her eyes travelled slowly round the room as if seeing it for the first time. 'Your Richard was good. I showed him the photos, Grandma Stringer's funeral after the ambulance left, told him I wanted something like that for my Bertie . . . four black horses with black plumes and a shiny black coach. He promised to fix it.'

'Well, I'm sure he'll do his best,' Lydia said, wondering how. Promises, promises . . . was it fair to promise things like that to a widow so recently bereaved?

'I've got to go and say goodbye to Bertie, haven't I?'

'Soon as you're ready I'll take you,' Lydia said.

'How kind. I haven't driven myself in the Bentley for such ages, I suppose I'll have to learn to drive myself all over again.'

It was quite dark when Richard came back that evening, driving slowly along Cedar Avenue. He hadn't meant to come back so soon. He had been dog-tired when he left, for one thing, tired all morning, but he had slept at the flat all afternoon and then phoned Sean. The call had revived him.

But life was so short.

Bertie's death had flattened him. Any death was unsettling, changed things in unexpected ways. The intimation of mortality seemed to quicken the quick, make every passing moment seem important, he had often noticed, even experienced it. But Bertie was a stranger, so why should he, Richard, be so affected?

All day he had been acutely aware of colour in the world round him, the mackerel pattern of the sky, the creamy Bath stone, the soft petal-pink and white of baby skin, the 'country cheerful' good morning of people in a small town like Bradford-on-Avon, the hum of the Astra, the stripe of the clean shirt on the seat beside him, the brilliant azalea pink of his travelling toothbrush.

If life was short, people should have what they wanted.

At times he felt like a Greek god, the kind who contrived to give people what they wanted. What did Lydia want? If she knew and told him he would certainly do his best to get it for her. What Margaret wanted was easier, a funeral for Bertie like Grandma Stringer's with four black horses and four black plumes and a shiny black coach.

It was why he had phoned Sean.

Well, yes, Sean said, they did have black horses with black plumes for the Dombey funeral scenes but he seemed doubtful at first. They were filming later this week. And yes, they did have a horsebox and it wasn't all that far to Bristol, a detour really, Sean said, slowly warming to the project. He was fond of his father and like him Sean loved to please people, especially women. He'd have a word with the assistant producer and ring back. Yes, life could be short and often was.

The house was in darkness as Richard came down the drive. Evidently Lydia was out. He ought to have phoned. He crossed to the front door, rang and waited, then pushed the key into the lock and let himself in, switched on the lights in the porch and hall. He must be careful not to startle her.

Being alone in Lydia's house was odd, a sort of violation. Did burglars feel like this? An unwashed plate lay on the kitchen table, rivulets of drying yellow egg and faint green stain, spinach perhaps? Sherlock Holmes, he smiled to himself. In many ways he was essentially domestic. He wandered across the hall and living room. A packet of small green stars lay on the table. What did it signify?

He found salad in the fridge and opened a small tin of tuna. They were partners now, weren't they, and he was used to getting his own meals? He heard the car on the drive, switched on the kettle and opened the front door.

'Glad you came back,' Lydia said, breathless. It was only half true. When tired she liked to be alone, was used to being alone now.

'Been out all day?' Richard said. 'Like some tea?'

'I would,' she said, dropping her coat on the hall chair. 'I took Margaret to the hospital to say goodbye to Bertie and then we did the undertakers, doctor, solicitor, bank, the lot . . .'

'Good for you.'

'Margaret feels responsible for Bertie's death.'

'The bereaved often feel that,' Richard said. 'It's a way of not accepting things have got beyond your control.'

'I suppose . . .' Lydia said, following him into the sitting room. Philistine he might be but he was also intelligent and highly intuitive. She sipped her tea. 'What's this about four black horses?'

'I phoned Sean, least I could do, got the promise of four black horses and a black coach when they've finished filming in Gloucester,' Richard said with an air of satisfaction. 'Well, two black horses and a black coach actually.'

'Won't there be a bill?'

'Black horses on me,' Richard said. 'Have to make the most of life while we're here, don't we?'

'How many times have you said that?' Lydia asked, putting down her cup.

'Said it nearly every week when I was in general practice,' Richard admitted. 'The thing about clichés is they tend to be true. Shall I phone Margaret, tell her about the horses?'

Later that night Lydia lay staring at the strip of stars between the curtains. For a bit Richard had held her warm in his arms but now he slept quietly beside her. Why couldn't she sleep? She was tired enough. Was she expecting a cry to disturb the dark night a second time? Annie's cry? But the baby wasn't due until February.

Unless it was early . . . Annie had been early, hadn't she?

Bertie's funeral was finally scheduled for two o'clock on Wednesday afternoon two weeks later at Canford Lane crematorium. In the interim Lydia's teaching started again but the house was quiet now and she painted when she could. The house and garden no longer absorbed her. Instead she painted a doll-like couple lying in bed side by side; outside darkness and a black-winged angel hovering at the window. The angel seemed to have claws. She supposed it related to Bertie and Margaret but how exactly?

Lydia and Richard had an established pattern now. Richard left early on Monday for his clinic and returned late on Thursday after Lydia's GCSE class. He shared the cooking, leaving his shirts in the linen basket once but then astonishing and wrong-footing her by doing all the ironing. Lydia went to talk to Margaret every day, Richard too when in residence.

His presence at the weekend eased Lydia's first meeting with Ruby, home from Hong Kong. She had invited the engaged couple for a drink on Saturday evening, ostensibly to discuss the wedding lunch arrangements. Ruby took to Richard at once.

'Do you come here often?' she enquired, flicking back her long red hair and smiling flirtatiously.

'Off and on,' Richard said.

'Cool. Didn't reckon on having two fathers-in-law. Still, it'll bump up the wedding presents. Like to see my list?'

'Ruby . . .' William murmured.

'What?' She tossed her head like a fractious pony. William did his best to talk over the lunch arrangements with Lydia, but his attention was riveted by Ruby.

'Hope Margaret's going to be all right,' Lydia murmured on the day of the funeral, getting into the back of the Astra *en route* to pick her up. It was a bleak late January day. 'I mean I hope the black horses won't upset her.'

'Should be cathartic,' Richard said, backing the car up the drive and dropping down to Margaret's. 'Treat people as helpless wrecks and they oblige you by becoming helpless wrecks.'

'So good of you,' Margaret said, emerging from the house in a crimson coat and Russian-style silver fox hat. 'Bertie loved me in red but I'm not sure it's quite suitable.'

'I think it's charming,' Lydia said.

'Becoming and cheerful,' Richard added, leaning over to open the door.

'So long since I've driven,' Margaret sighed as they drove into Canford Lane. 'Bertie loved driving the Bentley so . . .'

Moments later they passed a horsebox parked at the edge with a black coach beside it. Margaret gazed at it blankly.

'Funny place to leave a horsebox,' Richard prompted, swerving out to avoid it. Had Margaret forgotten? He caught Lydia's eye in the driving mirror. 'What's it doing there?'

'Bertie loved horses,' Margaret said vaguely. She had talked about the black horses several times the previous week but seemed to have lost the idea now. 'Perhaps there's a gymkhana, Bertie loved gymkhanas.'

'No gymkhanas in February,' Lydia said firmly as they swung through the gates of the crematorium and parked behind a line of cars. The bleak day seemed to have grown bleaker. Ahead of them was an avenue of leafless trees leading to the chapels at the far end. The Newtons and two other neighbours from Cedar Avenue were already there. Bertie's daughter had stayed home with flu.

'I know those people,' Margaret said, 'but I don't want to talk to anybody.'

'Sit on the seat a moment, you two,' Richard suggested. 'We're early anyway.'

'Horses – I think I can hear horses, or am I imagining?' Margaret said.

'Two black horses and a black coach like Grandma Stringer's funeral, don't you remember?' Lydia said. 'Richard fixed it with Sean's film company. The horses are Ebony and Beauty.'

'Course I remember,' Margaret said, staring at the gate. 'It's what I wanted, what Bertie would have wanted.'

A shiny black coach drawn by two black horses with black plumes on their heads came round the corner at a trot.

'Whoa!' the coachman in black top hat and frock coat shouted, slowing them to a walk. A murmur of surprise and excitement as they came up the avenue, ears pricked forward as people darted round them and cameras clicked.

'Beauty and Ebony,' Margaret murmured. 'Aren't they both so beautiful?' The cortège stopped by the second chapel and the coffin was carried in. 'I wish I had a sugar lump . . .'

'I think we should go in now,' Lydia murmured.

'How Bertie would have loved this!' Margaret whispered, her eyes, yellow-brown like topaz, glazed with tears. 'Ebony and Beauty, oh my Bertie . . . how I loved you.'

The priest was perfunctory but Richard had composed a kind of a oration from the bits of Bertie's life known to Margaret or deduced from the photo album. He delivered it with his usual aplomb but how much was true? Lydia wondered. Certain facts seemed incompatible. Did anybody know who Bertie was or where he had come from? But she kept such thoughts to herself and Margaret was delighted with Richard's version.

'Goodbye, Bertie, my little love,' Margaret whispered as Richard drove them away.

'*Adieu, Barbe bleue,*' Lydia murmured. '*Bon voyage.*'

CHAPTER TWENTY SEVEN

'A H, ANNIE, GOOD morning,' Dr Rinde-Smith said, swivelling
his chair towards her as she came into his consulting room.
'How are you? You've been looking so much better all this week.'

His cheerful smile suggested a conviction he didn't feel.

'OK,' Annie said flatly. She looked what she was, lethargic and
depressed. The window faced on to the street; sounds of traffic
filtered in from outside through white Venetian blinds. Annie
glanced up as a taxi swept past. She didn't want to stay but
where could she go? All she knew of London was Waterloo
station and Regent's Park Zoo and that awful hotel where she'd
worked.

Drina had gone and so had the babything. She didn't think
about it much, didn't think about anything much except the
silverything, the syringe pushed inside her which had started it all,
started the babything.

'Good, good,' Dr Rinde-Smith's head nodded vigorously as if
his energy could compensate for her lack of it. 'You've been here
some time, almost a month in fact. It's February now. We have to
decide things, don't we? Like where you want to go when you leave
here, back to your boyfriend or what? Life goes on.'

'Don't know.' Annie shook her head. She didn't seem to know
anything. Where was Jarvis, for instance? She had phoned him every
day until last week when she'd dialled and stood for hours listening
to the phone ringing in The Lotus but Jarvis had never answered.

Where was he? Had he run away?

'Perhaps you should go home to your mother then? Convalesce
for a bit, build up your strength, shall we say? Not that you're ill,
came through the pregnancy and birth with flying colours. You're a
strong, healthy girl, Annie.'

Lying little jade. No boyfriend at the moment, hadn't she
assured him? He would never have accepted her if Drina Spenser
had kept her cool. No contraindications but primigravida was never

advisable. But what could he do with the boys' school fees outstanding?

'Can't,' Annie said. Her voice was husky with disuse. The nurses were tired of her now, asking cheery questions but moving on before she answered, no more chats or walks round the block. Patients came and patients went but Annie just stayed.

'Why ever not?' said Dr Rinde-Smith.

'What I said to my mother, like I told her to *get lost, go away,*' Annie blinked rapidly.

'Please do not cry,' Dr Rinde-Smith said, articulating with a particular precision which usually halted the boys' wilder forms of self-expression. Annie stared at him dry-eyed.

'Mothers are very forgiving, poor dears have to be. Perhaps you should phone her and make your peace, apologise?'

'Can't,' Annie shook her head. 'I can't.'

'Well, you can't stay here indefinitely.' His voice had sharpened; patience had never been his strong suit. 'We need your bed and you need to get back to the real world.'

'What real world?' Annie muttered.

'Would you like me to phone your mother?'

Annie shook her head.

'Well, phone her yourself today then. Tell her to expect you tomorrow, Thursday. I'll drive you to Paddington to catch the three fifteen for Bristol tomorrow afternoon. Do you understand?'

If you wanted something done properly, it was best to do it yourself. The exigencies of the clinic had convinced him of that. Annie should travel first class and he'd have a word with the guard, ask him to see she got off at Temple Meads station, Bristol, tip him what . . . five quid about right?

'What about my money?' Annie said suddenly.

'It's in the safe, all ready for you. I'll give it to you when we get to Paddington tomorrow. All right?'

Early Thursday evening Richard unlocked the front door of Cedar Avenue. Amazing really, the third week into his relationship with Lydia and here he was arriving as casually as if he had been doing it for years. He came earlier each week, prowling round the house without his shoes, looking at things, taking a shower – Lydia's shower worked better than his – getting himself something to eat.

The current situation met his needs – well, some of them anyway – allowing him freedom and variety as well, best of both worlds. It was good for her too. She had relaxed a bit, looked better.

He kept right out of her studio, though, after the first time, kept away from her painting. Couldn't for the life of him see what she was trying to do and any comment, however well-intentioned, even grossly flattering, seemed to annoy her. He gave generously what he had to give, what he had always given his ladies, love, plenty of vigorous sex (*'Superbe!'* Chantal used to squeal), he gave appreciation, reassurance and an ever-listening ear.

It was what he was, a lover of life, a lover of ladies.

Course it couldn't go on like this. The house in Cedar Avenue had been sold, things would change. Lydia was looking round Bristol for a flat. Perhaps he could interest her in Bath. Anyway, she could stay with him for a bit and welcome, see how things went, whether they worked out.

Richard examined the kitchen shelves. Fried egg and baked beans or fried egg and spaghetti with grated cheese – which would he prefer? Suddenly the phone rang in the silent house.

'Is there a Mrs Kemp at this number?' an agitated male Bristolian voice asked. 'I'm ringing from the train station, Temple Meads. There's a young woman here, locked herself in our new facilities – the ladies' toilet, that is – says her name's Annie Kemp, seems very distressed . . .'

'Annie?' Richard said.

'You know this young lady, sir?'

'Yes, of course. I'll come at once.'

Flying through the dark evening because somebody needed him, a damsel in distress. It was what he had liked better than anything in the old life. He had grumbled, of course, his name on the practice rota more often than was strictly fair. Well, everything had its price. Disturbed nights made for fractious days but it was worth it all the same.

Would she know him, remember? Would he know Annabel from ten years ago? The railway man was waiting at the station entrance and led him down the wide stairs to the subway, then hovered uncertainly.

'Wait outside, shall I, sir? Stop other ladies coming in for the moment?'

'Annabel . . . Annie. It's Richard, Richard Foy.' He spoke softly, but his voice was always rich, full of feeling. Should have been an actor people often said, Shakespearean.

'Gone,' Annie whispered. 'It's gone.' A pause. 'Who are you?' Her voice dipped and fluttered like a maimed fledgeling. 'I don't know anybody . . .'

'You used to know me,' Richard said gently. 'A friend of your mother's from way back, and I know you. Remember that picnic we had on the Downs once, near the water tower? You and me and Lydia? You were about ten and we all played hide-and-seek and grandmother's steps . . .'

'Oh yes,' Annie said, and her voice was firmer now. 'William came too but not Marina. Where's . . . where's Ma?'

'Teaching at Park Lodge this evening. I'm staying with her at the moment. I can drive you home to Cedar Avenue if you like.'

'But I'm frightened,' Annie whispered. 'Scared.'

'What of?' Another long pause. 'Scared of what, Annie?'

'It's in my pigskin bag,' she whispered. 'All the money.'

'That's OK. I can lock it in the car boot,' he said. 'That's quite safe.'

A sob and then a click as the door opened. Annie peered through a narrow gap, swollen eyes pink above a voluminous black coat which almost reached her ankles. Not what he'd call a pretty girl, Richard thought. Possibly just as well.

'Dr Rinde-Smith says I got to be discreet,' she whispered as he steered her towards the stairs and out to the car.

'Does he indeed!' Richard said. Rinde-Smith, the name was familiar. Hadn't there been a Rinde-Smith a year or two ahead at medical school? Julian, was it, or Jonathan Rinde-Smith?

Annie gazed listlessly from the window as the car moved over the bridge towards Princes Street and the evening traffic.

'Your home town,' Richard said. 'Your mother will be pleased to see you. She's been very worried, you know. What about the baby?'

Annie shrugged. 'It got born a month ago and the Spensers took it. It was their baby.'

'Difficult for you,' Richard said.

'I didn't want it,' Annie said.

Ten minutes later she stood in the hall at Cedar Avenue. The way she gazed round was more like a visitor, Richard thought, but then no family was quite like any other family.

'What about a hot bath?' he suggested. 'Then you might like to go to bed. Your room's still just the same. I'll fix you some hot milk. Your mother won't be back until late.'

'OK,' she said. She seemed to accept him but her stare was blank, uncomprehending. The pigskin bag hung from her shoulder. She put it carefully on the hall chair, dropped out of the black coat, picked up the bag and tramped heavily upstairs to her bedroom, closed and locked the door.

Richard stood uncertain. He could hear her rooting about, the slamming of drawers. Five minutes later he went up and ran her a hot bath. He tapped on her bedroom door.

'Bath's ready, Annie.'

She didn't answer but back in the kitchen he heard her cross the landing a few minutes later and lock the bathroom door.

'Whatever's that?' Lydia said, dropping her briefcase on the hall chair, a breath of cold air coming in with her.

'Annie's coat,' Richard said gently. 'She's having a bath. They phoned from the station, I collected her.'

'Annie?' Lydia whispered. 'Thank God you were here, Richard. Is she all right?'

'Seems a bit confused,' Richard said. 'Says the baby was born a month ago. I said I'd do her some hot milk. You can take it up if you like.'

Lydia hesitated; her face had turned pale. 'But she . . . she'll be expecting you?' Her voice quavered; she needed time to consider what she should do, how she should be.

'Perhaps we should both take it up?' Richard said.

In the kitchen Richard explained and they listened like conspirators to Annie's feet on the cork mat, the gurgle of bath water, the bathroom door unlocked. Lydia heated the milk, Richard tapped on Annie's bedroom door.

'Annie?' he said, opening the door an inch. 'Your milk.'

'What?' She sat on the bed in a nightdress with her back against the water lily painting. She didn't look up for a moment. The contents of her pigskin bag were scattered across the bed in front of her, bundles of fifty-pound notes.

'Got to count it, haven't I? It's for Jarvis.' Annie smiled and looked up.

'Ma?' Her smile dwindled into uncertainty. 'Sorry I . . . I didn't *mean* to come home, Ma. Nowhere else to go, that's all. Sorry . . .'

'Course you came home, Annie. Where else would you go?' Lydia said. She held out her arms but Annie didn't move. 'I'm glad you've come, sweetheart,' she said in a cooler tone. 'Really I am. It's lovely to see you. Are you all right?'

'Course I'm all right.' Annie's voice was truculent now. 'Got ten thousand pound, it's for Jarvis. But I've got to count it first, then I'll phone him.'

'Would you like something to eat?'

Annie shook her head. 'Just leave me alone, will you? You can't make me do things, you know, not any more.' She went on counting.

'You know the house is sold?' Lydia said.

'Sold?'

'I have to move out end of March,' Lydia said. Somehow she had to draw Annie into the family again. 'Ruby and William are getting married, having their wedding lunch here afterwards. Did you know Marina was pregnant?'

'Course I didn't,' Annie said.

Lydia, waking in the night, was aware that Richard, flat on his back, was also awake. Other people's children, she thought – Annie was probably more than he bargained for. Across the landing sounds came from Annie's room: drawers opened and closed with a snap.

'What's Annie doing?' she whispered.

'Dunno,' Richard said. 'Searching for her lost baby? Trying to tidy her life?' He turned on his side. 'Go to sleep. She's not too bad considering. She'll sort herself out.'

'What did she mean, you can't make me do things? I never make people do things. I never have . . .'

'Go to sleep,' Richard said.

It was all very well, Lydia thought, Annie wasn't his child. But she did go back to sleep.

The following morning Annie appeared for breakfast. She

seemed composed and quite cheerful but afterwards went back to her bedroom. More sounds of drawers being opened and closed. It wasn't a situation Lydia could possibly paint in, so she got out the vacuum cleaner and began to clean the house.

Richard went round to see Margaret.

Mid-morning Lydia tapped on Annie's door. 'What are you doing?'

'Got to sort things out if the house is sold,' Annie said, opening the door. 'Throw stuff away.'

The contents of her chest of drawers were heaped upon her bed – all the toys, dolls, stuffies, the farmyard animals which had been William's once and which Annie had rescued from the dustbin. She had always kept everything. School uniform hung in the cupboard, clothes, kiddie things, girlie things, an uncool party dress, she didn't want Jarvis to see any of this. History, wasn't it? She was throwing away her childhood. People telling her what to do, what she wanted – who she was?

Everything was different now.

'I'm sorting things out, aren't I?' Annie said.

'There are plastic bags in the kitchen if that would help. Something to put your stuff in,' Lydia said.

'Yeah?' Annie looked at the floor. 'Sorry, Ma, what I said in Penzance, sounding off like that. I mean you can't help being like you are, can you? All that stuff about art school . . . can't remember what I did say but it wasn't your fault, you were only doing your best.'

'Best wasn't good enough, was it?' Lydia said gently. 'I guess it never is. I'm sorry too, Annie. Let's try and get it right between us now, shall we? You're still my daughter, sweetheart, you'll always be my daughter.'

'I've got to phone Jarvis now,' Annie said, and ran downstairs. 'Got to get hold of him.'

'Well . . . all right,' Lydia said. How frightened Annie looked, she thought. Why was she so frightened?

CHAPTER TWENTY EIGHT

For several days Annie stayed in her room, emerging at meal times, pale and silent. Otherwise the only sound was the occasional slamming of drawers. She didn't go out but she got in touch with Jarvis again, made protracted phone calls every evening and afterwards seemed more cheerful.

'Would you like to come and look at these two flats in Cotham, Annie?' Lydia suggested once, but Annie shook her head.

'She won't even talk to me,' Lydia told Richard. 'We used to talk such a lot.'

'Best leave her,' he said. 'She's been through a lot, probably feels she's let you down.'

And so she has, Lydia thought, but didn't really feel entitled to say or even think so. Unable to paint, she got out the vacuum cleaner and hoovered and dusted the house again. Wasn't Ed supposed to be coming to view the furniture this weekend?

She had already stuck green stars on pieces of furniture she wanted to keep. No need with the contents of her studio or the kneehole desk, but how could she make sensible decisions about bigger items when she didn't know where she was going to end up?

Who was to have the big old sofa, for instance, on which she could lie full length and often did? She had always been fond of it. She had tramped round various flats but the greyness of urban Bristol in winter depressed her. Could you get a green cottage for around £100,000? she wondered.

Richard was expecting her to stay at his flat until she got sorted. It was kind of him – Richard was kind – but was it an imposition, she wondered, and if so who was imposing on whom? Anyway it didn't seem likely there would be room for an extra large sofa in a small town flat.

At one o'clock, Lydia rang the bell for lunch.

'Bread and cheese, OK? I've got lettuce and tomatoes

somewhere,' she said. 'I'm cooking tonight. William and Ruby are coming, don't forget.'

'Fine,' said Richard cheerfully. It was his special talent to be able to enjoy other people's family life, Lydia thought.

'Jarvis is coming too,' Annie announced, arriving at the kitchen table and smiling round. 'He's on the road right now.'

'In that case do we need another trip to the shops?' Richard glanced at Lydia, eyebrows raised.

'Jarvis? Coming to stay here?' Lydia said.

'What's wrong with that?' Annie said. 'My boyfriend, isn't he? Phoned him yesterday.'

'Why didn't you tell me?' Lydia said, trying to fix his image in her head: swarthy, black hair, brown eyes, slight build, was it one earring or two? 'Good job I've got a really big chicken.' All my pretty chickens and their dam, she thought wistfully. 'We'd better make up an extra bed in Ed's study.'

'Why?' Annie went pink. 'Jarvis's coming in with me, course he is, what's it to you?'

'Annie . . . it's only a month since the baby . . .'

'You should certainly go to your doctor, have a check-up,' Richard said firmly, 'before you resume intercourse.'

'Yeah well, I do know the rules, Doc,' Annie muttered. 'Think we're at it all the time like flipping rabbits, do you?'

Ma's boyfriend, telling her what to do. Who the heck did he think he was?

'Course not,' Richard said. 'But some rules are better kept, hygiene is—'

'Know all about hygiene, thank you. Been there, seen it, got the tee shirt,' Annie said, getting up and putting two thick slices of bread in the toaster. 'Pardon me for living.'

She made herself a generous cheese and salad sandwich, picked up an apple and stamped up to her bedroom.

'Sorry about that,' Richard said.

'Not your fault. Little barbarian, don't know what's got into her.' Whose fault was it? Lydia wondered. Where had they gone wrong? Had she spoiled Annie? All that encouragement had been meant to boost her confidence but instead it seemed to have made her more disappointed, extra vulnerable.

'Typical child of the nineties,' Richard said, noncommittal.
'If you say so . . .'

Upstairs Annie ate her toasted sandwich slowly and decided she couldn't live in Cedar Avenue any longer. She couldn't live with anybody except Jarvis. She was all right now, so she could go back with him. She packed her pigskin bag and case ready, pushed everything else into black plastic bags. Now she wasn't staying it could all be chucked away, twenty years of her life. She didn't want to think about it any more. She piled seven plastic bags out on the landing.

It didn't take long.

After that her attention focused on the drive outside. Was there room behind the Astra for Jarvis's van? He had as much right to park as Richard, more because she and Jarvis were *probably* going to get married. What about William's Mini? Where was brother Will going to park?

'Annie?' Lydia called from downstairs later. 'Want some tea?'

'Tea up,' Richard echoed but she didn't go down. Later still Richard went out and parked the Astra over at Margaret's.

It was dark when from the bedroom window Annie saw William's Mini arrive. He and Ruby walked to the door.

'Annie?' they called from downstairs but she stayed where she was. Waiting like Sister Anne in the Bluebeard story, Ma used to read to her at one time. Waiting for the old van to creep in.

Finally it did.

'Jarvis?' Annie shouted, grabbing her coat and plunging downstairs with it flapping all round her like black wings. 'Jarvis?' Running out across the frost-sharp grass.

'Hello, Annie,' he muttered, getting out, tired, nervous and very cold as she flung her arms round him. 'Hello, love.'

'You're freezing,' she gasped. 'Absolutely freezing.'

'Heating's packed up in the old van.'

'Let's get in the house, quick.'

'Hang about.' Jarvis leaned in, grabbed his zipbag, and they sprinted across the lawn, slamming the front door behind them.

'It's Jarvis. Jarvis is here,' Annie called happily, holding tight to his left arm. She had never felt so ace, so mega-marvellous.

Lydia emerged from the kitchen.

'Hello, Jarvis. Good to see you again,' she said, and wished it was true. But glancing at Annie's joyous face she knew she must try to forget that other time in Penzance for everybody's sake. 'My goodness, what cold hands! You're freezing.'

'Heating's gone in the van,' Jarvis said, blinking in the brightness of the hall.

'This is Dr Richard Foy, friend of mine,' Lydia said. 'And my son, William, and his fiancée, Ruby.'

'Pleased to meet you,' Ruby said, smiling. Such a mischievous gleam in her cat-green eyes, Lydia thought, but banished the thought before Ruby could read it.

'Congratulations,' Jarvis said.

'Hi!' William nodded at Jarvis. 'Hello, little sister. You OK? We called but you didn't come down.'

'Waiting for Jarvis,' Annie said, still gripping his arm.

'Hello,' Richard said, taking his hand. 'My God, you're like ice! Where's the whisky?'

'Heating's gone in the old van,' Jarvis said. He tried to smile but his face was too stiff. 'Blinking thing, would have to go February.'

'Have a drink,' Lydia said. 'I've just opened the wine, letting it breathe. William and Ruby are getting married next month.' Her voice was too light, hectic. William glanced at her glass, her second or her third was it?

'Congratulations,' Jarvis said again. 'Fixed the big day yet?'

'I expect you're hungry. We'll be eating in a few minutes,' Lydia said. They were drinking too much, so was she. 'All my pretty chickens', she retreated to the kitchen, and refilled her glass.

Everybody followed.

'Went to the registry office today. Booked us in for the end of next month,' William was saying.

'Jarvis doesn't like wine,' Annie said, steering him after the others.

'Who says I don't?' Jarvis said, retrieving his arm and putting his hand in his pocket.

'I bet he does.' Ruby winked and took his other arm. 'I can read him like a book.'

'Jesus!' Annie exploded, her hand burrowing for Jarvis's. 'Piss off, will you?'

'Annie, please . . .' Lydia murmured, but everything was out of control except the chicken. She opened the oven door. 'Chicken's almost ready.'

'Spot of whisky, Jarvis, warm you up?' Richard said at his elbow.

'Thanks a lot,' Jarvis said. 'Just what I need.'

'What's the distance, Penzance to Bristol?' Richard enquired conversationally. 'Two hundred miles?'

'And the rest . . .' William said loudly. 'Three hundred more like.' Who did Richard think he was, lover-in-residence, mine host, husband-in-waiting? What about Ma and a cottage?

Jarvis sipped his whisky. 'Dunno the mileage, gauge went in the old van yonks ago.'

'Van's had it,' Annie said. 'Need a new one.'

'Teach you to drive?' Jarvis said.

'Deal.'

'Teaching Ruby to drive nearly broke us up,' William said. 'Where we eating exactly, Ma?'

'Dining end of the sitting room is where,' Lydia said loud and clear. 'Lay the table, please, Will. Let Ruby help you.' She had told the children lots of times that class really didn't matter nowadays, but she hadn't expected them to take her quite so seriously. Ruby and Jarvis, Jarvis and Ruby . . . but she mustn't think like that, couldn't afford to. Sow the seed and you reap the whirlwind.

'Certainly, madam,' William said, rattling the cutlery drawer. Ruby was bossy too. You had to get used to bossy women in the millennium. Too much female hormone in the water, they said. Wasn't that Ruby's third glass?

'Why are we eating in there when we never ever do?' Annie said, petulant.

'We're celebrating all being together,' Lydia sang out in desperation. 'We're celebrating William and Ruby's engagement and this large free-range chicken and all the trimmings cooked by me. Hope you're all right with chicken, Jarvis?' she added in her normal tone.

'Suits me fine,' he said. Her family wasn't so bad as Annie made out. Not snobs nor nothink. Pity he couldn't stop longer.

'Jarvis is a brilliant cook,' Annie said, hooking herself back on to his arm again.

'If only he'd got here earlier,' Lydia said, planting the roast chicken on its dish on the kitchen table and carrying it through. 'Plates, please, Ruby dear, hot plates under the oven.'

'Right,' Ruby said. 'What a keener you are,' she added to Richard, dishing up potatoes and peas. 'Make somebody a lovely husband.'

'What, no bread sauce?' said William, balancing the gravy.

'Don't start,' said Lydia. 'Just don't anybody start.'

A sudden silence.

'Would you like me to carve?' Richard said calmly. Could he see how gruelled she was, how fed up and utterly exhausted? Well, at least he had noticed.

'Looks like he's heard about your carving, Ma,' William said. 'One of the great non-wonders of the modern world.'

'Thank you, Richard,' Lydia said coolly. 'Please do.'

Later that night Dr Rinde-Smith woke in the small hours and thought of the smiling, well-heeled, blue-eyed Spensers who knew about bulls and bears and how to make a killing in sterling but did not necessarily know about the laws of biological inheritance, Mendel and the white and red pea flowers.

Should the twenty-thousand-pound boy's eyes turn chocolate brown in due course, a possibility much against the odds, very likely the Spensers would continue to smile.

Unless someone enlightened them, of course . . .

What had woken her so early when she been so tired? Lydia wondered the following morning. She had drunk too much, was that why she was so thirsty? She felt for her dressing gown and crept downstairs to make tea. Outside it was still dark grey, the heating had only just come on, Richard slept. How many more mornings would she wake in Cedar Avenue? Now William's wedding date was fixed, she could work it out . . . if she had the heart.

Annie was sitting at the kitchen table, the remains of a hasty breakfast, crumbs and cornflakes in front of her.

'Sorry, did I wake you?' she said bleakly, fair hair tumbling round her face. 'Jarvis has gone. Said to thank you for the dinner last night. Said you're a good cook, best nosh he's had for weeks.' Annie allowed herself a small smile. 'Kettle's just boiled . . .'

'Well, I'm glad you're still here,' Lydia said. 'You're really not well enough to go back yet, darling. I expect Jarvis wants to get on with things. Did you give him the money?' she added, trying to sound casual.

'Course.'

'All of it?'

'Course.' Her blue eyes flickered like butterflies, chalk hill blues, Lydia thought. 'Can't ever go back though, can I?' Annie said, and burst into tears. 'Didn't think . . . didn't think at all . . . only just realised, people saying *How's the baby?* and *Where's the baby?* How can I cope with all that stuff? They'd have me arrested, wouldn't they, an *emmet*, that's what I am, pinching their blokes, they don't like me anyway. Like I told Jarvis, I can't go back to Penzance. No way.'

'Jarvis was upset?'

'Course . . . ballistic,' Annie sobbed.

'But nobody has to know about the money,' Lydia said carefully. Annie should have what she wanted, entitled after so much. Marina and William had what they wanted. 'It's the money that's illegal. Can't you just say you had the baby for a woman who couldn't have one and gave it to her? Nothing wrong with that.'

'No, I can't.' Annie dabbed her eyes and got up. 'Can't face them all asking . . . whispering. Kettle's boiled . . .'

Lydia carried the tray upstairs. Richard was awake now.

'Jarvis has gone,' Lydia said, passing his tea. 'So has the money.' She sipped a minute. 'Annie suddenly realised she can't go back to Penzance, can't face all the questions, gossip and that. Quite possible Jarvis'll take the money and run.'

'Possible,' Richard said. 'In which case you'll have one distressed daughter on your hands.' He propped himself on his elbow, one hand holding the sheet over his scarred chest. 'Didn't strike me as that sort of bloke though . . .'

He sipped his tea.

'If Ed's coming about the furniture, I'll make myself scarce, get back to Bath this morning.'

'Well, if you like . . . but it's my half term next week,' Lydia said, trying not to feel dispirited. Was he trying to avoid Ed or had he had enough of Annie's problems? Even advocates of talking and listening could have too much of other people's children.

'I hadn't forgotten your half term,' Richard said, getting out of bed on the far side, dressing with his smooth, white back towards her. 'I was going to suggest you came over to Bath on Wednesday. Meet me for lunch at New Horizons and after that you might like to see the flat. I mean if you're talking about splitting the furniture you ought to look round at least.'

'All right,' she said. 'How's my pieris?' She had given it to him for safe-keeping – just until she found a new garden.

'Fine. I give it lot of TLC.'

What was going on between them? Lydia wondered. What was he up to? He was cool all right but was his cool just taking her for granted or indifference either way? He had been good last night, indispensable. But sometimes she wondered if she really wanted him or if she just wanted him to want her.

'Thanks for helping me out with yesterday,' she said.

'All in a night's work.'

He left after breakfast. 'See you Wednesday then? New Horizons half-past twelve? Keep an eye on Margaret for me.'

'I always keep an eye on Margaret,' Lydia said.

'I know you do. You're a wonderful woman. Bye, Annie,' he shouted up the stairs. Who was it said women came in three sizes: 'young,' 'not so young' and 'wonderful'? Lydia thought wryly. Something about the way Richard sprinted across the lawn to his car on Margaret's drive suggested the joy of escape, or the pleasure of deceit.

Why hadn't Jarvis phoned? Annie stared at the ceiling where horrid possibilities hovered like moths. Was he still on the road, had the van broken down, an accident, lying in a pool of blood, stitched in some hospital bed? She got up and opened the bedroom door. The heating was off and the cold of the house folded round her like a shroud. She lifted the phone and tapped in the number, heard it ringing in The Lotus far away. Ringing and ringing. She put it down and dialled again.

'Annie?'

'Jarvis. You promised you'd phone.'

'Been down to Keppels Head.' His voice was thick, lumpy like porridge. 'Bought a van. Blue Ford, off of Jim Trewin, H reg, goes like a rocket.'

'What about the bills, rent, council tax?' Annie whispered. She could see him swaying in the dark passage. 'He'll get us evicted.'

'Don't you worry your head about bills, you just get yourself back here, girl. Stand by your man. Right?'

'But, Jarvis—'

He slammed down the phone.

CHAPTER TWENTY NINE

'WHAT SHALL I do with these?' Annie said, standing at the top of the stairs the following day with a bulging plastic bag in either hand. She had tried to phone The Lotus several times but nobody answered. 'There's seven altogether.'

'We'll take them down Whiteladies Road to one of the charity shops. Sure you want to throw all this away?' Lydia looked at them wistfully. 'I always grieve for my rejects afterwards. Once I even went and bought my old tee shirt back.'

'Typical! Can't let anything go can you, Ma?' Annie said. Would Jarvis even remember the phone call she'd made last night? He had been quite drunk. Would he phone? When would he phone? Suppose . . . suppose he never ever phoned?

'Dad's coming round this morning, by the way,' Lydia said.

'Dad?' Annie flushed. 'Whatever for?'

'Look round and decide what furniture he wants to keep,' Lydia said. 'You know how he is. Anyway, come down, will you, Annie, I want to talk . . .'

'Not again?' Annie said, padding downstairs in her bedroom slippers with a plastic bag in either hand. 'I can't be what you want, Ma, I'm not like that. And I never found out what I really really want because you kept telling me.'

'I'm not sure that's quite right,' Lydia said, but the words had a horrid familiarity. They could have come from her own head, her own mouth, had she been bolder; the things she didn't say to Mother still lurking there. Too late to liberate them now, but at least Annie didn't have that problem.

'Course it's right. All that crap about my amazing sense of colour . . .'

'I did think you had talent, Annie,' Lydia said. Was the world divided into people denied their sense of worth either by too much maternal encouragement or too little? 'But I promise not to say it again. Being grown up is when you stop blaming people.'

227

'Leave it out, Ma.'

'You can stay here until William gets married, if you like. After that we both have to go . . .' Lydia glanced towards the garden. The snowdrops were almost over, early daffs just starting. 'If I've got to live somewhere, I fancy a cottage.'

'What cottage?' Annie said suspiciously.

'Cottage in a wood. Red Riding Hood's grandmother's cottage would suit me fine. You can stay with me as long as you want. Do you still think about the baby at all?'

'Not much. Born early, no fingernails . . .'

'You were early,' Lydia said. 'Runs in the family. Nobody believes you. Doctors just think women can't count . . .'

'Yeah?' Annie smiled. 'Dr Rinde-Smith was like that. Never believed me. Course, I did tell him loads of porkies.'

'Porkies? Like what?'

'Told him I hadn't got a boyfriend, didn't I? Well, he wouldn't have taken me otherwise . . . I mean, Jarvis was up the weekend before and other weekends before that.'

Perhaps it *was* actually her grandchild, conceived before the in-vitro fertilisation, Lydia thought, but didn't say. Much better not. Such secrets disclosed spread endless trouble.

The front doorbell rang.

'That'll be your father.'

'Didn't tell him anything, did you?' Annie whispered.

'Course not, I promised not to, didn't I?' Lydia opened the front door. 'Morning, Ed.'

'Last look round the old homestead,' he said, stepping inside. 'Oh, Annie! What are you doing here?'

'Hello, Dad. What's it look like?'

'Annie's staying for a few days,' Lydia said.

'What about art school? How you getting on?'

'Dropped out a year ago,' Annie said.

'Surprise, surprise,' Ed said, glancing at Lydia. 'Nobody bothered to tell me.'

'Ma didn't know,' Annie said. 'I didn't tell anybody.'

'So what you doing now?'

'Bit of waitressing,' Annie shrugged.

'Suits you, does it? Height of your ambition?'

'Who says I got ambition?' Annie muttered.

'Would you like a coffee, Ed?' Lydia intervened.

'No time, thanks.' Ed glanced at his watch. 'Some of us have a job to do, a living to earn. I'll have my stuff collected from the study after the wedding. I came to measure the sofa. Not sure it'll go into our flat.'

'I could easily have measured it for you,' Lydia said.

'Rather do it myself,' he said, taking a tape measure from his pocket. 'Accuracy has never been exactly your forte. Ten feet . . .' he murmured. 'Too big I'm afraid.' He brushed at the sofa back fastidiously. 'Good deal shabbier and grubbier, than I remember, I have to say.'

'Like the rest of us,' Lydia said.

'Speak for yourself.' They looked at each other. Calculating. What was between them now? Anything, something, nothing?

Had he overreacted to that silly business of hers ten years ago? Ed wondered. Still, standards were standards; somebody had to maintain them.

Better out than in, Lydia thought, Ed was still wonderfully good-looking, but handsome is as handsome does.

'I put green stars on the stuff I want to keep,' she said.

'So I see. How do you feel about the baby?'

'What?' Lydia blushed. 'What d'you mean?'

'Marina's baby, our first grandchild?' His look was keen; what was going on?

'Oh, fine,' Lydia said.

' 'Scuse me, I got to make a phone call,' Annie said, leaving the room, closing the door behind her.

'She all right?' Ed murmured. 'Looks a bit pale.'

'She never has much colour.'

'Boyfriend trouble?'

'Possibly,' Lydia said.

'Oh well . . . I'll just take the stuff in my study, the dining table and chairs, and the easy chairs,' Ed said, snapping his tape measure shut. 'What about the kneehole desk, no green stars on that?'

'Everybody knows that came from *my grandmother*,' Lydia said.

'Just asking.' Ed paused at the door. 'Got yourself a flat yet?'

'Not yet. Been looking round but doesn't seem much point until we get the house money. I'd only get gazumped.'

'Up to you. What about William and Ruby getting married?'

Lydia shrugged. 'Up to them, isn't it? Will was really wretched when she went off to Hong Kong.'

'Knows how to play her cards, that one,' Ed said, opening the door. 'Let's hope she teaches William a trick or two.' Annie was sitting with the phone against her ear. 'Well, see you at the wedding. So long, Annie. End of an era, eh, Mrs Kemp?'

'Start of an era,' Lydia said, closing the door behind him.

'Don't think he likes me,' Annie said, putting the phone down.

'He has trouble showing his feelings, that's all,' Lydia said. 'Why don't you go out for a bit, get some fresh air?'

'Isn't any fresh air left, just carbon-polluted stuff . . .' Annie said, retreating to her room. But she did go out soon after, walking right across the Downs, tufts of grass all springy under her feet, calling The Lotus from the privacy of a call box. But the phone rang on and nobody answered.

Where was Jarvis? Somebody must know. Who?

Annie phoned Clover who worked at the laundrette in Chapel Street three days a week. The Lotus was closed all right, Clover said, had 'Closed' on the door for weeks. Sorry, but she hadn't seen Jarvis, hadn't seen no blue Ford van but that Jim Trewin did use to have a blue Ford van. Kids and blokes, same difference, had to keep your eye on both.

Why didn't Jarvis phone? Annie wondered. How long could this go on? Suppose he had run away, where would he run?

'Here we are then,' Richard said, pausing on the front steps. 'This Englishman's castle, Albert Place.'

Lydia had left the car at Temple Meads and come by train to avoid the problem of parking in Bath. They had lunched at New Horizons. She hadn't mentioned her earlier visit to his flat and now it was impossible. Could you be too close in a close relationship, she wondered, feel stifled? Everybody was entitled to their secrets – fantasies too fragile to risk derisive comment, yearnings too discreditable to be exposed. She gazed up at the tall façade. Something seemed to be expected.

'Looks OK on the outside,' she said.

'Solid Victorian, suits me fine. You can keep your speculator-built Georgian,' Richard said, opening the heavy outer door and closing it carefully behind them.

'Wait there,' he said, walking forward down the dark passage to press the time switch, bending to unlock the panelled door on the right she already knew. 'Home Sweet Home.'

She followed him across a small hall into a high-ceilinged room with an elaborate plasterwork cornice. Could I live here? she wondered, staring round. Bath was more beautiful than Bristol but just as urban. She could still hear traffic passing. The rest of the room was sparsely furnished with a small table in one corner, a Habitat sofa, chairs and a shabby Axminster carpet.

'Had some good stuff at Chippenham. Alison went in for antiques a bit,' Richard said, seeing the room with Lydia's eyes. 'Fen took most of it when she got a house. Wasn't really bothered at the time, only too pleased . . .'

'Indulgent Papa, that's you.'

'Suppose I am,' he said, but he seemed surprised. 'Indulgent husband too . . . if I get the chance,' he added with a sideways look. 'Cold? I turn the heating off when I go out. I'll put it on again. Bedroom's there.'

She followed him back across the hall to a small room which looked over the garden, almost filled by a brass double bed, mahogany wardrobe and chest of drawers.

'Kitchen's three steps down,' he said. It was small too, but well equipped, probably the original scullery, she thought. A door led out to the back garden.

'Everything else is down here,' Richard went on. 'I call it a flat but it's a maisonette actually.' She followed him down a flight of steep stairs to the basement. Bathroom and two bedrooms, only the tops of their windows above ground level. One bedroom looked over the drive in front, the other over the garden. I couldn't live here, she thought. Well, not for long.

'Spare rooms are for visitors. The children come sometimes, well, Sean . . .' he said. 'But you could have one as a studio, or both, if you like?'

'Too dark,' Lydia said. 'Anyway I probably won't be here for long. Garden's nice, that thatched summerhouse. Where's my pieris?'

'Come and look.' Richard pulled back the bolts on the back door eagerly and they walked across the grass.

'But you've planted it!' Lydia said. What cheek! Did he think she was going to stay indefinitely? Did he think he could make her?

'Better for it, room for its roots. Shrubs don't do that well in pots.'

'They do all right,' Lydia said, but what was the point of being churlish? 'Amazing summerhouse.'

'Isn't it?' Richard said enthusiastically. 'Somebody's mother-in-law lived out here, didn't get on with her daughter-in-law, so they had electricity laid on and stuck the old dear out here. There's an outside lavatory and washbasin at the back of the house, old-fashioned but still functional. I could get the electrics and everything checked out if you'd like to paint here, make it your studio?'

'Poor old mother-in-law,' Lydia said, peering through the window at a rusty Baby Belling and some garden chairs. 'Too small and dark for a studio, Richard. Not to mention the vibes, all that misery hiding in the timbers. I'm freezing, let's go in.'

'Pity,' Richard said, bolting the kitchen door again.

'Not really. Easy enough to rent a studio in Bath.'

'I was thinking of having a resident wife,' Richard said. 'Nice to come home to.'

'Tough, you'll have to advertise,' Lydia said. She was prepared to love him but not prepared to marry him, that was the truth. Playing games, she thought, but what did she want, what did he? 'Shall I make tea?'

'Rather make love,' Richard said, swinging an adept arm round her shoulders. Tactics, she thought. Was he trying to make her like the flat? 'Give the bed a surprise.'

'In the afternoon?' Lydia murmured. Wasn't the bed well used to surprises?

'You never used to be so stuffy,' Richard said, closing the curtains and dropping his jacket on the chair.

'That was a long time ago,' Lydia said, undressing more slowly, glad the room was darkened. It was still cold but here in his flat, the way her heart was thudding, was more like the other time, the long-ago time.

'God, it's freezing,' he said, and his arms stretched out to meet her as she slid between the sheets.

'You taste of coriander,' she whispered.

'If I'd known you were coming I'd have baked a cake,' Richard said through chattering teeth.

'Who needs cakes?' she whispered as his fingers stroked her breasts but wasting no time, moved on. Richard had never been one for prolonged preliminaries. 'When they've got you?'

She kissed his scarred chest, used to it now, feeling no fear. Feeling nothing but the warmth of his body, the strength of his arms, the wet heat as he pushed into her . . . like drowning, she thought, drowning in hot wet velvet . . . like dying. Like dying and dying again . . .

'OK?' Richard said presently.

'Very good,' she said. 'Even excellent . . .'

'Tea break.' He got up. 'Milk or lemon, Mrs Kemp?'

'Milk will do nicely.' A few minutes later he deposited the tray on the bed and climbed in beside her. The room was warmer now.

'How's Annie?'

'Not so good. Jarvis hasn't phoned.'

'Can't she phone him?'

'He's gone. There's nobody at The Lotus.'

'Think he's done a runner?'

Lydia shrugged. 'Hard to say but I'd better get back.'

'Annie?' she called, opening the front door in Cedar Avenue two hours later. For a moment she thought she had been burgled. The seven plastic bags had been dropped over the banisters and broken into a ragged pile. A postcard lay on the hall table. 'Jarvis phoned. Can't go back to Penzance so he's found this place at St Ives, wants me to look. Last train 4.15. Will phone. Love Annie.'

It was five o'clock.

CHAPTER THIRTY

M ARCH WAS A good time for a wedding, Lydia thought, standing at the window the Friday evening before. It didn't encourage self-deception like the blue skies and abundant roses of June. On the other hand was self-deception a necessary ingredient for the celebration of an enterprise as perilous as marriage at the end of the twentieth century?

But with spring beginning and summer ahead, perhaps William and Ruby would work things out. Despite her misgivings Lydia's spirits began go rise in anticipation. Marriage was for generous love and the birth of a new generation. It was recognised by every human society. Only the mean-spirited refused to celebrate its hopeful purpose.

She had made an effort with Ruby since the engagement, inviting the young couple for supper, smiling hopefully in Ruby's direction, as well as inviting the Fields, her parents, over. She had made a special effort with the garden too, planting out polyanthus in reds and pinks along the border, behind them daffodils shone like gold stars against a background of well-established evergreen shrubs.

March would be a good month for her to leave Cedar Avenue too, Lydia thought, a chastening but stimulating month, especially if she had decided where she wanted to go.

What time was Richard likely to arrive?

Lydia couldn't actually bring herself to attend the registry office ceremony – maternal tears would only be an embarrassment for William, poor, good-hearted, innocent boy – and Mrs Barley, the caterer's, early arrival was sufficient excuse.

The sitting room was already set up with twenty stacked gold chairs and two trestle tables, later to be covered in white. The family dinner table was all wedding presents one end and the tray for champagne which Margaret had presented the other. The large sofa and two armchairs were pushed against the wall. Ed had arranged for a firm, 'Good Move', to collect his furniture on Saturday after the festivities were over.

Thank God for Mrs Barley and her two daughters, who were bringing the food early tomorrow: poached salmon, green salad, new potatoes, followed by crème brûlée, strawberry ice cream, coffee and chocolate mints. Mrs Barley was experienced and calm. 'Garden's looking ever so nice,' she had said. 'I'm moving out by the end of the month. Pity I can't take it with me,' Lydia said. 'You getting divorced? Our mum's divorced,' the younger Barley girl said. 'That's enough, Beryl,' said Mrs Barley.

If Lydia was ambivalent about the bride, at least she was composed about the wedding lunch. All she had to do was write the names on twenty place cards for William, Ruby, Rodney best man, Alice from the nursery nurses college, Ed, Leonie, Marina, Jeremy, Izzy, Margaret, Bill and Sarah Newton, old Mr Beavis, Mother, Vera, the two Fields and daughter Tracey, Richard and herself and decide who should sit next to whom.

The kitchen was Barley territory now, surfaces covered with alien glasses, plates, cutlery. Lydia managed to find a tray of her own and was searching the fridge for a remembered slice of ham, when William's Mini crunched on to the drive.

'Hello, you two look blooming,' she said cheerily, though it occurred to her mid-sentence that they looked mutinous.

'Hello, Mrs Kemp,' Ruby said, getting out. She was wearing her blue uniform, her hair released like a red waterfall down her back.

'Call me Lydia, please . . .'

'Lydia then. Mum and Dad are really looking forward to meeting you again tomorrow.'

'Is Richard here?' William said warily.

'Not at the moment, but he's coming tomorrow, of course. It's chaos here at the moment,' Lydia said as they followed her into the kitchen. 'Everything's arrived. Did you want to see me about something special?'

'No,' said William.

'Yes,' said Ruby.

'Looks like we're even getting married on the wrong foot,' William said.

'Married? You should be so lucky,' Ruby snapped, but turned to smile at Lydia. 'Thing is, my wedding dress was only finished yesterday – loads of gorgeous white lace, very trad, looks a treat, a real picture according to my mum . . .'

'Get on with it,' William said.

'Like I say my dress is absolutely fab now but it won't be if I have to go to the registry office in William's Mini. I mean, how could anybody get in and out of that old rust bucket in a cloud of white lace?'

'Well, I suppose . . .' Lydia began.

'No way she's settling for your Fiesta, Ma,' William said. 'It's white Rolls Royce or nothing for Miss Ruby.'

'I'm not like that, William Kemp.'

'Stop it, both of you,' Lydia said firmly. 'You've got wedding nerves, that's all, everybody gets them. Why can't Ed collect Ruby? Nothing wrong with arriving in his immaculate BMW, is there? Give him a ring, Will. He'll be home by now.'

'That be OK, Rube?' William said sulkily.

'Long as it's got white ribbons on the front,' Ruby said, flopping on to a chair as William went to phone, closing the kitchen door. 'Nearly broke it off, didn't I? None of you Kemps think anythink of me . . .'

'Oh, Ruby, that's not fair. I was just going to ask if there were any bits of furniture you'd like.'

'Kind of you but I don't fancy old stuff myself. But I'll be a good wife for William, you'll see. He needs pushing, else he's not going anywhere, know what I mean?'

'I think I do,' Lydia said slowly.

'Maybe we should go back to Hong Kong. It's where the money is. Don't fancy working all my life, not when I've got a man to work for me. Sitting by the pool and working on my tan will suit me nicely, thanks.' Ruby giggled conspiratorially. 'Don't let on I said that,' she added as the phone went down.

'Dad says he'll collect you in the BMW tomorrow, Ruby,' William said. 'All right?'

'But I've got to have white ribbons,' Ruby said.

'Dad said he'd put them on if we get them, but how can we when the shops are shut?'

'Got friends down the market, don't you worry,' Ruby said. 'I'll be waving like the Queen, won't I?'

'Better get off then,' William said. 'See you tomorrow.'

'Yes.' Lydia watched as he backed the Mini up the drive. She had been chilled by Ruby's saying William needed pushing. How could a girl, supposedly in love, talk like that? But what to do? William had been so miserable without her, which alternative was worse? It was too late to back out now.

Lydia watched as the garden darkened. Would Richard ring? He usually phoned about ten o'clock the nights he was away. But he might not phone tonight. A week after her visit to his flat he had suddenly said he couldn't do with all this coming and going. He wanted to be settled. She had been surprised. She had enjoyed the partings, phone calls, reunions and mini honeymoons. She thought Richard had too.

The phone rang. 'Thought you'd like to know we've arrived safely, Lydia,' Mother said hoarsely. 'Vera and me.'

'Yes, thanks. Journey all right?' Lydia said.

'Vera's a good driver, but the traffic's dreadful. Friday and Saturday are the worst, Vera says.'

'But the hotel's OK?'

'Made us very comfortable, haven't they, Vera?' Mother's voice faded as her head turned away. 'I was just telling my daughter about the traffic.' Mother's voice came back. 'See you at the luncheon . . .'

'Take care, Mother,' Lydia said, putting the phone down and resuming her train of thought. Was Richard determined to stay put, live at his flat for ever and ever, or what?

The phone rang again.

'Ma?' Marina always phoned on Friday nights again now or explained in advance if she couldn't. Marina was reliable.

'How are you, darling? Everything all right?'

'Quite all right,' Marina said. 'Saw the doctor Thursday. You know that kneehole desk which came from my great-granny, can I have it?'

'Yes of course,' Lydia said, ashamed of her disappointment. What was the use of keeping things? 'And I thought you might like the white garden furniture from the terrace.'

'Thanks, Ma. Yes, I would. Anyway, expect you're busy. See you tomorrow then. Bye for now.'

Lydia sighed but she didn't have to worry about Marina any more. Marina knew what she wanted. She didn't even worry about Annie much, the baby gone and Annie painting the walls of the café at St Ives, ready to open in April. Annie had slipped rein. Tomorrow she would stop worrying about Will too. If marriages didn't work out, you got divorced. So what?

It didn't look as if Richard was going to phone.

Alone was safe in a way but alone was chilly. How quickly you forgot the cold black hole side of it. Richard might want to be part of her life but did she want to be part of his? And what about painting, what about compromise? Did he expect her to give up everything for a relationship which might not work out? Could she take such a risk?

Why hadn't he phoned?

The following morning Mrs Barley and her daughters arrived, each carrying a silver dish on which lay a huge and handsome poached salmon carefully decorated.

'How marvellous, how beautiful they look!' Lydia said, pausing to admire – it was a celebration after all – before backing the Fiesta out of the garage so they could bring their food-laden van close to the house.

A March wind chivvied clouds across a pale blue sky. The next-door drives could be used for parking but Cedar Avenue was still going to be somewhat congested.

She hoped Richard would be first. She hadn't seen him since he left early on Monday, but at twelve o'clock guests began to arrive. Ed with Ruby was closely followed by William with Leonie and Rodney, then the Fields.

'How lovely you look!' Lydia said as Ruby came through the front door in a froth of white. 'Truly lovely.'

'Beautiful girl, you got there, beautiful girl, my daughter,' said Mr Field. Traces of red hair flecked his short-cut grey. 'Most beautiful girl in Weston-Super-Mare.'

'Oh Dad . . .' Ruby said.

'Don't you *oh Dad* me, my girl. Everybody says it . . . the photographer even. My friends call me Vince, right?'

'Have you met Rodney, my best man?' William said, grabbing Rodney's arm as he tripped on the doorstep.

'Whoops! Sorry, folks . . .'

'Still staggering from the stag night looks like,' suggested Vince Field.

'Kept swigging at his hip flask in the registry,' Ruby said as William steered him to a chair. 'Really embarrassing!'

Mrs Barley began to circle with glasses of red and white wine, while Beryl dealt with coats to the cloakroom and her sister steered ladies upstairs to powder noses.

'Over here, waitress dear,' Rodney called, taking a glass in each hand.

'That's quite enough, Rod,' Lydia said. 'Have you had any breakfast?' If only Richard would come.

'Given breakfast up for Lent,' Rodney said.

'Doesn't the best man have to make a speech?' Vince whispered.

'Lovely the tables look!' said Mrs Field.

'Lovely girl, our Ruby.'

'You said that a dozen times already, Dad,' said Tracey.

'If you're jealous, girl, so you should be.'

'Stop it, the both of you,' said Mrs Field.

'Congratulations, you two brave Kemps!' Izzy said, arriving and kissing them both. 'You look gorgeous, Mrs Kemp.'

'Doesn't she? Thanks for the, er, mixer, Izz,' William said.

'You can tell he does the cooking our place,' Ruby said.

'I hope we're not late. Vera got lost,' Mother said at the door. 'What a really lovely dress, Ruby dear – Mrs Kemp, I should say.'

'Three Mrs Kemps now,' Leonie said.

'You can have too much of a good thing,' Ed murmured.

'I did not get lost,' Vera said. 'I was misdirected.'

Had she said twelve o'clock to Richard or half-past? Lydia wondered.

'Congratulations, my dears.' Margaret, in crimson coat and silver fox hat, kissed bride and groom enthusiastically.

'Thanks for the really gorgeous . . .' Ruby began.

'Dishes,' William said. 'Le Crueset, last us a lifetime.'

'Congratulations,' Marina said, kissing them both. 'Hope you'll be as happy as we are.'

'How happy is that?' William said.

'Cheeky!' Marina said.

'Ecstatic,' Jeremy said.

How pretty Marina looks. Pregnancy suits her, Lydia thought. The kneehole desk would be a sort of prize.

'Better get the meal started, Ma,' William whispered, glancing at Rodney.

'But Richard isn't here yet.' An accident? Even good drivers had accidents sometimes.

'So?' William said. 'Anyway I can hear a car now.'

'I think we'd better start lunch, Mrs Barley,' Lydia said.

'Right you are.'

'Find your places, everybody,' Lydia said. But the slow footsteps coming down the drive belonged to old Mr Beavis.

'Congratulations, you young Kemps,' he said, raising Ruby's hand to his lips. 'You're a beautiful girl, my dear. Feather in his cap, shouldn't wonder. Blessing of Ceres and Juno be on you both.'

'Thank you, Mr Beavis, and thanks for the, er, lovely crystal decanter, was it?'

'Who is Dr Richard Foy?' Mother asked, peering at the place name beside hers.

'Doctor friend of Lydia's, expect he got held up,' Izzy said.

'Who's Ms Isobel Simmons then?' Mother said, peering the other way.

'Me.' Izzy sat down but her hand flew to her neck. 'More or less.'

'All right, Rod?' William said, levering him towards his chair.

'No . . .' Rod murmured. His eyes closed as his face fell forward on to the plate of salmon.

'Hell!' William said, putting an arm round Rod's shoulders as Jeremy supported from the other side. 'Upstairs.'

'Do start everybody,' Lydia said.

'Very nice behaviour, I must say,' whispered Mrs Field, passing the new potatoes.

'Boys will be boys.' Ruby's radiant smile extended over both tables. A smile of such particular charm had to mean something, Lydia thought hopefully.

'Not in my day, I'm glad to say,' Mother said.

'I do admire you, Margaret,' Lydia murmured, sitting beside her. 'You're marvellous, you know. I'm not talking about the champagne, generous though it is, I mean the way you manage to be happy whatever happens, even . . . after Bertie.'

'Heavens!' Margaret's eyes blinked and widened. 'Well, Bertie's gone but the love is still there, the love between us. My dear mother was a happy person, perhaps it's inherited? Anyway, where's Richard?'

'Late,' Lydia said.

If he doesn't come, if he doesn't come at all, I shall store my stuff and go to Izzy's for a bit, she thought. It was best to have a plan, be prepared.

There was subdued clapping as William and Jeremy came back.

'Sorry about that, ladies and gentleman,' William said.

'OK?' whispered Ruby.

'Fairly.' William smiled into her eyes. The phone rang in the hall. 'Probably for me,' he said, jumping up. 'Hi, Annie . . . Thanks.' His voice joyous and exalted came through the open door. 'Well, we're just having lunch actually . . . OK, OK . . . thanks anyway.' He laid the receiver on the hall chest.

'Ma, Annie wants a word, says it's urgent.'

'Urgent?' Lydia moved swiftly, closing the sitting room door behind her.

'Annie? You all right?'

'Course,' Annie said. 'Just phoned to give you the number at St Ives. I was thinking I'd phone every week . . .'

'Good. But I'm only here for a day or two now, not sure where I'll be after that . . .'

'Oh well . . . Anyway, Jarvis wants to speak to you.'

'In the middle of William's wedding lunch?'

'Er, Mrs Kemp?' Jarvis said hurriedly. 'Hello, Mrs Kemp?'

'Call me Lydia, Jarvis, please . . .'

'Right, Lydia. Won't keep you, congratulations to William, by the way.' He sounded breathy, nervous. 'The thing is, Annie and me . . . now we got this place St Ives, we was thinkin' about gettin' married, so I wanted to ask you, Lydia, I am askin' you, for your daughter's hand in marriage. Er, that all right?'

'It's fine by me, Jarvis, if it's what Annie wants,' Lydia said.

'Course it is,' Annie said.

CHAPTER THIRTY ONE

As the barleys cleared the tables, William tackled the gold-topped bottles, champagne corks popping and flying.

'Mind the lights,' Lydia cried. But how well he was managing, she thought, how happy he looked. She decided to keep quiet about Annie and Jarvis for the moment. Was it her idea or his that Jarvis should ask for Annie's hand? Either way it was quaint, no point in arguing, and baby or no baby, Annie wasn't everybody's money.

'I'm paying for all this, I hope you realise,' Ed whispered to Leonie. 'But nobody mentioned champagne.'

'He is your son,' Leonie murmured.

'So I am informed,' Ed said moodily.

'Well, he does look rather like you.'

'First toast,' said Ruby, jumping to her feet and raising her fizzing glass. 'To me and William on our wedding day and the great life we're going to have together.'

'Great life!' the guests murmured, raising champagne glasses and some eyebrows.

'As you see my wife's right out of order already,' William smiled engagingly. 'However, owing to the unfortunate indisposition of the best man,' faint titters, 'it falls to me to propose a second toast to anyone I like. So here's to my beautiful bride, Ruby Kemp.'

Glasses raised. 'Beautiful bride, Ruby Kemp.'

'Thirdly I have to thank my parents, Edward and Lydia, for all they have done to make this wedding lunch possible.'

'Edward and Lydia,' Jeremy said and everyone sipped.

'Fourthly Rodney having done his best to *liberate* the proceedings, I shall continue the good work.' Lydia had never seen him so light-hearted. 'Champagne up and I want you all to offer your recipe for a happy marriage in one sentence for the benefit of Ruby and me.'

'His idea, not mine,' Ruby said.

'Starting with Grandma,' William said.

'I'm the grandma,' Mother said. 'Married twice, two happy marriages, did everything for James and he did everything for my girls. Get married and stay married, I say.' She glanced at Lydia as she sat down to clapping.

'More champagne for Grandma,' William said. 'Leonie, your recipe?'

'I hereby agree with every single word my husband is going to say,' Leonie said, raising one hand.

Laughter. 'Knows which side her bread is buttered.'

'Vera?'

'Pass,' Vera muttered. 'Never got married.'

'Likewise.' Mr Beavis's voice was quavery. 'Engaged to a girl in the Wrens once, bombing raid on Portsmouth killed her. That finished me.'

'Poor old soul,' Mrs Field murmured.

'Vince?'

'What can I say with the wife here?' Vince said. 'Next?'

'Pass,' Lydia said. 'But Jarvis has just asked me for Annie's hand in marriage.' Clapping all round. Quarter past two, Richard wouldn't come now, she thought.

'Did Annie accept? The girl's mad. Champagne, Ma?' William said.

'He wants to put us all under the table!' Grandma said.

'Margaret?'

Margaret stood up. 'I've been married three times but Bertie, my third husband, was my first love,' she said in a small clear voice. 'He has died but he's still with me, he'll always be with me.'

'Poor lady, shame, isn't it?' Vince said.

'Dad?' William said.

Ed stood up, squared his shoulders and cleared his throat. 'Marriage, fidelity to one's partner, is the basis of a civilised society, necessary for good order and the responsible rearing of children.'

'Hear, hear,' said Vince.

'So how is it that today the UK has the highest divorce rate in Europe, more single parents than any other country, vandalism, violence, a rising crime rate, a television devoted to crime, sitcoms all about fashionable fornication? Let us ask ourselves where this is leading.' Leonie was tweaking the back of his jacket.

'I said one sentence, Dad,' William said, and Ed sat down.

'He spoils everything,' Ruby muttered. 'A wedding day is for good luck and congratulations, not that stuff . . .'

'He can't spoil today, not for us,' William whispered, squeezing her hand.

'But Ed's right, you know.' Sarah Newton began to clap.

'Course he is,' Bill said, clapping too.

'I'm right with you, mate,' Vince said, as the clapping crescendoed round both tables.

'It's not fair,' whispered Ruby. The clapping faltered as her sister, Tracey, a gawky fifteen-year-old, stood up.

'Aristotle says "Marriage is the assassin of love," ' she said breathlessly.

'Brains of the family, this one,' her father winked.

'So what we ought to wish William and Ruby is a quick divorce to save their love,' Tracey added, and sat down.

'Eh? What you on about, girl?'

'I think it was Aristotle *Onassis* said that, actually,' Jeremy said smoothly into the ensuing silence.

'And being married is really nice,' Marina said quickly.

'Thank you, darling,' Jeremy said.

'Your turn, Izzy,' Lydia said.

'But she's not married,' Grandma said.

'Yes, I am,' Izzy said, producing a gold ring suspended on a tape from round her neck. 'Proof positive.'

'Chris?' Lydia said.

'Married last December. Officially I'm Mrs Isobel Gage.'

'Congratulations,' Lydia said. 'Why don't you wear it on your finger like everybody else?'

'Marriage is a secret society,' Izzy murmured. 'By the way, you can kip at my place until you find somewhere if you want.'

'Thanks.'

'But today's *my* wedding day,' Ruby said plaintively. 'Not Izzy's or Annie's.'

'What's this, tears before bedtime?' Alice said with a giggle.

'Lucky if we get to bed at all this rate,' Ruby said. 'Start my new job Monday. As for my little pig sister . . .'

'In the old days the bride and bridegroom went off on their

honeymoon. It made a nice climax,' Grandma said.

'Lucky things!' Ruby rolled knowing eyes.

'Then everybody knew when it was time to go home,' Grandma said.

'Hush up, Gran,' William whispered, steering Ruby towards the front door.

'It's been lovely, a really nice occasion,' Sarah Newton said. 'But we must get back to the children.'

'Or our child-minder will be on strike,' Bill added.

'Think that's my taxi,' Mr Beavis said. 'Wish you every happiness, young Kemps.'

'Thank you, sir.'

'Can I take the kneehole desk now, Ma?' Marina said.

'Feel free.'

'If you could just help Jeremy get it to the car, Will?' Marina said.

'In a minute,' William said as guests departed in a flurry of good wishes. 'Rodney seems to have done a bunk.'

'Not surprised, ashamed to show his face,' Ed said. 'Want a lift home, Ruby, if you're worried about your dress?'

'Doesn't matter now, does it?' Ruby said.

'What happens to all the used wedding dresses?' Tracey said.

'Cut up for christening robes in my day,' Grandma said. 'Come along, Vera.'

'Thanks for everything, Lydia,' Ruby said as the last guest departed.

'Thanks, Ma,' William said. 'Last night in the old home?'

'Not quite. Got a few more days.'

'Where you going anyway?'

'Haven't decided yet.'

'Well, don't get miserable.' He glanced at Ruby. 'She could come to our place, couldn't she? I mean . . . ?'

'Course,' Ruby said.

'Don't be ridiculous,' Lydia said. 'Anyway, there's a lot of clearing up.'

'Take care then.'

Mrs Barley snapped the legs of the trestle tables flat and carried them to the van. The Barley girls followed with stacks of gold chairs. Boxes of crockery had already gone.

'I think this is what we owe you,' Lydia said, holding out Ed's cheque. 'Thank you all so much, you've been wonderful.'

She waved as the van backed up the drive and turned away along the avenue.

It was almost dusk. She phoned Richard's flat and getting no answer left a mild, 'What happened to you?' on the answerphone.

Could he have been caught up in some emergency? It was possible but somehow it was too neat an explanation to be credible. Was he trying to teach her a lesson?

It didn't sound like good-natured Richard but we all had our breaking point, our wounded vanity, men especially, and he had proposed marriage to her twice and been rejected.

What was wrong between them? How come you never knew how much you were going to miss people until they were gone?

Now she was alone, alone in a quiet house, Lydia thought, it was an expectation rather than a condition. There was an arctic chill about the descending March evening. It would be good to know how things stood but perhaps she never would.

Richard listened generously to other people's problems, gave sensible advice but that didn't mean he was clever with his own. Perhaps she would never see him again.

At six o'clock 'Good Move' arrived and carried away the entire contents of Ed's study and the old rug, then the dining table and chairs, the two easy chairs. Afterwards there was little left in the sitting room except the big sofa, the old rug, the television and an air of devastation, castor dents in the carpet, a pale square where the kneehole desk had stood for twenty years.

Upstairs there were things to do, the cot to be dismantled and wrapped in plastic, green stars applied to the bits of furniture she wanted to keep, her painting equipment to be packed up and the paintings themselves, but Lydia was tired.

Tomorrow would do.

She wrapped herself in the rug and lay full length on the sofa. Inside the house was full of echoes, children's voices, a guinea pig's squeak, but she didn't want to stay any more. It was time to leave Cedar Avenue. It wasn't her place any more, she *wanted* to leave.

Outside she heard the whirr of the swimming pool cover and

the faint splash as Margaret slid into the water. Her first swim of the year. Love was gratitude, Margaret said, gratitude and admiration to and for Bertie.

Had the wedding party saddened her? Water was a lonely medium, sad cold stuff, rising every year, islands lost, Bangladesh flooded, Atlantis drowned.

Lydia slept.

It was late when she woke, a car on the drive. Footsteps. She knew at once, of course she knew, even before he let himself in with his key.

'Richard?'

'That's me.' He crossed the hall, switched on the light. 'What's the matter now?'

'Nothing,' she said, sitting up. 'I think I fell asleep. What happened to you?'

'Something came up,' he said vaguely. His eyes evaded hers and she knew it wasn't true. Better not to probe. He was entitled to secrets he didn't want to disclose, as was she.

'Got to be out of here in the next few days.'

'I know.'

'Feels all right,' she said, but her voice sounded brittle. 'Feels like I've gone already. Holroyds move in next week.'

'I know,' he said.

'I've been thinking about us,' Lydia said suddenly. 'I think we should get married, Richard.'

'Now she tells me,' he muttered. But the grey eyes which met hers had a hint of shrewdness and more than a hint of triumph. Was this just what Richard intended? she wondered, prepared to forgive him. After all, she had messed him about, hadn't she?

'What's wrong with now?' Lydia said. 'Unless you have other plans?'

'No other plans,' Richard said. 'What else do you think?'

'Well, I don't think I can live without you . . . I mean I don't want to . . . but I can't live at your flat, not for long anyway. It's too dark, so I'll get a cottage with a garden near Bath. I mean you can come to my cottage when you like but we don't have to live together all the time. I mean Mary Wollstonecraft lived in her own house and her husband lived just opposite . . .'

'Who she?' Richard said.

'And Margaret Drabble and whatshisname live five miles apart.'

'Aren't any cottages near Albert Place.'

'There's nothing wrong with your flat. I won't mind living there for a bit, long as you don't mind?'

'Be my guest.'

'Well, I'd rather be your wife, if that's OK with you?'

'Quite OK.'

'But I need a cottage with lots of good north light.'

'Perhaps you should go to art school next year,' Richard said. 'Bath or Corsham, if you can get in.'

'Why shouldn't I get in?' Lydia said.

'Competition is fierce.'

'And I need to be on my own quite a lot . . . I hope that's all right with you?'

'Give us both time to pursue our respective hobbies,' Richard said.

'Painting is not a hobby,' Lydia says. 'It's my life. Anyway, what's your hobby?'

'Well, it's always been "the ladies",' Richard said. 'OK?'

'Absolutely not,' Lydia said. 'Absolutely no ladies.'

'I'll have to think of something else,' Richard said. 'Like golf . . .'